IT WAS LIKE RADAR

The moment she knelt beside the bed, Jess's nose turned toward the cup of coffee in her hand and twitched at the rich, dark scent.

"Good morning," Charley crooned. She let her fingers scrape along his bristly cheek while teasing him with the aroma wafting from the cup.

"Hi." It was a low sexy rumble.

"I brought coffee to tame the savage beast."

His mouth curved softly. "Thanks." As he dragged himself up to a half-sitting position against the headboard, Charley climbed onto the bed and straddled his denim-clad thighs. Interest piqued, he played with the hem of the T-shirt she was wearing.

"Isn't this mine?"

"All of it's yours." She let that linger. "What would you like first?"

Jess drew her down for a leisurely kiss, one that was sleepily sensual. Then he drank deeply and sighed. "Ummm. Good coffee. Good kiss. Helluva way to start the day."

"Breakfast of champions," she returned with a saucy wiggle of her hips.

Jess took another sip, letting his thumb rub along the inside of her thigh in distracting circles. "Something on your mind, Charley?"

DANA RANSOM

Love's Own Reward

ZEBRA BOOKS
KENSINGTON PUBLISHING CORP.

ZEBRA BOOKS

are published by

Kensington Publishing Corp.
475 Park Avenue South
New York, NY 10016

First printing: September, 1992

Printed in the United States of America

For Debbie Macomber,
my friend and mentor.
Your advice made all the
difference in the world!

A special acknowledgment
to my technical advisors:

Orysia, for showing me
how to shop the Mile
and survive parking.

My brother-in-law, George,
for translating
science into English.

One

My God, he's going to hit that car!

Just as the thought shot through Charlene Carter's mind, the eighteen-wheeler shifted lanes. Crowded from the pavement by the diesel-snorting semi, the driver of the compact ahead of her had no choice but to take to the shoulder with a hard wrench of the steering wheel. The truck sped on, with a rumble of massive metal and a rattling vibration. The driver never saw the devastation left in his wake.

Charley had seen it hundreds of times in her early-morning commute to work. A reckless driver cutting lanes, tired, in a hurry, not checking his mirrors as carefully as he should. Usually the result was an angry blare of the horn or a sudden swerve and vigorously-mouthed curses. This morning it was worse. Much worse.

The small car struck the shoulder going close to seventy. Loose gravel flew as tires fought for traction. The rear end spun and Charley could see the driver hauling frantically to correct it. But not in time. In that second she could see the female passenger scream as Charley's car passed. It seemed the woman was staring right at her through the side window, her eyes huge, terrified, begging for assistance. Then the image was gone as Charley stomped on the brake, struggling to bring her own vehicle to a safe stop.

She saw the impact in the rearview mirror. Somehow that made it more horrifying, that narrow glimpse of harsh reality. The careening car slammed broadside into an overpass abutment. She could hear the raw rend of metal, the shattering of glass, even with her windows tightly closed. The passenger side crumpled like a can. The horn sounded, but the eerie wail was cut brutally short as the car skidded and flipped, once, twice, then rolled to rest on its side in the gully of the median.

Seconds passed. Charley's fingers were frozen about the steering wheel. A fierce tremor started in those cramped hands and spread rapidly up her arms until her very teeth chattered with shock. *My God!* Just like a scene from a made-for-TV movie! Only the dark smoke billowing from the grassy valley was real. Terribly real. That was what shook her from her stupor.

There were people in that car!

Charley never remembered shoving her car into park. The engine was still running when she leaped out and dashed onto the highway. Traffic had come to a complete halt by then, but she wasn't aware of the confusion. She never even looked before sprinting across the rubber-burned blacktop. All she could think of was that woman's petrified face.

Charley rushed forward and could see the wheels were still spinning. The passenger side of the car, from bumper to front door, was a mass of twisted metal. Steam and an awful gassy smell came from the wreck. The rear door. Charley's thoughts were working on some primitive level. They were clear now, completely panic-free, even though her chest hurt from the hammering of her heart. Maybe she could reach the people from the back seat. Losing her shoes, ripping her pantyhose, she crawled up, using the buckled trunk lid for footing. She managed to wrestle the heavy door up and open. It would only go halfway before catching on the bent frame. But it was far enough.

It never once occurred to her to worry about her own safety. There just wasn't time. By lying on her stomach, Charley could lean inside the crushed car. The stench of fuel was even stronger inside.

"Hello? Are you all right? I'm going to get you out."

There was no response from the front seat. But from the shadows of the back came a whimpering moan. A child.

Charley stretched down toward the little figure belted in behind the driver's seat. Her fingers fumbled with the fastener. The hot scent made the air almost unbreathable by then. She started to cough. So did the boy. There was a click and the belt dropped away from his middle.

"Can you grab onto my arms?" Charley cried. Her balance was precarious. She wasn't sure she could lift the child out by herself. She caught a thin arm and pulled upward at an awkward angle. The boy began to cry in great, catching sobs. He was heavy.

"Help me! You have to help me!" Charley ordered frantically as she lost her grip on his forearm and was left with only his jacket twisted in her hand. "Help me! Give me your arms. Reach up to me. Come on now."

"Mommy!" the child wailed in pain and terror.

"First you, then I'll get her. I promise. I promise." Charley began to slip. She felt the cut of sharp metal. "Give me your hands!"

Then he reached up to her, wrapping his little arms around her neck, twining desperately, chokingly. Wriggling backward, she dropped from the car to the grass, stumbling with the boy in her arms until she caught her balance. And she ran. The smell of fuel was overwhelming. The punctured engine hissed and seethed. When she'd gotten him far enough away, she found other hands reaching for him, relieving her of the burden of his weight. But not from the burden of his terror-stricken cries.

"Mommy! Mommy!"

It was madness. The first thing Charley saw when she turned back toward the car was fire. Flames snapped out from under the hood and spread hungrily down to the gas-puddled grass. But she couldn't see the flames as clearly as she could see that woman's face.

"Mommy!"

Charley was running. Several people grabbed at

her coat, but she jerked away, continuing her race toward the flaming car. It was burning fiercely by the time she reached it. When she grabbed at the doorframe, she was vaguely conscious of heat searing her palms. Adrenaline surged. She could hear her own heart thundering in her ears, rivaling the frantic rasp of her breathing and the snap of the fire enveloping the front of the compact.

Inside, the car was thick and dark with smoke. She could barely see, so she felt her way along the hot vinyl. The woman was dangling from her shoulder harness, her torso bent over the buckle. Charley couldn't reach it.

"No!"

The woman was wedged between the bucket seats. Charley used her shoulder for leverage, trying to lift the woman's still form and release the seat buckle. She slipped. Momentum began to pull Charley inside the car, when something snagged the band of her skirt. Strong hands began hauling her back and out. Away from the woman and her husband.

"No," Charley could hear herself screaming. "Let me go! I can save them! I have to save them!"

But fresh air was suddenly cold on her face, and through tear-blurred eyes she could see the car become a ball of fire as she was carried away. She fought wildly.

Then she was overcome by coughing. Her lungs burned until she felt as if they would explode from the tearing pressure. She couldn't struggle anymore. There was no strength for it. Her knees gave, and if not for the arms encircling her, she would have collapsed onto the grassy median.

The car burst like a detonated bomb. Bits and pieces of twisted steel showered down, fiery comets that sizzled as they struck the ground. Stunned, Charley watched the tragedy—helpless and heart-broken. A terrible despair rose within her, swelling her smoke-clogged throat and trapping the wail of anguish inside. Shock and grief shuddered through her, and she sagged into surrounding male arms. It was a warm, protective embrace, isolating her from the horror. Stinging tears distorted the sight until it was completely obscured by a leather-clad shoulder.

"Shhh," came a low, husky whisper close to her ear. "You did everything you could. No one could have saved them. No one could have saved them."

That soothing caress of sound was the last thing she remembered.

"How is he?"

The nurse paused in pumping the blood-pressure cuff and smiled at the pale young woman. "They flew him to Ann Arbor this morning."

Charley moaned. "He's worse?"

"Oh no, no. Nothing like that," the nurse soothed quickly. "It's just that the grandparents thought he'd get better care at a bigger hospital. All his signs were stable. Thanks to you."

Charley sighed in relief. Then a small swell of disappointment rose. She had hoped she'd be able to see him. Chris Osgood. She hadn't known his name until three days ago, when she'd woken up in this bed with her hands mummified in bandages. She'd seen his picture in the paper. A sweet-faced six-year-old. Right beneath the photos of his parents. The people she hadn't been able to rescue. She swallowed hard and closed her eyes. Right under the massive headlines that changed her life.

"Are they still out there?"

"Who? Oh, you mean the vultures? Thick as thieves. It's not every day they have a real live hero in their midst."

Charley's lips curled in a wry disclaimer. "I'm no hero."

The nurse tugged the Velcro to release the pressure cuff. Her voice was warm with admiration. "Could have fooled me."

She'd fooled them all. She, Charlene Carter, simple lab assistant, the new John Wayne of the highway. The guardian angel of a small boy who just happened to be the only surviving grandchild of one of the richest industrialists in Michigan. A fearless Samaritan braving death to rescue a stranger. That's how the press painted her in their bold banner headlines. Some hero. So tortured by nightmares of fire and fear that she couldn't sleep without medication. So haunted by that woman's eyes that Charley couldn't close her own without seeing them. So overpowered by the shadow of her own brush with death that she couldn't speak of the accident without falling into fitful tremors. She couldn't read about it in the papers. She couldn't watch it on television. And if she'd been trapped inside that burning car, would they have likened her to Joan of Arc? Would that have sold even more papers?

Charley squeezed her eyes more tightly shut and forced the image from her mind. The hospital psychologist had taught her how to suppress the panic, how to control it. But it wouldn't go away. She'd asked about the man who'd pulled her out of the overturned vehicle, the stranger who had saved her life. But in all the confusion no record had been made of his name. So he would go without thanks while she was weighed down with reward.

Five hundred thousand dollars' worth of reward.

"Are you sure you want to be released this afternoon, Miss Carter? It probably wouldn't hurt to stay another day. I'm sure there won't be any problem with the insurance."

Charley almost laughed. Paying for her hospital stay was the least of her concerns. The Osgoods had seen to that with their overwhelming gift of thanks.

"I just want to go home and get back to normal." But was that going to be possible?

For three days, ever since she'd been confined to this hospital bed, she'd been swamped with requests from the press. Interviews. Pictures. In-depth features. At her insistence visitors had been barred from her room. But that didn't keep the media from flocking outside, from pumping the nursing staff and even the janitor for information. Didn't they understand that Charley just wanted to put it behind her? Couldn't they see that she'd done nothing noble? Why wouldn't they let the horror of it die along with Chris Osgood's parents?

Because of the money.

"Leave those bandages on and keep them dry until your follow-up next week. In the meantime, get that prescription filled right away. You're probably not feeling anything now, but I won't lie to you. When that shot wears off, the next few days are going to be pretty miserable. Take what you need to control the pain. Healing time varies with burns, so you'll just have to be patient. You were lucky, Miss Carter. There was little tissue damage, so you should be itching like crazy with new skin in about a week. Don't scratch." The nurse looked sternly at her patient to make sure the orders were understood. The young woman nodded vaguely. The medication had her drifting nicely. "Have you signed all the papers? Is someone coming to pick you up?"

Charley felt a brief tug of hurt as she said, "I've called a cab." She knew why Alan wasn't coming. She knew all the reasons by heart. But that didn't lessen the ache of abandonment. Couldn't he find the time to be there when she needed him? That wasn't fair of her, but then, she wasn't feeling particularly unselfish. Her hands throbbed behind the blunt of painkillers. Her courage faltered at the thought of facing those reporters alone. She just wanted to escape to the safety of her own quiet world.

"Your limo's here, Miss Carter," called the young black orderly maneuvering a wheelchair into place for her. "First-class service right to the front door. Got everything?"

"Just what I have on." A co-worker had brought her the change of clothes and slip-on shoes. The pair she'd worn the day of the accident were beyond repair. The nurse had helped her into the pull-on skirt and button-front blouse. Charley's hands were fairly useless, but she was learning to adapt by slow, uncomfortable degrees.

"What about all your flowers and cards?"

Charley glanced at the elaborate sprays adorning every available surface of her room. Get-well notes had come in by the hundreds. Almost all from strangers. "Could someone box up the cards and send them to me?" The nurse nodded with a smile, "Take the flowers to the children's unit," Charley suggested. "They could use the cheering up." It would take more than flowers from people she didn't know to raise her own spirits. Someone might as well enjoy them. Besides, it was all she could do to hang on to her purse and place her feet one in front of the other. Her pain medication acted on her with the subtlety of an animal tranquilizer. It would have dropped a rhinoceros. But that powerful drug dulled the edge of her anxiety as well as her discomfort, so she was grateful for it. Otherwise, she never would have found the fortitude to seat herself in the wheelchair. Some hero!

She dozed during the ride down the elevator. It made a pleasant whirring sound, soothing her senses in tandem with her lethargy-producing pills.The cab should be waiting. All she had to do was remember her address. Then she'd be home. What a divine thought. She'd take the phone off the hook and sleep for a week with no one to disturb her. She was smiling serenely as the doors shushed open. Then her pleasant dream was shattered by explosions of light.

Charley shrank back into the chair like a startled doe confronted with the brilliance of oncoming headlights.

"Who let you bastards in here?" the orderly growled at the reporters swarming the elevator bank. He ducked his head against the flare of flashbulbs and muscled the wheelchair through the crowd. They were quick to give him room or be run down, then trailed along like hounds on a scent.

"Miss Carter, how are you feeling?"

"Free Press, Miss Carter. Can you comment on what the last few days have been like?"

"This way, Miss Carter. I need a picture."

"What are you going to do with the money?"

"Yeah, how are you going to spend it?"

"Another picture, Miss Carter."

"Over here."

"What were you thinking when you ran back to that car?"

Charley shook her head. "Please, I'd rather not—"

"Did you know who they were when you went back to rescue the parents?"

That question shocked her, penetrating the film of confusion slowing her brain. She stared up at the reporter who was elbowing close to push a microphone in her face. She met the man's eyes. They were bright, avid with the morbid curiosity of the general public, searching for a cynical story angle.

"No," she managed to mumble. My God, how could he think it would matter? "Please . . ." She tried to turn away from the thrusting hand mike and was instantly blinded by another flash. "Please . . ."

Faces began to blur. The noise grew to an awful roar. Charley closed her eyes, wishing the press would just go away, that they'd respect her pain, that they'd leave the gruesome facts alone. She heard the click and buzz of the hospital doors opening and the intensity of sound struck her like a physical force. The size of the media tripled as members of radio, television, and newspaper staffs jockeyed to get near enough to shout their questions or snap a picture. The microphones shoved at her claimed an alphabet soup of call letters. She couldn't hear any one clear question, just a loud babble of discordant voices in ever-increasing volume. It buffeted her into a daze of desperation. The orderly bent to ask her something, but she couldn't understand him above the clamor of the crowd. Frantically she tried to see through the press of bodies, looking for the means to escape, but there were too many people, all mashing tight to form a solid barrier. From the chair she couldn't tell if her cab was waiting in the circular drive. She'd have to stand.

There was no strength in her legs. She had to push herself up using the arms of the wheelchair for leverage. Instantly she felt a reminding jolt of agony as her palms pressed down. She dragged herself up and was immediately engulfed. A heavy camcorder smacked into one bandaged hand. Pain swirled up, blurring her eyes, then was quickly muted by the drugs deadening her system. She managed a hesitant step forward, and all sense of direction was lost.

"Miss Carter . . ."

"Over here!"

"Did you name the amount, or was that what Osgood offered?"

"WYZ, Miss Carter. Could you tell our listeners—"

". . . already dead when you went back for them?"

Charley's head swam. She blinked rapidly against the glare of camera lights, against the fogging pull of her medication. *I'm going to faint,* she thought in a hazy panic. *I'm going to be sick right here on national television.* Her stomach roiled. A cold sweat broke out on her face, and her limbs began to quiver. And suddenly she couldn't move. She stood in a glaze of bewildered horror, not knowing what way to go, how to flee the barrage of questions.

Firm hands cupped her elbows in the same second she feared her legs would no longer support her.

"Miss Carter? I'm parked right over there. I've been waiting for you. Let me get you out of here."

Her cab. Thank God! She surrendered control of the situation to the owner of that confident voice. Abruptly she was being moved purposefully through the crowd. Vaguely she heard the annoyed grumbles and the anxious last-minute shout of questions. Weak with gratitude, she glanced around and up to see the face of her rescuer. She got the indelible impression of piercing gray eyes, eyes that could look right into the soul from beneath a slash of brooding brows. Angry eyes.

That puzzled her. Even through the mist of uncertainty clouding her mind, she wondered why this man was so upset with her. But that was silly. Probably the drugs. What reason could he possibly have to feel one way or another about her?

Then she felt herself falling into the front seat of a car. Not the back, she noticed in a dreamy blur. The door shut and there was blissful silence. The roar flared briefly again when the driver's door opened, then there was just the purr of the engine.

"Where to?"

Groggily Charley gave her address and let the cottony balm of the sedatives envelop her. She was going home.

Two

Jess McMasters studied the entrance of the hospital from the front seat of his car. They'd already started to gather—the curious, the media. The walk was like a snake pit of electrical cables. Every opening of the mechanical doors moved the crowd in a rhythmic tide, surging forward eagerly, ebbing in disappointment. They were waiting for the same thing he was: a chance to talk to Charlene Carter. It didn't bother him that she wasn't giving interviews. He wasn't worried because he knew something they didn't—he knew the lady.

Jess gave the plastic top of his convenience-store coffee a practiced toss onto the dash. While he sipped the scalding brew, he leaned against the driver's door and propped one long leg up on the seat. He was used to waiting. Part of his job was waiting—for the right person, for the right moment, for the right story, for the right slant. And here he had it all. Charlene Carter was exactly the kind of item he was known for. For the past two years his features in *Metro Magazine* covered the gritty and the glittery of the Detroit area. He was respected for his journalistic style. He was feared for his unbending honesty. "Cynicism," some called it. "Candor" was the term he preferred. His exposés touched on gang violence, political corruption, urban renewal scandals, the nasty and preferably hidden habits of the wealthy and the powerful. So his editor had been understandably surprised by his request to do a story on Charlene Carter. Until Jess explained his angle. Then he could swear he heard the man salivating through the lines of Michigan Bell.

Charlene Carter was the day's hero. She'd rushed into the fires of hell to effect one rescue and attempt another. A noble act that had paid off handsomely to the tune of five hundred thousand dollars. That was the value Detroit industrialist Benjamin Osgood placed upon the life of his grandson. Apparently Miss Carter agreed. Because she'd accepted the money. And, in doing so, shattered every cherished belief Jess McMasters had held since the fateful day of the crash.

It was the bravest damn thing he'd ever seen. She was only a little bit of a thing, so delicate she might have been confused with a girl. He could remember every finely-cut line of her face as she'd dashed in front of his stopped car. So small and yet possessed of a courage that put the rest of them to shame. While others watched, himself included, she'd scrambled into that compact, heedless of the danger, to bring out the little boy. And if that wasn't enough, she'd gone back toward certain death in an effort to save the kid's parents. She couldn't, of course. Jess had known that the moment he saw the fuel ignite. But it hadn't stopped her from trying. God, she'd fought him like a madwoman when he'd pulled her away, barely seconds before she would have been engulfed in the same fiery ball that consumed the car. Such amazing strength in such a tiny package. He'd been awed by her. Until this one had played out before his disbelieving eyes, he'd shunned stories of heroism. He'd felt the frantic beat of her big, big heart against his chest. He'd felt the helpless trembling of her despair as he held her in his arms. And never had anything touched him so strongly, so powerfully, so tenderly as that moment. As that woman.

Why had she taken the money?

Dammit, why had she failed him? He saw so much ugliness, so much greed. He wanted to believe such unselfish goodness was possible. He wanted to believe the tears he saw on her face were genuine, for her anguish over others instead of her own pain. He wanted to hold on to the emotions that filled his soul with such poignant possessiveness as he'd cradled her close and tried to give her comfort. In that brief slice of time she'd reached inside him and torn out his heart. And then broke it by proving all his illusions false. Charlene Carter wasn't a saint willing to throw down her life to save another's. She'd been quick to snap up the fee for her bravery. In his jaded eyes that made

Miss Charlene a mercenary, not a Samaritan. And Jess hated her for it. Because he'd wanted to believe.

Jess had followed the details with a bitter interest. She'd met Ben Osgood from her sick bed and had taken his reward. Then she'd closed herself off from the opinions of the world by refusing all calls, by turning away all visitors. As if she felt she didn't owe them any explanation for her greed. Well, dammit, she owed Jess one! And he was going to get it. Then he was going to shout to her adoring public how she'd manipulated a child's tragedy and a grandparent's grief and gratitude into financial gain. Because they had a right to know that they'd been tricked, just as Jess had been tricked into thinking Miss Carter, was something special.

From the commotion in front of the hospital, he knew all their waiting had paid off. He cranked down the window and pitched out the remains of his cold coffee. The Styrofoam went over the seat back. Jess turned the key to bring his engine to life. And he watched.

The sight of her was like a fist to his gut. So small. As small as he remembered. And looking dangerously fragile in the wheelchair with her hands swaddled in white. Quickly she disappeared in the rush of newspeople and Jess was relieved. It gave him a chance to take a steadying breath, to quiet the sudden thunder of his heart.

"Get a grip, Jess," he muttered through the achy fullness in his throat. He couldn't afford to forget what this woman was. Hauling hard to drag up every vestige of his professional objectivity, he put the car in gear and edged up the circular drive into the center of the circus. She'd played them just right. By refusing information, she'd whet the press's need to know. He could well imagine her holding queenly court from her wheelchair, milking their sympathy for all it was worth. How he hated hypocrisy. Nosing his bumper toward the curb in front of an Eyewitness News van, he got out and shouldered his way through the tightly-woven throng. No one paid him any attention. Everyone was focused on Charlene Carter.

Again she knocked his logic out from under him. She wasn't in the wheelchair playing to the press with her taped hands. She was on her feet, tottering like a newborn foal, her wide, dark gaze sweeping the ring of faces, brushing by his without recognition. Her eyes were glassy with shock, and she was panting like a woodland animal run to ground. That look cramped his emotions up in a vise of protective fury. Couldn't they see they were scaring her? No way did she deserve this after all she'd been through. He could still remember the frail feel of her bones, the scurrying beat of her heart when he'd held her. She'd been so helpless yet so amazingly brave. That same fascination skewed his reason now, a tender compulsion to wrap her in his strength when hers was at a weary ebb. He found himself barging forward, ignoring the muttered curses of those he elbowed out of his way.

What if she wouldn't come with him?

When he cupped her elbows, he could feel her trembling, and that shivered right through to his guarded soul. He spoke to her, pitching his voice low and steady, a life preserver of calm in the sea of insanity around them. And she grabbed for it in desperation. She was so weak and disoriented that it was easy to steer her where he wanted. She made no protest.

Then she looked up at him, through eyes dark and luminous with relief, and he felt his heart take a hard ricocheting glance off his ribs. At that instant he wanted the reward of her gratitude more than he needed his next breath. And it was crazy. He knew it. But he couldn't control it. She held some compelling charm over his sterner sensibilities, and it shook him right to the core.

"Hey, J.T.! Let us have a taste of your exclusive, will ya?"

Jess didn't respond to the shout from the crowd of his compatriots, but it did serve as the necessary shock to bring him back to reality. To who he was and who she was. He couldn't forget again.

At least until he slid in behind the wheel of his car and looked over at the small figure crumpled in his passenger seat. She mumbled her address, then sank into oblivion upon a trusting sigh. She was too out of it to do up her own belt, so he reached across to strap her in. As metal clicked in metal, he glanced up into her face and was arrested by what he saw. Her eyes were softly closed, her lips gently parted as if in a deep natural sleep.

This was how she would look if he woke up next to her in the morning. His insides took a nasty turn. Damn, she was beautiful. Dark auburn strands framed skin of porcelain quality in casual disarray, making his fingers itch to brush them back into place. Her finely-etched features had been branded on his memory since the first time he'd seen her. Flawless. Delicate. Without artificial enhancement. But more than that. There was a vulnerable sweetness to her that pushed every button of his male guardian instincts and made him want to shelter her for the rest of his days and nights.

You're losing it, Jess.

He drew a deep, tight-chested breath and straightened away from her. Angrily he started the car. It screamed away from the curb, scattering reporters like hens in a chicken yard. He took no satisfaction from their looks of begrudging defeat. He felt no victory in snatching their prize feature out from under them. He was too busy trying to put a lid on the frantic scramble of his emotions.

Charlene Carter rattled him right down to the foundations. And that scared the hell out of Jess McMasters.

Coffee.

Charley could ignore the tease of sunlight and the sound of rattling pans but not that rich, full-bodied aroma of fresh-dripped coffee. She breathed it in, letting the scent tantalize her nose and stir her sluggish brain. A jump-start of caffeine was exactly what she needed.

A leisurely stretch dragged her toes beneath her covers with an unusual ease. In some surprise, she realized she was still wearing her pantyhose. Then came the sharp stab of remembrance through her hands. And contentment parted like the Red Sea.

Who made coffee?

She sat up too quickly, and the room moved in dizzying waves. Her sheet dropped away, and she was further confused to find herself clad in a lacy full slip and bandages. Not exactly her usual sleeping attire. She pressed fingertips to her throbbing temples, trying to force-feed logic into a stagnant mind. The hospital. She remembered leaving. The cab. Then nothing. How had she gotten inside? Undressed? In bed?

And who made coffee?

It came to her all at once with pleasure. Alan. Of course. Alan had come to take care of her. And a good thing, too, or she might have spent the night sleeping in the foyer of her apartment building. Never again would she take those painkillers full strength. It was like stepping in front of a truck.

The sound of pots and pans clanking in her kitchen was intriguing enough to coax her from the comfort of her bed. The lingering effects of the drugs made movement slow and concentrated, but she managed to find her terry bathrobe and slip it over the bulky wrappings on her hands. She avoided the mirror on her dresser. Thank goodness Alan wouldn't mind how she looked. Appearance had never mattered all that much to him. She couldn't believe he'd take time off work at this most critical point of his study just to be with her. That knowledge warmed her, making up for his failure to visit the hospital. There, she'd had competent others to care for her. Here, she had no one, and his consideration touched her heart.

She was smiling as she shuffled zombie-like down the hall and took a turn into her narrow galley kitchen. Then drew up short.

Confronting her was the nicest denim-molded backside she'd ever seen.

Whoever was rummaging about in the vegetable crisper of her refrigerator, it definitely wasn't Alan Peters!

Charley must have made some noise, for the forager called back cheerfully, "Good morning. How do you like your eggs? Over easy or scrambled?" He straightened and turned. With one look at her stunned features, he nodded to himself and said, "Scrambled."

Charley's mouth opened and closed several times in soundless wonder. Who on earth was this absolutely gorgeous man taking control of her kitchen with more natural ease than she'd ever managed? She just stared. She couldn't help it. His untidy brown hair looked finger-combed back from a moody brow and startlingly gray eyes. An overnight stubble darkened his firm jaw and made his mouth appear disarmingly soft in contrast. A white cotton sweatshirt clung to his broad shoulders and exposed very masculine forearms where its sleeves had been shoved up to the elbows. From beneath the hem of the blue jeans she'd already noticed in far too much detail, his feet were bare. "Ruggedly bed-rumpled" was the only way to describe him. And that evoked a more alarming question.

Where had he spent the night?

Noting her confusion with a slight lift of that mobile mouth, he turned back to the refrigerator. "How old is this milk?" When she didn't answer—couldn't answer—he popped open the spout and sniffed. His head jerked back as if a snake had jumped out at him. "Never mind." He upended it in the sink. "Why don't you go sit down? I'll have things ready in a minute."

Obediently Charley stumbled to the breakfast bar and collapsed on one of the high stools. She knew her jaw was sagging. She could feel the slack weight of it as she struggled valiantly for a stabilizing breath of air. She made a half-strangled noise like a sink gurgling.

"Coffee?" He was already pouring. She stared at the steaming mug in blank amazement. "Cream? Sugar? Though God knows if you have any."

"Black's fine."

"Ah, she talks. Good. If your hands are bothering you, that's your prescription on the counter. I filled it for you last night." At her distressed shift of expression he soothed, "Don't worry. You were dead to the world. I figured it would be safer to leave you than to haul you around in a wheelbarrow."

Charley's mind was still laboring. Emotions were dulled. When she should have been having hysterics, she found herself only mildly bewildered. No, she definitely didn't want to take any more painkillers. She already felt as stupid as a stump. All she could think of to say to him was, "You undressed me."

He smiled. It was a very slow, very wide, very sexy smile. "No need to thank me. It was no trouble at all." He was still grinning when he began to crack eggs into one of her little-used skillets.

Wait a minute. Just wait a minute, Charley thought. *There's a man in my kitchen who I've never seen before. He's making me breakfast in his bare feet. He's talking about filling my prescription and taking off my clothes as if he's been doing it for years. And I'm sitting here with a cup of coffee when I should be dialing 911!* Except she didn't feel threatened. Whoever he was, he could have done anything he wanted to her while she was knocked out cold. For all she knew, the entire Detroit Lions backfield could have filed through to have carnal congress with her. She'd have no way of knowing. But she didn't believe he'd taken any unfair advantage. And she didn't think he meant her any harm. So that left one last question.

Who was he?

"Here you go," he was saying as he slid a plate

in front of her. "This ought to perk you up a little."

Charley looked down at the eggs dressed up beneath several spoonfuls of salsa and framed by triangles of buttered toast. Then up at him as he dropped onto the opposite stool to take up his fork. As if sharing breakfast was the most natural thing in the world. He took a bite and sighed in appreciation.

"Dig in. Nothing's worse than cold eggs."

His eyes. Gray and clear.

"If the meter's still running, I'm going to have one heck of a tab," she mumbled.

"What?"

"You're the cabdriver from the hospital." Then she was less sure. "Aren't you?"

"No. I'm sorry." He put out his hand, and she reached for it unthinkingly. He caught just the tips of her fingers and curled them into his palm. It was a wonderfully gentle gesture. "I'm Jess McMasters." He waited as if that would mean something to her. Then his brow furrowed. "You don't remember me."

Charley examined his regular features. How could she forget such a face? "No. I'm sorry. Should I?"

He gave a tight smile, shuttering something behind that cool steel gaze, and shook his head. "Just from the hospital. I gave you a ride home in my car."

"I thought you were . . ." Charley broke that train of thought. Good Lord, he could have been anyone! She'd gone along with him as compliantly as a lamb. Thank heavens the only thing wolfish about him was his smile.

"I hope you don't mind that I made myself at home. You weren't in any shape to take care of yourself, and I had no idea who to call. So I just made you comfortable and bunked out on the couch in case you needed someone."

Charley could feel her features growing as hot as the salsa. She thought of him carrying her from the car, up three flights of stairs, tucking her into bed after stripping off her skirt and blouse. Of his big hands and his intense eyes on her while she was unaware. Of him moving about her apartment with an intimate familiarity that even Alan didn't share. It was disturbing. But it was strangely exciting.

Seeing her delightful flush of color, Jess was prompted to say, "I'm sorry if that undressing business embarrassed you. Had my eyes closed the whole time. Honest. I thought you'd rest better—well, hell, now that I think about it, I probably could have hung you up in the closet, and you wouldn't have cared a bit."

That teased a small smile from her, but her mind was still cluttered with ill-fitting puzzles. She stared at this handsome stranger and she had to wonder . . .

"Why?"

"What?"

"Why would you go through all that trouble for me? I don't understand. I don't know you, yet you've done things for me that no one else thought to do. Start from the beginning. What were you doing at the hospital?"

Jess took a minute to sip his coffee and compose his thoughts, then said smoothly, "I was visiting a friend and kind of stumbled into the middle of your little media party. You looked like someone who needed rescuing and I've always been a soft touch when it comes to helpless women."

Something was wrong with the way he said that. Charley couldn't pinpoint it. There was a rougher edge to his voice, a colder glint in his eyes. Something. She wasn't sure it should matter. But she knew it did. She pushed on with her questions, hoping for more clues about who and what Jess McMasters was.

"So you picked me up like a lost stray and brought me here. How did you get in? Where did this food come from? I know I didn't have eggs, and I've never bought salsa. Where did you get my prescription?"

He grinned at her with a disarming smugness. "I'm a resourceful kind of guy, Miss Carter."

Charley smiled back. "I think you're a very nice man, Mr. McMasters."

He looked uncomfortable with that claim. His stare lowered to his coffee cup, and the muscles of his face tightened. Modesty? Almost but not quite. What exactly?

"Your eggs are getting cold."

Charley stopped trying to figure him out. He'd

been there when she needed someone. Why make more of it than that? Mainly because handsome men didn't ordinarily pay her much attention. Oh, she got her share of interested inquiries, but none of them followed through. *She* wasn't interested in games of courtship, and that put them off in an instant. They wanted more joie de vivre in their women, not the studious quiet of a Charley Carter. The male ego was a fragile thing. It wasn't that she didn't want to coddle it; she just didn't know how. She'd never been good at personal relationships. What was it about Jess McMasters that made her feel her luck was about to change?

"Not hungry?"

She shook herself from her musings and made a concentrated effort to eat. Easier said than done. The simple effort it took to pick up a fork brought the sweat of pain to her brow. She had always taken the free movement of her fingers for granted until every little bend, every tiny twist, woke an incredible agony. By the time she brought the first forkful to her mouth, her hand was trembling.

Jess watched, his expression pinched. He'd never have believed the simple act of eating breakfast could be so heroic. He could see how much discomfort she was in, yet she kept going, without complaint, without reaching for the numbing crutch of painkillers. When she finished, he was nearly as breathless as she was.

"I'll clean up in here if you want to put yourself together." He said that gruffly, and Charley was reminded of how she must look. While he gathered up their dishes, she excused herself and headed for the bathroom.

Jess leaned against the sink and exhaled raggedly. This wasn't how he'd planned it. Oh yes, he was close to Charlene Carter. Too close. He'd carried her curled trustingly in his arms. He'd felt the enticing softness of her skin and watched the way her slow breathing rocked the filmy bodice of her slip. He'd watched for a long, long time, until he couldn't even name the disquieting emotions wadding up within his chest. He'd spent the evening wandering about her cluttered little apartment, poking into personal things she doubtlessly wanted to keep secret. And he felt guilty doing it. That was a first. He wanted to despise her. He wanted to call her on her less-than-honorable greed, but somehow the anger got lost whenever he was with her. He turned the water on full blast and began to savagely scour their plates. Didn't she know how to take care of herself? For the love of Mike, there wasn't even any food in her icebox except a couple of freezer-burned microwave dinners. How had she expected to feed herself? He slammed the faucet off and stood still, with eyes closed.

He wanted to get a story. That was his reason for being here, for spending the night on a too-short couch. Not because he was *nice*. He wasn't here to play housekeeper to a woman who could now afford a staff of servants to wait upon her every whim. What was wrong with him? No one had ever accused him of being *nice* before. He didn't even know anyone who used the word "nice" in normal conversation. He flung the tattered dishrag into the drain. No more Mr. Nice Guy.

Then he heard the shattering of glass and a soft cry. And Jess went running.

Three

She was leaning against the tiled wall of the bathroom with shards of a broken drinking glass scattered about her bare feet. When she turned to him, he was struck by the teary frustration in her face.

"I'm sorry. It just slipped. I couldn't hold on to it."

"Don't move. You'll cut yourself. I'll get it."

She stayed where she was, her breath laboring with agitation while he crouched to pick up the pieces and dump them into the plastic wastebasket.

"There. It's all right. No harm done. Just a glass."

She gave a hiccuping sob and stared down at her bandaged hands. "It's more than the glass. It's everything. I can't seem to manage the simplest things. I can't brush my teeth. I can't comb my hair. I can't even wash my face. I hate being helpless. I just hate it." She sucked a long, shaky breath and let it out with a contrite smile. "I'm sorry. I'm usually not such a baby."

"Which do you want to do first?"

She blotted her eyes on the sleeve of her robe. "What?"

"The teeth, the hair or the face?"

Her dark eyes went round. "Oh, you don't . . . I didn't mean for you to . . ."

"Now don't be such a baby," he scolded mildly.

"Mr. McMasters—"

"Jess," he corrected as he soaked and soaped her facecloth. "Shut your eyes."

"Jess—"

"Better shut your mouth, too."

While she stood with eyes closed and mouth frowning, he lathered her cheeks and chin and nose, trying to concentrate on each individual part rather than the enticing whole. It wasn't easy. With her skin freshly scrubbed and glowing, he was more aware than ever of the full curve of her lips and the dark sweep of her lashes.

"Hair next. Turn around," he ordered somewhat hoarsely.

Charley turned and sighed as he pulled the stiff bristles through her fine hair. She'd never known how wonderful it felt to be pampered. It made the humiliation easier to handle. He was being so good about all of it that she couldn't object to placing the currently impossible tasks in his capable hands. When he revolved her to face him once more, her eyes were still shut, and she was smiling slightly in contentment. Then she felt the distinct warmth of his breath brushing upon her lips. He was going to kiss her! Her mind registered the shock, but her body refused to respond. *Let him,* all her senses whispered in hope.

But then he was leaning back, and her eyes flickered open. The coldness was back in his gaze. She was sure of it now. And she still didn't know why. All she knew was the flutter of disappointment within her breast because she wouldn't get to feel the sweetness of his mouth on hers.

He was reaching for her toothbrush.

"Don't even think it," she warned with a strained laugh. "If you could squeeze out some of the paste, I can take care of the rest."

He did, then handed her the brush. She took it gingerly. "Sure?"

"Yes. Now thank you very much, but get out of here. I can manage everything else."

The hard glint was gone from his eyes. A teasing warmth was there in its stead. "Are you sure you won't need my help in the shower sometime in the near future?"

"I'll let you know, Mr. McMasters." She pushed at him with her knee, then used her toe to shut the bathroom door behind him. She found that she was quivering with an odd excitation. Shower, indeed. Her heartbeat seemed to skip several repetitions imagining it.

Charley managed her teeth and the change into a comfortable jogging suit without any challenging fasteners. Her hands ached fiercely, but she was proud of her scant accomplishments. She would do all right. Without Jess McMasters. And that brought a slightly wistful sigh. It had been nice, though. Very nice.

He was standing at her balcony slider finishing the last cup of coffee. She paused and let herself admire him, from the back of his head, over his wide shoulders, down his straight back and firm seat to long legs and athletic shoes. She eyed them sadly. She'd liked his bare feet. There was a kind of forbidden thrill in thinking of a man's naked toes tangling in her carpet. One she might never have again. Alan rarely visited her apartment. Too risky. And she didn't think his bare toes would be quite as provocative. Not a very charitable thought, but a truthful one. She couldn't picture Alan without his shoes and socks. He wasn't the type. Nor was she, and it was time she remembered that.

"Well, Mr. McMasters, I want to thank you for your kindness."

He turned, his brows elevated in surprise. "That has a rather final sound to it."

"I really appreciate all you've done, but I have to get to work and—"

"Work? You can't possibly be—"

"Just checking in, not doing any manual labor," she reassured him. She liked the thought of his concern. And the way it wrinkled the bridge of his nose just between his eyebrows. "I have some lab results to check, and it can't wait the full three weeks my doctor insists I take off."

"So you're throwing me out."

She blushed. "Well, not anything quite that rude."

"Politely asking me to leave, then. How are you going to get to work? Have you thought of that? You can't drive."

"I'll call a cab." There was an angle of stubborn independence to her chin. That delicate little chin he'd washed with soap and water.

"At your service," he told her with a roguish smile.

"Really, I can't—"

"Of course you can. You're at the university, right? That's what I read anyway. That's where I'm going, too. I . . . um . . . teach in the English department."

That wasn't a lie. He did have a night class once a week, instructing a group of bored underclassmen who thought journalism would be an easy credit. Not in his class. He didn't believe in easy As or sloppy work, a professional quirk of his that was the first lesson he taught. So if it wasn't a lie, why did he feel so churlish when her features lit with pleasure?

"Do you? Then we're practically neighbors."

Jess forced a smile that didn't reflect the sour state of his emotions. "Yeah. Something like that. Come on, neighbor. I'll give you a lift."

Part of Charley was ridiculously glad she didn't have to say goodbye to Jess McMasters, at least for a little while longer. The other part was thinking ahead to realities she'd let escape her. Like the reporters. And the money.

It was then her phone began to ring. And it rang four more times before she could leave the apartment. With each call Jess watched her color fade to a whiter shade of pale as she stammered her excuses. The haunted look was back in her eyes, the hunted panic back in her rapid little breaths. So the next time the phone shrilled, he yanked it up off the cradle.

"Carter residence," he growled in the receiver. "Miss Carter will not be giving interviews until further notice, so if you'll just leave her the hell alone—" His words broke off. His tone softened with chagrin. "Oh. Sorry. Yeah, just a minute." He passed the phone to Charley. There was an unmistakable tension in the lines of his face. "For you. It's personal."

She took the phone from him and hesitantly said hello. Then her features warmed with an intimacy that cut through Jess's heart. He wasn't aware that his teeth were grinding, only of a sudden ache along his jaw as he listened without appearing to listen.

"I'm fine. Thanks." Charley's eyes flirted up to Jess and away. "A friend," she told the man on the other end of the line. "No. You don't know him. Okay. I will . . . Don't worry . . . Okay, go ahead and worry. See you soon. Love you, too."

Jess's gut had writhed into a series of hard knots, and that last phrase jerked it tight. Until Charley hung up the phone and explained with a small, fond smile, "My brother," and his insides unraveled in relief. "Guess I'm as ready as I'll ever be."

The phone rang again, and her body snapped rigid.

"Don't answer it," Jess advised.

"I really should—"

"No, you shouldn't. Not if you don't want to. Where's your coat?"

He helped her on with it while the insistent rings continued into the dozens. Then the silence was almost as disturbing. Charley swallowed the feeling of invasion. Tonight she would get an answering machine to screen the calls. That would be the first thing she'd buy with the Osgood windfall. Rather ironic when she thought of it.

"Let's go."

They went down the back stairs of her building and made a wide loop to where Jess had parked his car. Charley stiffened when she saw several unfamiliar men lingering outside her usual exit.

"Don't look at them," Jess warned as he handed her into the car. But she couldn't help it. These strangers were pushing their way into her privacy, and the intimidation they forced upon her was slowly giving way to a simmering resentment.

"Why won't they leave me alone?" She didn't know she'd said that aloud until she discovered Jess's piercing stare upon her. There it was again. That glittering chill quickly masked by his smile.

"Just doing their jobs. Ignore them."

"Ignore them," she muttered. She sighed heavily and let her head rest against the back of his seat.

Ignore them. How? She couldn't answer her phone, she couldn't walk to the dumpster, she couldn't open her drapes without being confronted by their probing stares. Was that their job, to force her into hiding as if she'd done something wrong?

Then she started as Jess's knuckles lightly skimmed down her cheek. He didn't say anything. He didn't even take his eyes off the road. But that fleeting touch conveyed a wealth of reassurance. How could she help but be heartened? She'd survive it. Just as she'd get by with the limited range of motion in her hands. There were those who had to adjust to worse. Realizing that pulled her from her gloom of self-pity. She sat up in the seat and reached out to tap her fingertips on the hard curve of Jess's thigh. When he glanced at her, she smiled. He grinned back.

"Good girl."

Those two words were an admiring caress. Confident in her control, Charley found herself looking forward to getting back to the staid normalcy of her life. A premature hope, she found. For there they were. She saw them the minute Jess turned into the parking lot of the building where she worked. Swarms of them staking out the entrances with their camcorders shouldered and their microphones ready. She made a sound of stark dismay.

"You want me to take you back home? Maybe you need a little more time to prepare yourself for this." His voice was carefully neutral, distant after the warmth of a minute before. He was staring straight ahead, not at her.

An angry irritation firmed alongside the flutter of her nervousness. "I don't want to go home. I have work to do. But I can't talk to them now. I just can't. Jess . . ." She let that trail off, looking to him hopefully, already relying upon him as if he were a lifelong friend instead of a stranger who'd brought her home less than twelve hours ago.

"You're going to have to, Charlene, sooner or later."

"Later, then," she insisted. "And it's Charley."

"Okay, Charley. I'll get you past them, but you have to do something for me. Have lunch. I'll pick you up at eleven. Unless you have other plans."

Other plans? She thought of Alan and almost grimaced. No, not likely. "I have to eat, and you've already seen what I have at home."

"Pretty pathetic," he agreed.

Charley flushed and murmured, "I'm not very good on the domestic front."

"No kidding." He was sizing up the front of the building with a practiced eye. "There a custodial entrance to this place?"

"Around the side, I think."

Within minutes he'd slipped into the rear loading zone, out of sight of those hovering at the front, and came around to help her from the car. Charley smiled her thanks as she stood. She came barely to his shoulder. Again he was struck by how fragile she was. Feeling that twang of protectiveness cloud his better instincts, Jess took a step back, looking grim.

"You won't fool them forever. You'll have to come and go a different way every time."

"You sound like you know what you're doing, Mr. McMasters."

"I'm a—"

"Resourceful kind of guy," she finished for him. Then she touched his sleeve shyly with the tips of her fingers. "Yes, you are."

"Eleven," he reminded her sternly.

"I'll be ready."

And she watched him walk away with a decided breathlessness.

"Charlene, where are those muscle-tissue studies? I've been looking for them all morning."

Brusqueness was nothing new from the research fellow she worked under. It was Alan Peters's single-minded dedication that had drawn her to him almost two years ago. When he was in the middle of a project, he had all the sensitivity of sterile gloves, so Charley didn't expect him to drop everything to greet and gush over her. But a look would have been nice. A word of concern would have been appreciated. Especially since he was her unofficial fiancé.

"I need those figures, Charlene. Think you could find them for me?"

He stood in the center of the lab with a look of exasperated impatience on his face that she'd once thought endearingly boyish. This morning he looked just plain petulant.

"They're in my office," she told him quietly. "I'll get them."

Even as he nodded, he was turning, dismissing her. And it hurt. This morning it really hurt. Maybe it was because her burns throbbed so miserably. Maybe it was because of Jess McMasters's unexpected kindness. Whichever, she was blinking back moisture as she walked to her cubbyhole. Habit had her forming excuses for his indifferent behavior. He discouraged any type of personal display in the lab. There, they were researcher and assistant. He didn't have to warn her of the consequences should their relationship become common knowledge. Bad form, he said. A black mark on his chances to move into a senior position. A doctor did not carry on with his assistant. It wasn't professional. For nearly two years she'd listened and let him talk her into agreeing to the clandestine meetings after hours, to the hurried promises of what would come when he'd published enough work to gain notice. But staring down at the file where it lay in plain sight on top of her desk had he chosen to look there, Charley didn't feel terribly agreeable.

She jumped when his long fingers curled over her shoulders. "Hey, I'm sorry about that. You know how I get when you're away. I can't seem to get anything accomplished. We're a team. You know that. I really count on you, Charlene."

She'd just started to smile, feeling a little better,

when he added, "When will you be back to work?"

"Two, maybe three weeks. It depends on how fast I heal."

Alan's hands dropped away. She could imagine his scowl without having to witness it. "That was a dumb thing to do, Charlene. You could have gotten yourself killed. You couldn't have picked a worse time to be off, right when I need you the most."

The angry blur returned to her eyes. Picked? As if she'd chosen to broil her hands just to inconvenience him. Charley bit her lip to hold back words to that effect. They'd be counterproductive. He'd sulk and she'd end up apologizing, and she was in no mood to travel that familiar road. She drew a deep, diplomatic breath. "I won't be gone all that long. Besides, I can still help out, unofficially."

He made a disbelieving noise. "Like you're going to be any help when you come in dragging that entourage of camera nuts behind you. You wouldn't have believed some of the questions they asked me when I got here this morning. I had to call campus security to keep them out of the lab." Then he paused and said tersely, "What have you told them?"

"Nothing. I haven't told them anything." She lowered her head and went through the motions of meticulously straightening the haphazard stacks of papers on her desktop.

"Well, I don't need to warn you about the press. They can take the smallest thing and turn it into tabloid fodder. It will be better for us all if you don't even mention the lab."

"I won't, Alan."

"Good." He completely missed the clip of her tone. "Now, let's get some work done, shall we?"

Charley picked up the file and took another cleansing breath.

"Hey, did you forget the time?"

Charley brushed aside a stray lock of auburn hair as she glanced up at Jess. He was freshly groomed and garbed and more handsome than she'd remembered. It would have been easy to dismiss this morning as a product of an overmedicated mind—except here he was. And she couldn't ignore the very real snap of anticipation she experienced at the sight of him. "Is it eleven already?"

"Looks like it flies when you're having fun. What have you been doing? Cataloging the national debt?" He frowned down at the huge pile of data sheets she'd organized in her cramped work space.

"Just taking care of a few loose ends." She rolled her shoulders and tried to ease the nagging discomfort. She was thrilled by his intervention. For the last hour complaining nerve ends had made an impossible distraction, and having Alan stalk up to glare over her shoulder every few minutes hadn't helped one bit. Jess was one welcome blessing.

"Well, tie them up in a quick bow, and let's get

going. You look like you could use the break."

As he fit his hand under her elbow to assist her to her feet, Alan came screeching to a halt outside her door.

"Charlene?" His voice bit with accusation.

"Alan, this is Jess McMasters. Jess, Alan Peters."

The two men did quick summaries of each other. *Egghead,* Jess concluded. *Jock,* Alan sneered.

"You're not leaving, are you, Charlene?"

"I'm taking her to lunch," Jess interjected smoothly.

Alan's pale gaze stabbed at him with dissecting precision, then he turned to Charley with a wounded lift of his sandy brows. "I thought we'd get a little something later on. There are some things we need to discuss, Charlene."

"Maybe tomorrow, Alan. I really need to get away, and I did promise Jess lunch."

"Jess," Alan spat. "Who is this guy, Charlene?" he blurted out. "I don't remember you ever talking about him."

"Oh, we're very close," Jess drawled as he settled his dark glasses on his nose with an arrogant flair.

"He's a friend, Alan."

"I've been taking care of her since she got out of the hospital," Jess clarified just to enjoy the plentiful hues of red that colored the tall, slender scientist's face. *Where were you?* was his unspoken challenge.

Charley awkwardly tugged Jess's arm before the two of them came to blows. She couldn't imagine what had gotten into them. Alan was normally so civil, and Jess hadn't struck her as the belligerent type. "I'm famished, Jess. If you need anything, Alan, just give me a call at home."

The researcher scowled and said nothing.

"What's with your boss?" Jess demanded as he smuggled her out the service door.

"He and I are sort of . . . engaged," she mumbled reluctantly.

"That sounds sort of . . . vague."

Vague. Yes, it was. Very vague. She found herself brooding over it while he maneuvered his car out of the lot. Her sudden dissatisfaction was a surprise because she had the utmost admiration for her fiancé's work. And had been content with their arrangement until . . . until when? She darted a glance at her driver and experienced an uncomfortable revelation. Since Jess McMasters had come into her life. That was startling enough to make her purse her lips until after they'd been seated at a dimly-lit campus restaurant. And her mood didn't lighten when he launched his first question.

"So if Doc is your fiancé, why are you at lunch with me instead of him?"

The last thing she wanted to do was explain her situation with Alan to Jess. For one thing, it was personal. For another, she was aware of a sudden embarrassment that she'd never recognized before. What would he think of her if she told him the truth? That she was good enough to ply with kisses in a storeroom or at a distant research seminar but not to take to lunch in a public restaurant? She wasn't sure she understood it, so how could she expect Jess to?

"It's complicated," she said simply.

"And none of my business," he concluded for her. He accepted a menu from their waiter and turned to a less intimate topic. "So, Miss Carter, what does your boyfriend think of your sudden riches?"

Subtly Jess reached down into the pocket of his coat and switched on his voice-activated tape recorder.

Four

The money.

She kept thinking that if she ignored it long enough it would go away and she could get back to her well-planned life. But she knew she couldn't. She'd been given an incredible opportunity and she knew she shouldn't shirk it. It opened doors she'd never thought would be accessible. Only now she had to make certain she used the right ones. Ironic, she thought. She'd always believed that lots of money would alleviate worry, not increase it tenfold.

"Or is that none of my business, too?"

There was an unmistakable tartness to his tone that Charley was quick to ease. She didn't want to alienate Jess McMasters. He was the only friend she had right now, and she needed one badly. "No, it's not that. We just haven't had the chance to discuss it, is all." She gave an expressive sigh. "He's the only one who isn't dying to know the particulars."

Jess's voice softened with what she took for

sympathy. "We don't have to talk about it if you don't want to."

But suddenly she did. With him, she did. For some reason she felt a strong kinship with this handsome stranger, an intuitive link that told her he would understand. Unburdening her soul was not something she was comfortable doing, not to her family, not to Alan. But something in Jess McMasters's encouraging half-smile crooned, *Trust me,* and she wanted to.

"It's all happened so fast. I haven't had a chance to take it in. I'm used to having five dollars in my pocket and a couple of hundred in savings. Now all of a sudden I need a tax consultant, and everyone imaginable is crowding around with their hand out. You can't imagine . . ."

"No," he said softly. "I can't."

Their salads arrived and Charley was faced with the torturous task of controlling her fork. After several bites the effort didn't seem worth it for a few pieces of oil-drenched lettuce. She set her fork aside. "It's funny. I used to watch these big lottery winners whining about the horrors of having money. And I used to think, 'I should have it so bad.' Now I can see what they were complaining about."

Jess was chasing a tomato around the edge of his salad bowl, so he didn't look up right away. Finally he asked in a steely voice, "Why did you take the money, Charley?" Then his gaze lifted. She'd seen knife blades with a duller edge than the one in his eyes. For an awkward second she could almost feel that look pressed to her throat, then he smiled slightly to ease the intensity crackling from him. "Planning to take some exotic trips, buy a condo on the coast, pick up a sports car or two for starters?"

Her chuckle was low-pitched with amusement. It did funny things to his insides.

"Sorry to disappoint you, Mr. McMasters. I hadn't considered anything quite so glamorous." And amazingly she hadn't. Since Ben Osgood had presented her with the unexpected reward, her mind had been spinning in half a million directions. But never had she thought of squandering it on herself. Frugal habits of a lifetime were hard to push aside. She lived from paycheck to paycheck on a carefully-regimented budget. She even carried a calculator to go grocery shopping—on those odd occasions when she did. Now she wouldn't have to pinch pennies. Quite a concept.

"You don't look like the type to invest it all in stock portfolios," Jess was saying. His manner was relaxed now, openly friendly, as if he hadn't skewered her with his piercing stare seconds before. "Please don't tell me you're going to put it in your savings account to gather five percent for the next fifty years."

"What would you do, Jess? If it was yours?"

He blinked, taken totally off guard. Was she evading him or baiting him? His answer came out in a low, self-righteous drawl. "I wouldn't have taken the money."

Stupid, Jess. Real stupid. He could see the impact of his words. She stiffened slightly at the criticism, and all the animation blanked from her face. In the instant her gaze lowered to her nearly-untouched plate, he saw hurt swimming there, and it was a brutal slash to his conscience. He mentally scrambled to make up for it.

"But if I did," he began with a forced lightness, "I'd probably do something terribly self-centered like chuck my day job and rent some incredibly atmospheric loft where I could work on the great American novel and ignore the outside world. I'd have one of those slots in the door where my meals could be slipped in, so I'd never be distracted by such an ordinary thing as leaving my computer to eat."

She smiled, but it was remote, not like her earlier expressions. *Come back to me, Charley. Come back to me.*

"You're a writer."

Careful. His grin was crooked. "When I was little, all my friends wanted to be professional ball players. I wanted to be Michener."

"So," she began, sparing a quick smile up at their waiter as their meals were deposited, "why aren't you?"

Why aren't I? "Too practical, I guess. I let a little thing like paying bills get in the way of suffering for best/sellerdom." *That, and a greedy ex-wife.* But he wasn't here to talk about himself. Casually he shifted subjects again, trying to restore her accessible mood. "So now I teach instead of do. What about you? What do you do in that cute little lab coat? Trying to find a cure for the common cold to put a zillion over-the-counter drug companies out of business?"

You're losing her, Jess. Instead of responding to his playful banter, she grew more distant, more quiet. Like a turtle retreating into its shell.

"Nothing quite so vague as that," she answered solemnly. "We're researching juvenile diabetes. It's been kind of an obsession with me ever since my brother was diagnosed with it twelve years ago."

"I'm sorry." His fingers slipped over hers for a quick, supportive press and she melted. He could see the crisp reserve thaw as she soaked up his tenderness like a thirsty sponge.

"Oh, please don't be. Robert would hate that. He absolutely refuses to let anyone feel sorry for him. So I do what I can in ways he can't object to." She shrugged off her noble intentions with a little laugh. "He's a great guy. You'd like him." As she said that, her gaze canted up shyly and the connotations smacked Jess in the chest like a baseball bat to the ribs. He sucked in a quick breath.

"I'm sure I would."

He tackled his meal with single-minded vigor. He didn't want to meet her brother. He didn't want to hear about her noble causes. He didn't want her to smile up at him as if he were some wonderful nice guy. Those things were too taxing on his jaded heart. He had to push them away if he was to do what he'd set out to do. To find out why she'd taken the damn reward. He didn't want to like her. It messed up his focus.

Once he'd cleaned his plate in brooding silence, he glanced up, then stared in alarm.

"Charley? Hey, are you all right?"

There was no point in lying. She could feel the tension gathering between her brows in deep furrows. Her jaw was tight with it, her eyes pinched with it. She hurt. There was no pretending. "I'd like to go home, Jess," she said in a small voice.

"Do you have those pills with you? Charley?"

She made a face but produced them from her purse. He regarded the label. "Two, it says." He twisted off the top.

"One."

"Two!" He shook them out and leaned across the table. "Open." She received them reluctantly, then he sat back with a satisfied smile while she washed them down with water.

"I don't know what you're looking so smug for. You'll probably have to drag me out of the car and put me to bed."

"No problem."

Then he smiled, a wide, suggestive smile that made her throat feel as though the pills had stuck there and suddenly grown four sizes bigger. "Let's go, then, before I turn into spaghetti."

When they wound their way through the aisle of booths, she heard the whispers. She pretended not to, but she did.

Is that her?

I saw her picture in the paper.

All that money just for saving a kid she didn't even know.

She walked faster.

Charley could feel the medication working on the drive back to her apartment. First there was a blissful relief of the gnawing pain. Then that numbing sensation continued to spread, seeping along her limbs in a trail of useless relaxation until it reached her mind. Thoughts slowed and grew dreamy. She rolled her head on the back of the seat and looked at Jess. He looked dreamy, too. She was smiling rather foolishly when he turned into her complex and came to an abrupt halt.

"Charlene, you have company."

In response to his curt statement, she turned from her study of his profile to follow his displeased stare. And she gasped in dismay.

"Oh no."

News vans blocked her building entrance. A group of bored reporters milled restlessly upon the soggy grass. Waiting for her.

"They haven't seen us yet. You want me to turn around?"

She nodded jerkily.

When they were back on the main road, he cast a quick look at her. She was slumped in the seat, her eyes closed, her lips thin with distress. "Where to?"

"I don't know," she said miserably. "A hotel, I guess. I need someplace quiet so I can pull all this together."

"I have just the place."

It took about fifteen minutes to reach the quiet suburb where yards sprawled beneath the spread of giant still-bare maples. She was fuzzily aware of a bungalow-style house with a big open front porch and a mailbox that was overflowing. As Jess guided her inside, more disjointed impressions. Oak trim, wood floors, bright yellow kitchen with checkerboard linoleum. All that was missing were Ward and June Cleaver, she decided tipsily.

"You can sack out in the spare room. The sheets are clean. Bathroom's right there. You need something, you just holler."

"Who lives here?" she asked groggily.

"I do."

Charley stumbled. A house. That meant family. A wife and kids. Did he have them tucked away someplace in that sea of linoleum and old wood? She didn't want to think so and blurted out, "Are you married?"

That seemed to take him aback, then he shook his head. "Not anymore. Here you go."

He stripped the covers off a terribly inviting bed, and she went down into its wonderfully-soft embrace without a whimper. She felt his hands on her ankles as he lifted her feet, shucked off her shoes, and swung her legs onto the mattress. "Sleep tight."

"Thank you, Jess," she mumbled into the pillow. "You're a nice man."

"Yeah, right."

She felt, more than heard, him leave the room. She wiggled slightly, making a comfortable hollow, then sighed. Heaven. From the other room she heard the sound of another voice. A female voice. She frowned and tried to gather her sensibilities.

"Hi, Jess. It's me. Aren't you ever at home? I'll be in town for a couple days. Give me a call." Then that same throaty voice listed off a series of numbers, and Charley realized he must be playing back his answering machine.

"J.T., it's George. Got tickets for the Pistons. Call if you're interested." A beep, then another sultry message.

"Jessie, hi. Lose my number? I miss you. You left your jacket here the other night. Come and get it."

"It's Joanne. How are you? Haven't seen you around. Still make the best lasagna in town? You know me, always hungry for more. Call when you have an appetite."

"Jess, pick up." Silence, then the gruff male tones continued. "Just checking to see how the piece is coming. Have you managed to—" There was a loud click as the machine shut off. Then a heavy, engulfing silence she couldn't pull up from.

I miss you.

Call when you have an appetite.

Charley yawned and muttered a few choice expletives. "Call me," she mimicked in the same husky timbre, then gave an indelicate snort. With her eyes closed and her conscious drifting, pictures formed in that cottony void of thought. Images of herself draped in diamonds and sequins with a tuxedoed Jess McMasters on her arm. They were getting out of a gray stretch limo in front of a huge pillared mansion. She was tipping the driver with a fifty-dollar bill.

Then there were women there, gorgeously garbed, tugging at Jess's arms.

Come and get it.

Call when you have an appetite.

Jess McMasters, maybe you're not such a nice guy after all.

A scream. Charley could hear it clearly across the distance that separated them. The woman's scream as her mouth twisted with horror and those eyes reached for her in a desperate signal.

Charley bolted upright. Springs creaked softly beneath her, and then there was just the sound of her own ragged breathing. Her panicked gaze swept the room. It was dark and the shadows loomed deep and unfamiliar. Where was she?

She couldn't lie back down. The terror was there in those damp, almost knotted sheets, waiting for her to close her eyes again. So she wouldn't. It would be too much, twice in one night. But then she didn't have to close her eyes to see the face, to hear the silent scream.

Charley placed her bare feet on the floorboards. They were cold, but the shock was what she needed to clear some of the wool from her mind. Breathing in quick, jerky gasps, she came up off the bed to totter dangerously, then attempted a few awkward steps. When she was sure she wouldn't fall, she moved out into the hall and toward the faint light spilling in from the street. Her toe caught the edge of the sofa, and that sharp jolt of pain was all it took to start the flood of tears she'd dammed up since the day of the accident. She stood in the middle of the strange living room on one foot, dampness coursing down her cheeks, soundless sobs contracting her chest in a hard rhythm. She cried for them all: for the woman and her husband, for the little boy who was suddenly all alone, for herself because she'd never had the time before. For the pain and the fear and the nightmare that wouldn't go away. For the confusion that wouldn't leave her mind and the changes that were tearing her life apart. There seemed no end to those tears, to her grief until . . .

"It's all right."

He'd come up as quietly as a shifting shadow. Without thinking of hesitating, Charley stepped into his embrace. *How well we fit,* was her first coherent notion, her head in the curve of his shoulder, her hips against the long, hard line of his straddled thighs. He held her without offering comment or compassion because she didn't need them. She needed this, the wordless comfort of his strength, the security of his arms around her, and the sturdiness of his chest as a resting place. And for a fleeting second it seemed so very familiar. Then his hand rose to lightly touch her hair, fingers moving slowly to ply its silken texture between them. And the mood altered, subtly, disturbingly. Charley leaned away but not out of the circle of his grasp.

"I'm sorry," she muttered, unable to look up at him. Her apology was as rambling as her flustered thoughts. "I didn't mean to wake you. I didn't know where I was and I stubbed my toes and I had this awful dream. I'm sorry to be such a b-baby."

His palm curved to the shape of her jaw, tipping her head up even as his thumb drew down on her chin, bringing a part to her lips. His voice was unnaturally husky.

"Baby, you're the bravest woman I know."

And he was kissing her.

Charley wasn't prepared for it. Her gasp was soft and wondering as his mouth sought hers. From the way he jerked, he was just as surprised by the sudden sweet contact. But he was quicker to recover. The kiss grew in intensity from gentle seeking to urgent taking, and Charley was helpless to do more than ride out the wild surge of sensation. She was limp and breathless by the time he finished.

"Jess . . ."

"Don't say anything," he rumbled gruffly as he brought her back into the safety of his embrace. She could feel his racing heartbeats and quick, uneven gulps for air and sanity. And for some reason his loss of composure calmed her.

What was he thinking? Jess squeezed his eyes tightly shut and tried to ignore the soft tickle of her hair beneath his chin. How had things gotten so carried away? He'd brought her here to his home to provide her with a harbor in her sea of stormy troubles, to coax her into lowering her guard, not to seduce her or lose himself in the process. Her tears undid the best of intentions. The feel of her against him broke the fetters of control. It was crazy. His heart was chugging away like an engine gathering steam. His kiss had rocked the foundations of passion. Yet she stayed in his arms, trusting him when he couldn't even trust himself.

"You'd better get back to bed," he said hoarsely. It was a warning. He wasn't sure how much more of her innocent temptation he could stand. He wasn't expecting her reply.

"No." Fright trembled in that single word, and his mood jerked in an instant from desire to tender reassurance. She took a shaky breath, fighting for courage. "I think I'll sit up for a while." Until her demons left her.

"I'll sit with you."

"You don't . . ."

But he was already leading her to a big fabric-covered recliner. He surprised her by sinking onto its wide seat without releasing her. As he kicked up the footrest and at the same time leaned back, she found herself nestled quite snugly into his side. And after experiencing the sturdy pillow of his chest, she had no inclination to move or seek a softer comfort. It was a long while before she could sleep again, however. Not because of the pain in her hands, not because of the dream. Because of his kiss.

Should she be lying with him like this after experiencing what she had in his arms? What had that been, exactly? Nothing short of cataclysmic, she concluded with a sigh. He'd sucked raw sensation right up from her soul. Oh, it wasn't as if she'd never been kissed, but compared to the scorching sensuality of Jess, kissing Alan had all the excitement of photocopying research findings—all rote movements expended toward a predictable end. She wasn't being fair to Alan, she knew. He was nothing like Jess. He was serious, dedicated, detached from the distractions of passion. Jess McMasters *was* passion. Everything about him seethed with it, from his wide, lazy smile to the glittery brilliance of his stare. It simmered beneath the smooth surface of his words and shook through the restrained forays of his touch. He wasn't satisfied trying to improve life from the other end of a microscope; he wanted to live it. That made Jess McMasters uniquely appealing to her reserved position on the sidelines of living. And dangerous. Because he hadn't wanted to stop with just the kiss.

And neither had she.

Everything was so steady in her relationship with Alan. They knew what to expect from each other, their roles well defined and sensible. She knew on any given day, at any particular time, exactly what he'd be doing or thinking. No surprises. She'd liked that about him. She could count on him implicitly, and for one raised in a regimented world, that was very important to her. He might not have the fire of a Jess McMasters, but neither did he upset her world with these rifts of panicky emotion. He had never in the two years of their acquaintance demanded what Jess had in that searing kiss—that she take what he gave and return it in kind. A frightening concept. A temptation she didn't dare explore. Because though Alan might not ignite the same spark of response, she owed him her faithfulness. And that meant denying the hornet nest of feelings Jess stirred up inside her.

He hadn't meant anything by it, she told herself sensibly. He was used to inspiring women to a frenzy of longing, with his charismatic looks, with his casual confidence, with his smoldering sexuality. It was part of his nature but not necessarily part of his intent. His kiss said he wanted her at that moment, but that didn't mean he would feel the same way next week, the next day, or even the next hour. He was a man of the impulsive moment, and she couldn't be like that. She needed the stability of long-range plans. She evaluated risks until they became certainties. And Jess was a risk she couldn't take because there was nothing certain about him. She wasn't like those throaty-sounding sirens on the phone, content to wait for his mood to shift in their favor. She demanded an amount of commitment, and she sensed he wouldn't give it. He wasn't a staid, dependable Alan Peters. He'd swept into her life on an unexpected wind and would blow back out just as freely. And she couldn't afford to let him carry her heart away with him. He was dangerous. Because when he'd kissed her, she'd been willing to throw all logic aside. She'd been willing to grab at the risk just to ride that wild wind for the night. Because she'd wanted to make love with Jess despite all that reason told her.

What if she used the money to become the kind of woman who could hold him? It was a brief, whispering thought just on the edge of falling into slumber. What would it take to have Jess McMasters? An eclectic loft and the freedom to explore his creativity? A facade of sophistication only money could buy? Surely it wasn't a dowdy researcher in a rumpled lab coat whose idea of culture grew in a dish. What? She had the resources. What she lacked was the experience. What would it cost to make a man like Jess love her?

Five

Something was burning.

The hot, unpleasant scent jerked Jess from a heavy sleep. He woke to confusion. There was an ache low in his back, and his neck was cramped to one side. How had he come to nod off in his chair? He'd wakened at the computer keyboard on more than one occasion, but he wasn't normally the recliner type. It was reserved for the evening news, nothing more. He read his morning *Free Press* in the bathroom while shaving or at the table over his first of countless cups of coffee. He wasn't sedentary enough to enjoy lingering in the cushy chair. Sue had bought it for him several Christmases ago. Just another sign of how little she'd understood him.

His nose wrinkled. Toast. That's what was burning. Then he remembered the warm little figure tucked into his side all night and he smiled. Should he go and see what kind of disaster she'd made of his kitchen, or first, call the fire department? He gave a long, lingering stretch and snapped the footrest down. Still smiling, he ambled-toward the smell of smoke.

"Disaster" was a mild description. She was like a four-year-old in the kitchen. A very sexy-looking four-year-old. Opened cartons of milk and juice tottered precariously on the edge of the counter. One of his gourmet whisks leaked egg yolks all over the top of his stove, where she'd laid out an odd collection of pots and pans. What was she planning to use the double boiler for? Butter sizzled and smoked in one of his best coated sauté skillets awaiting the potatoes she'd managed to whittle down into skinny parings. The bread wrapper was dangerously close to melting against the hot edge of the pan.

" 'Morning," he called out cheerily as he scooted the bread to one side.

"Oh!" Charley jumped, her fingers opening reflexively. The egg she'd been holding burst on his linoleum. She stared down at the mess in dismay, then slowly lifted her anguished gaze to his. Then she scowled. "What are you laughing at? I was trying to make you breakfast."

Still chuckling, he advanced into the disaster zone, turning off the burner, popping up the blackened toast, and turning off the coffee maker where a steady stream of clear water ran through an empty filter. Then he turned to her where she stood, a trembling wreck in the middle of the culinary carnage. She looked crestfallen. Everything inside him turned to mush.

"Oh, baby, I wasn't laughing at you," he said softly, although the humor quirking his mouth belied his words. "It's been a long time since anyone's wanted to make me breakfast. It's . . . nice. Now, get out of my kitchen and let me finish up before you burn the place down." He took the sting out of his words by leaning forward to glance a kiss off her brow. Then he gave her a no-nonsense push out.

"If you expect breakfast from me, in the future you'll have those neat little microwavable deals in the freezer," she told him haughtily as she picked her way around the egg remains.

Grinning, Jess said, "I'll pick some up at the store."

Charley stopped dead, her face fusing a becoming crimson. She was talking about starting the day with him as if it would become a habit. And he'd accepted without pause. Feeling as if she'd just taken a handful of her painkillers, she moved numbly to drop into one of his Windsor dining-room chairs.

She watched him work the kitchen with a practiced efficiency. He cleaned up her clutter and started over with clean countertops and a properly-filled coffee filter. Part of her was admiring the view. The other was spinning frantically.

She'd never waked beside a man before. Asleep, Jess McMasters was beautiful. Relaxation erased all the sharper angles from his face, and the curve of lashes resting softly upon his cheeks lent a heart-clutching sweetness to contrast with his rough morning stubble. She'd headed for the kitchen in a mad scramble, seeking its frustrations to distract her from a more subtle agitation. Then he'd kissed her again, just a brief brush of his lips that branded her brow like a hot iron. Didn't he know what damage he could do with such casual intimacies? Suddenly she was glad for the pain in her hands so that she had something on which to concentrate other than the way Jess's gray sweatpants clung in sculpting swells whenever he moved. For heaven's sake, she was a scientist. It wasn't as though human anatomy held any mysteries for her. Still . . .

"Here you go."

Charley glowered enviously at the puffy omelet that oozed diced potatoes, peppers, onions, and grated cheese. He puzzled over her reaction. "Not hungry?"

"It would be like destroying a work of art," she observed with a wry twist to both words and smile. "How did you learn your way around the kitchen?"

"Self-preservation. I enjoy a good meal, so I had to make do. I think of it as therapeutic, you know, all that mashing and chopping. Great way to relieve stress. In warmer weather, I grow my own vegetables and parsley." He paused with a hesitant pride of accomplishment. "I like digging around in the dirt. Bet you think that's a silly thing for a grown man to admit to."

Somebody had. That was all too apparent as he awaited her response. He was coiled defensively for her opinion. Guarded shadows clouded his stare. Who had hurt him with their scorn? Charley vowed right then she wouldn't follow suit.

"No," she said softly, warmly. "I don't think it's silly at all. Spoken by a woman who watches bacteria multiply for a living."

"Ah, so that explains the inside of your refrigerator."

"Very amusing." She was more than willing to let him tease her if it would bring back the animation of a moment before. She took a bite of his creation and savored it. "This is great. A man who can cook and cultivate. Your wife was one lucky woman."

The light went out of him. Her thoughtless words pulled the plug. So that was it. Now Charley knew who had torn the heart and soul from Jess McMasters. And she felt an overwhelming dislike for the woman she'd never met.

"No. Sue liked to eat out. She didn't have time to watch water boil." His voice was chillingly quiet. With his stare focused on his plate, Jess ate in silence for several minutes while Charley struggled for something to say. How she wished she was clever at conversation. Never had she felt so inadequate as at this moment when she wanted desperately to reach out to him.

"I'm sorry, Jess," she murmured in an uneasy attempt at compassion. He looked up at her with a tight-lipped smile. The raw sorrow of that look broke her heart.

"Hey, it's no big thing."

Of course it was.

"Any children?" Charley blundered onward, then cursed her clumsiness.

He shook his head. "No. She didn't have time for that, either. I like kids. I think of them as smart little adults who haven't formed any bad habits yet."

Charley felt an urge to cry. What kind of woman could turn away from this treasure of a man? If he was hers . . . She severed the thought she had no business thinking. He wasn't hers. He wouldn't be hers. There was no point in continuing the hypothesis.

"It's Friday," he announced suddenly. "Got plans for the weekend?"

"Other than changing my name and identity to escape the press?"

He gave her a crooked smile. "Yeah."

"Oh, I don't know. I'm tired of hiding out. I have to pull myself together and face them with some answers. Only problem is, I seem fresh out of them. I have to be at a civic award presentation the Monday after next, and just thinking about it gives me hives. I'm not good at public speaking. I'm basically a social washout when it comes to people."

Jess started to scoff. Then he saw the very real distress in her averted gaze. So he shifted gears.

"Isn't there someplace you can go for the weekend? Sort of a mini-vacation to let things cool down around here? By the time you get back, you'll be old news, and they'll have moved on to something else. Then you'll have a nice quiet week to work on your speech."

"You think so?"

She sounded so hopeful that he almost caved in with guilt. Almost. His smile was smooth and convincing. "Sure. That's the way these things work. Where can I take you?"

She had an idea but quickly dismissed it. "No, I can't ask you. You've done too much already. I'm sure you have better things . . ."

"Not a thing. Honest."

What about the sultry-voiced Joanne and your other panting girlfriends? She didn't say it. Suddenly she was arrogantly pleased to have surpassed them in his attention. That should have been warning enough for her to back away from his offer. She shouldn't have cared where she stood in Jess's rankings.

"A weekend away." How good that sounded. And she did know just the place where she could regroup and return to take a stand before the press. She remembered the barrage at the hospital and tried to hold to that confidence. If only she wouldn't freeze up. Like hounds, they could scent fear and would be merciless. She could feel her stomach tensing, readying for a blow. Then Charley forced a redeeming breath. She wouldn't think about it now. That was three days away. Three days for her to heal and grow strong. A real hero. She was smirking when Jess called her on her thoughts.

"What?"

"Nothing. I was just thinking how heroic I am. Those reporters are going to be very disappointed when I get lockjaw."

"Hire a press secretary to handle it for you," he suggested noncommittally as he began to clear the table.

"But that would cost—"

"What do you care? You can afford it." That sounded almost angry, and Charley looked to him for an explanation, but he'd already turned toward the kitchen.

"I have other plans for the money."

"Like what?"

"I'll show you. Pack a bag."

They were still there. Jess counted one, two, no, three of them lingering outside the apartment complex. He cut the engine, glad he'd insisted Charley stay at his place while he went to fetch her things. She was going to attempt a shower. Better he not be there. He'd be too tempted to offer his assistance. After she'd gone to putty in his arms over that kiss, he knew it was wiser to keep his distance.

"Hey, Jonesy. Kind of far from home, aren't you?" he called to the cameraman who was cooling his heels at the complex's security door.

"Hi, J.T. Same goes for you. What are you doing here?"

He dangled a set of keys. "Visiting a friend." He let go a wolfish grin and the other man laughed.

"Lucky you."

"What's going on?" Jess gestured to the others with a lift of his brows.

"Oh, some celebrity story. We're beginning to call her the Invisible Woman." His gaze sharpened as Jess unlocked the door. "Hey, how about letting us slip in with you."

Jess smiled. "That wouldn't be ethical."

"Ethical? Since when do you give a hang about ethics, you son of a—"

Jess pulled the door shut until he heard the firm sound of its lock.

The phone in Charley's apartment was ringing when he opened the door. In two long strides he reached it. "Hello?"

There was a pause, then a clipped voice. "I'd like to speak to Charlene."

"She can't come to the phone right now. She's . . . busy."

"Who is this?"

"Who is *this?*" Jess could imagine Alan Peters

seething with fury, and it pleased him to no end. The line went dead. Grinning, he replaced the receiver and went to pack Charley a bag.

"Where are we going?"

Jess thought it a logical question since he was behind the wheel and she was dozing contentedly in the seat beside him. It helped to concentrate on the road. It distracted him from the memory of how she'd looked coming out of his bathroom with her hair wet and sleek and her soft curves concealed by the generous folds of his Lions jersey. That had knocked him for a loop, and he'd yet to stop spinning. He was very particular about the ladies he allowed in his shower in the A.M. hours, and Charley looked so at home that it would be easy to slip into the routine of thinking she belonged. That he had to avoid. By the end of the weekend he would have all his answers. He would say goodbye and write his story, then go on to something else. Because that's what he did for a living. And Charley couldn't be more to him than just another interview.

Except she already was.

From the moment she'd run back to that burning car, she was already more to him than he could comfortably admit.

Charley opened her eyes and glanced around for landmarks. "Almost there. Take the next exit." Then she closed her eyes again. Jess had talked her into taking one of her pills, and it gave her a nice numbing aura of serenity. She let her mind drift until she heard Jess downshift and the sound of a different paving material grinding beneath the wheels. "Take a left. It's just up ahead. Turn at the arch."

Jess followed her directions and was soon pulling into a neat compound of log buildings set back into the pines. "Looks like Boy Scout camp."

"You were a Boy Scout?"

"Where do you think I learned to be such a—"

"Resourceful kind of guy." She grinned and straightened in the seat. "I don't think it was from the Boy Scouts."

As the car rolled to a stop, they were approached by a slightly-built man. His features split in a broad smile as he recognized Jess's passenger.

"Charley! How's my girl?"

She stepped out of the car and right into the man's arms. Jess got out a bit slower and observed the two as they hugged enthusiastically. Something gnawing and unpleasant twisted in his belly and knotted up around his throat. His eyes narrowed into glittery slits. Who was this guy? Another boyfriend? Someone whom she trusted enough to come to for refuge. Jess had grown used to being the one she depended upon, and he wasn't sure he liked the invasion of territory.

Then the young man looked over at him curiously and Jess's hostility melted. He didn't need to be introduced. The similarity was striking between brother and sister.

"Robert, this is Jess McMasters. Think you can put us up for the weekend?"

Robert advanced around the front of the car with his hand extended. His clasp was firm. "Hi, Jess. Yeah, sure, Charley. It's not the Ritz, but then our rates are better. Grab your gear and follow me."

Jess got their bags and walked behind the two Carters. So this was the brother. He didn't look like someone suffering from an incurable disease. There was too much spontaneous life to Robert Carter. He was small and wiry, nearly sizzling with energy. And Jess liked him immediately, just as Charley had predicted. There was a direct, "don't hand me any crap" attitude about him that Jess admired in a man, and if he wondered over this stranger's relationship with his sister, he passed no judgment. At least, not yet.

Jess stepped into Robert's cabin and said the first thing that came to him. "Wow!" From the outside the structure seemed small, but inside, the spaces soared to an awe-inspiring peak of rounded logs, glass, and fieldstone. One whole wall was windows, interrupted by a huge stone fireplace. Before its hearth lay a sheepskin rug, and Jess was taken by the wildly erotic image of Charley stretched out naked on that fleecy nap with the firelight bronzing her skin. He hauled his stare away from that site of wicked fantasy to study the rest of the cabin.

The ground floor was one big room with a loft over the kitchen and eating area. The decor was rugged Adirondack rough-cut logs and boldly-woven geometrics. It was a place where a man could lose himself to leisure and long, quiet nights, and Jess fell in love at first sight. He could picture himself busy at the computer keyboard in the overhead loft and Charley down here waiting for him in front of a roaring fire with a meal of cheese, bread, and wine—something she didn't have to cook. It was a wonderfully-vivid illusion, and it did funny, cramping things inside his chest.

"That all right with you, Jess?"

"What?" He turned to Robert and was dismayed to feel heat crawl up his neck and cheeks. It wasn't as though the man knew what he was thinking about his sister. Or was it too obvious to everyone but Charley?

Robert smiled tolerantly. "I said you can bunk down here on the couch, and Charley can take my room upstairs. I'll find other accommodations." He gave a bawdy wink, and Jess grinned in response. Yeah, he liked Robert Carter just fine.

As Jess gave his bag a toss toward the end of the couch, a loud bell gonged.

"Just in time for lunch," Robert announced.

"Come on. We can't keep the tribe waiting." At Jess's puzzled look, he asked, "What has Charley told you about this place?"

"Nothing."

Robert gave his sister a severe glower. "Well, I hope you weren't expecting a luxury resort. Welcome to Camp Carter. I like to think of it as juvenile diabetes boot camp. C'mon. I'll introduce you to the troops."

The troops were a group of adolescents and preadolescents who, if lunch was any indication, were as rowdy as any other kids their age. The teenage boys shook his hand with grown-up sobriety, and the girls were outrageous flirts. He'd catch them staring at him and grin to send them into gales of nervous giggles. The place had a charming atmosphere that was a mixture of Scouting and the marines; strict regiment wrapped up in relaxed good humor. Robert was the driving force. That was plain to see. The kids were drawn to him as if he were some kind of smiling messiah. He treated them with a gruff affection and controlled his small staff with a velvet fist. He would have done any general proud.

Over the midday meal the troops were lectured on the proper quantity and content of the food on their plates in jovial but nonetheless serious fashion by a pretty brunette. From the looks she cast at Robert, Jess figured out where Charley's brother meant to find lodgings and said so to

Charley while they were walking alone in the vast wooded acres stretching out behind the cluster of cabins. She looked properly shocked at first, then had to agree.

"Rob's always liked the ladies. I think he feels pressured to enjoy them as much as possible in case later on he can't."

Jess wanted to ask what she meant by that, but her expression had gone so sad and introspective that he opted for silence instead. They walked for a time on the soggy bed of pine needles until they came abruptly to a clearing. There in its center was a small, crystal-clear pond, and on the other side Jess could see the cabins of the camp. They must have gone halfway around. It was a beautiful spot. He could picture the kids squealing and splashing in the water during the warm summer months. He drew in a deep lungful of cool spring air, tasting the tang of pine and loamy earth.

"This is paradise," he declared quietly. When Charley shot him a wondering glance, he grinned self-consciously. "I was born and raised in inner-city Chicago. I was sixteen before I found out that grass was nature's ground covering instead of concrete. So humor me if I go all gushy on you."

Charley smiled warmly up at him, and his heart staggered. It was more than he could take, this pristine place, this enigmatic woman. He dragged his stare away from hers to look out over the small lake, trying to dredge up some degree of control. Just when he thought he was successful, she delivered a one-two punch to put him out for the count.

"Remember when you asked what I was going to do with the money?"

"Yeah," he mumbled cautiously.

"It's going here, in this land, in those kids, in my brother's dream."

Six

"For as long as I can remember, Robert's been talking about a place where kids could go to come to terms with their illness. I don't know how different things might have been for our family if we'd had one when Robert was diagnosed."

They had come to a weatherworn gazebo situated to give the best view of the lake. Jess imagined the sunsets would be gorgeous from this angle. Charley leaned her elbows on one of the rails and stared wistfully across the water toward the cabins.

"Our family fell apart," she said sadly. "You can't imagine how awful it was." Jess came to stand beside her, not touching but close enough to lend support. "It hit him when he was twelve. He and Dad had been inseparable. Dad saw him as having a career in the family business. Dad's chance for immortality. They spent all their time together doing man-things, you know. Then one day Robert went from a healthy, athletic boy ready to carry on my father's dreams to the critical list at the hospital. His pancreas had shut down, and his blood sugar shot through the roof. No warning or explanation. That was the hardest on Dad. No one could tell him why Robert. Type I isn't inherited. It's nongenetic and spontaneous. There's no known cause and no cure. There's been speculation that it's caused by a virus with a link to chicken pox or mumps, but the virus can't be isolated. Dad blamed himself, then Mom, then the whole world. He finally just took off after Robert had been home for a couple of months. He couldn't handle it. Dammit, Jess, none of us could."

He put his hand on the back of her neck, gently massaging the wads of tension knotting there, coaxing her by his silence to continue.

"Mom overreacted, too, in the other direction. She smothered Robert, fussed over him every minute of the day. The entire focus of her life was on how much he ate and when and what his sugar level was and did he get his insulin. She was a complete wreck. No one could convince her that Robert wasn't going to die at any second. Everything we did revolved around him."

"And you resented the hell out of it," Jess supplied softly.

She looked up at him in surprise, denial defined clearly in the set of her features. Then she blinked and that surprise turned inward. "Yes," she confessed with an equal quiet. "Yes, I did.

Not Robert, never Robert, but the disease that distorted our lives. In a way, I can understand why Dad ran. It was so frustrating at first, and later there was always the fear that something would go wrong, that we'd make some mistake and lose him. But Robert, he was the brave one. He never let it get to him. He just charged right on with whatever he wanted to do and let us worry. That's why this place is so special, so important to us. We take kids like Robert when he was diagnosed and pull them out of the smothering family unit. For two weeks we teach them diet and exercise and the fact that they have control. That's the key. They have control. They love Robert. He's a living example of how to succeed and beat the odds. What he's doing is important and worth every penny I can give him."

"So you're going to give it all to him."

"Oh, I don't think he'd let me do that. You don't know him well enough to see what a proud man he is. If he knew that I was working to—"

"To what?"

She took a breath to slow her want to pour out the whole truth. She wasn't quite ready for that. She didn't want to overwhelm Jess with all her emotional baggage. Enough had been said for one day. "We'd better start back. It gets dark out here real early, and dinner is like clockwork. A minute late, and dinner's gone."

As much as he wanted to detain her and demand the rest of the story, Jess let her go. He followed at a slower pace, trying to cull all the information she'd given and what he'd picked up between the lines. He had a pretty good picture of what it was like for a young Charley. Scared, isolated, her needs overlooked in favor of her brother's. Sure she'd want to strike back. He admired her immensely for not taking her anger out on Robert. She worked through it another way, by attacking the cause, not the result. No wonder she panicked when her feelings were laid bare for the inspection of strangers. She wouldn't know how to react as the center of attention. She'd always been the silent support behind the scenes, not the dynamic focus. That was Robert. He had enough charisma for both of them. Of course she would run back to a blazing car to save a stranger. She'd been a rescuer all her life. It was ingrained.

Now what the hell was he going to do?

He was spared from finding an immediate answer. Robert swooped down upon them and sucked up all their energies with his relentless enthusiasm. When he wasn't pushed into taking part in the camp activities, Jess was content to sit back and observe them. Especially Charley. Something happened to her around those kids. She blossomed and the beauty of the transformation was breathtaking. Thick emotions jammed up around his heart, making his chest feel so heavy he could barely breathe. There was a paralyzing ache in his throat, and by the evening's end he was doing well to nod and force a smile. Robert and his bubbly girlfriend, Shelly, escorted them back to the cabin and refused to leave before midnight. They gathered around the fireplace, sitting cross-legged on the sheepskin rug and telling the most outrageous stories until their sides were sore from laughter. Then, without warning, Robert seized Shelly by the arm and bade them a brisk goodnight.

Still smiling, Jess shut the door behind them, then turned to be confronted by the pulse-stopping sight of Charley before the fire. The blaze burnished her hair to a dark, molten flame, and he felt a similar heat race through him. That pagan image of her stretched out before the flames returned like a sock to the solar plexis. At that moment a sane man would have run, not walked, to spend the night in the safety of his car. But there was nothing sane about the storm of sensations gathering inside him. Nor about the pull of inevitability that drew him across the room.

Charley's gaze lifted to his, and she smiled, completely unaware of her allure, or of the danger she was in. She was so damn naïve that Jess hated himself even as he sank down on his knees and caught her innocently-inviting face between his hands. He hauled her up against him, securing her lips before a startled squeak of sound could escape them. He drank of her sweet, unpracticed response like a man who'd thirsted long and turned down many a drink until he'd found the one that would quench him. She could. He knew it the second he reached deep to taste the inside of her mouth and she made a soft noise that spoke of surrender and simple satisfaction. God, it drove him to the limits of reason.

Jess wasn't sure what happened. Maybe in his eagerness his fingers clenched too tightly in her hair. Maybe in his impatience his kiss grew too rough. Or it could be she was alarmed by his body's ready indication that he was anxious to rush more intense intimacies. Whatever it was, her willingness became reluctance. He felt it, but it took a while for the rest of him to obey the signals from his mind to let her go. The instant his grip slackened, she lunged back and scrambled to her feet. He didn't look up. He didn't dare, too afraid of what she'd see carved into his expression. It was bad enough to hear the frantic slap of her feet as she ran up to the negligible safety of the loft. He dropped face first onto the rug and groaned his frustration into its thick wool. For a long while he didn't move. He was afraid if he did, he'd go up after her and that wasn't what he wanted. At least he told himself it wasn't. She'd made herself clear enough for an idiot to understand.

Idiot. Jess, you're an idiot. Spend all this time

getting her to trust you, then try to jump her bones the minute she lets her guard down. Swift move. A real class act.

He flopped onto his back and fixed an unregistering stare on the high peak overhead. His palms were damp. His pulse was going crazy. *Geez, you're in worse shape than one of those lusty adolescent boys next door. Calm down! It's not as if you haven't had a woman in years.*

It was then it struck him. It wasn't just any woman he wanted. It was this woman. Maybe he'd known it all along, and that's why he was so desperate to pursue this story. To find some flaw in her too-good-to-be-true sincerity. So he could safely push her out of his thoughts, out of his foolish heart. If she had a fault, it was that she cared too much for others and not enough for herself. Was that a flaw? He didn't know. What he did know was that he was wrong in his harsh assumptions. There wasn't a selfish or greedy bone in Charley's exquisite body. That was the problem. He was scared to believe in her, in the good he saw there. Scared right down to the wary depths of his soul. He'd trusted once. He wouldn't be twice the fool. Not over a woman.

Only maybe, his subconscious whispered traitorously, just maybe, this one might be worth the risk.

* * *

Charley huddled on her brother's big, soft bed and struggled to slow her panting breaths. She listened. It was very quiet below. She fought against the urge to crawl to the rail and peek down. Finally she heard him get up, heard the sigh of the couch cushions and the thump of his shoes on hard wood. Then the silence lengthened into long listless minutes. And Charley wanted to die.

Coward, coward, coward. You wanted him! You know you did. She could chide herself all she wanted, but that wouldn't change the fact that she'd panicked when he'd pressed her. Everything had suddenly gotten so intense, so overwhelming. And she'd run. Just as she'd run from the reporters. It wasn't Alan. She realized that with some degree of guilt. Her quasi-fiancé was no roadblock to her desire for Jess. Alan wasn't even a speed bump. She would have shoved him aside without a thought for the sheer pleasure of ripping off Jess's clothes and rolling on the rug with him. The only thing stopping her was Charley Carter.

A man like Jess wouldn't settle for a woman like her.

He felt sorry for her. She'd touched on a protective note in him, and she was taking shameless advantage. It was worse now that he'd seen the camp. She could see it intensifying in his gaze throughout the day. She'd snagged his sympathies, and now he was flapping restlessly at the end of the line. It wasn't fair for her to hang on to him, to be dependent on him. He had a life to get back to, one that satisfied him, one that didn't include her. She'd let him take care of her and had wallowed in hedonistic luxury under his pampering attentions. He'd made her breakfast. He'd even offered to brush her teeth for her! She was so desperate, so needy, she'd sucked him into her life before he'd had a chance to consider saying no. But he would. Eventually he would grow tired of playing nursemaid to helpless little Charley Carter, and then where would that leave her? With her emotions foolishly raw and exposed. Robert wasn't the only one in her family with pride. She couldn't let Jess see how much he'd come to mean to her. That would only force more responsibility upon him. She wouldn't make him feel obligated anymore. She had to protect them both from that unpleasant trap—his pitying, her grasping. And that meant backing away from what she wanted most.

But then, she was used to making sacrifices.

"Rise and shine, buddy. We don't allow any lazybones around here."

Jess glared up at Robert Carter and growled a favorite expletive. Lord, he hated cheerful people before he'd had his first cup of coffee. Grumbling every inch of the way, he yawned and stretched and dragged himself off the couch, hoping a shower would resuscitate him. It was then he cast a quick, uneasy glance toward the silent loft.

"Oh, she's been up and about for a couple of hours now," Robert informed him. "And if you want breakfast, you'd better get a move on."

Jess made a face and an anatomically-impossible suggestion before shuffling off to the bathroom. Robert's laughter didn't make him feel any better. Neither did the savage pounding of the water. It couldn't wash away his guilt over what had happened before the fire. He'd put a panic in Charley, and there was no excuse for it. All that was left for him to do was find her and plead temporary insanity. No woman should look that good with firelight playing through her hair. Would she believe him and forgive him? Could things go back to the relaxed, comfortable way they were before? He hoped so.

But he was wrong.

Charley steered a wide path away from him. It was almost funny the lengths she went to to avoid being alone with him. She volunteered to teach a nutrition class in the morning and an exercise program in the afternoon. The kids adored her, Robert confided proudly. *So do I,* Jess confessed to his tormented soul.

Was she being a bigger fool by hiding from him? Charley wondered, but she couldn't bring herself to confront him. He was going to apologize for last night. She could see it in his face. She didn't want his apology. She wanted him to tell her—Oh, she didn't know what she wanted. He certainly wasn't going to break down and admit he just couldn't help himself because he was so crazy in love with her. He would mumble something about hormones going out of control or some sweet insincerity about its being the magic of the moment. But he wouldn't tell her what she wanted to hear, so she didn't want to listen. Did that make her scared or just plain stubborn?

Even though she kept a careful distance, Charley was ever aware of Jess McMasters. He was one hard fellow to ignore. He'd caught the roving eyes of all the female staffers, and the camp girls melted into rapturous sighs whenever he glanced their way. He didn't need her drooling over him, too. She kicked a chair out of her way and earned a startled look from her brother. She glared at him and stomped away to the camp kitchen.

She'd always liked teaching. She spent her summer vacations here helping Robert. Somehow there was a greater sense of accomplishment when working with people than with lab animals and slides. Alan scoffed at that, and perhaps he was right that she could do her best work in the lab. But she did enjoy the classes, giving hope to those like Robert. It filled her heart the way nothing else could. At least that's what she thought until she came out of the classroom cabin and bumped squarely into Jess. And her heartbeat tripled in an instant.

"Charley—"

She tried to wiggle from his grasp. "Please, Jess. You don't have to say anything."

"Yes, I do. I wanted to explain about—"

"No. Don't. I don't want to talk about it."

The beseeching edge of her despair must have reached him because his grip on her forearms gentled and his look lost its intensity. "All right, but let's talk about something else, then, shall we? No more dodging me like you've done all day. There's no need for that. I'll behave."

I don't want you to behave! She would have liked to scream that at him, but she didn't. She had her emotions firmly screwed down. Instead, she gave him a narrow smile and asked, "All right, what would you like to talk about?"

"Alan Peters."

"That's—"

"Don't you dare tell me it's none of my business!"

Charley stared up at him in angry frustration. Her chin firmed belligerently. "All right, Mr. McMasters, what is it you want to know about Alan?"

Jess backed down, bluff called. He scrambled mentally for a way to ask without sounding like a jealous fool. Which he was. "How did you get hooked up with the likes of him?"

"For your information, Alan is a very respected researcher. I'm very fortunate to be working with him."

"I'm not talking about work, Charley."

She was afraid of that. She expelled a ragged breath. "If you're determined to pry open my personal life, can we do it somewhere a little less conspicuous?"

He wasn't about to let her off that easy. Cuffing her upper arm with his hand, Jess marched her back to Robert's cabin. She tugged loose and went to plop down on the front porch glider, purposely assuming the center of the seat so he couldn't join her. Grinning wryly, Jess went to lean against the rail.

"Okay. Talk to me, Charley."

She eyed him in irritation, the way he stood there arrogantly with arms folded patiently across his chest, one ankle crossed over the other.

"Shall I start at the sordid beginning?"

He waved a casual hand for her to continue.

She sighed fiercely. "Fine. All right. I was finishing up my degree and supplementing my income by teaching diabetes-education classes at the hospital. Alan heard me speak and asked if I'd consider giving up the lecturing to assist in his research. He had a fellowship at the university and a healthy grant, so he could offer more than I was getting at the hospital. But I didn't want to give up the practical to go into the theoretical. Until the funds were cut for my program. Then I didn't have much choice. I needed the money to—I needed the money. So I started working with Alan. Satisfied?"

Jess scuffed his toe against the smooth porch boards, studying the grain with apparent concentration. "So when did the big romance happen?"

Big romance? Hardly that. There'd been no explosive passion, no grand declarations, no feverish excitement. Not like with Jess. She was glad his gaze was averted at that moment. "It just sort of evolved while we were working together. There were a lot of long hours, we shared the same dedication to the study. We made a good team, and Alan suggested we continue that outside the lab. He said when he'd published enough to get a senior position, we could be married. I don't suppose you understand that."

Oh yes. He understood very well. Alan Peters had himself a sweet little setup. A smart woman who would run things for him at virtually slave wages and be content with his vague notions of love and future. *Charley, baby, can't you see he's just using you?* But she wouldn't hear that, not from him. He could tell by the defensive glint in her dark eyes.

"Then you have everything you want, don't you?" he said quietly.

Everything? Charley gave him a long look. No, not quite. But enough. She wouldn't complain. She never complained. "Yes, I do. I'm going to marry a man I respect for his views and his work, and I'm going to help my brother make a go of this place."

"And what about you, Charley? What do you get out of all of it?"

"Me?" She stared at him rather blankly as if he'd suggested a foreign concept.

"Yeah, you. Are you going to be happy being Mrs. Alan Peters, working for him and watching mold grow in a dish?"

"Y-yes, of course I will be."

"That's what you want, is it?"

"What I want isn't what's important, Jess." How could she explain it to him? She grew frustrated trying.

"Yes, it is. To me it is. And it should be to you. Who told you you shouldn't want things for yourself? Not Robert. Alan? Your mother? Charley, they were wrong. There's nothing wrong with asking for things for yourself, for doing what you want."

"Some lecture from a man who'd rather teach than do," she parried with frightening accuracy. It was a thrust right through the heart. She hadn't meant to hurt him. She'd only wanted to protect herself and her safe ideals. He'd threatened them, and she'd struck back, wounding him in the process. His expression became unreadable. She could feel the tension in him even across the distance.

"Damn you, Charley. You hit hard."

The quiet anguish in his tone was too much. Without a reply, she left the swing and fled for the security of the cabin.

Feeling utterly defeated, Jess went to sit on the front steps, letting his forehead rest upon arms folded over his knees. In trying to prove his point, she'd turned it back on him with a vengeance. And she was right. Who was he to judge her? Instead of lessening her burdens, he'd only added to them. What a thing for a nice guy to do. But no one other than Charley had ever accused him of being that. And only Charley could make him look upon the success he'd made of his life and see it as a failure because he was doing exactly the same thing she was—pretending he was happy.

A timid shuffle of sound pulled him out of his grim musings. Jess looked up to see a boy of about 8 or 9. He offered a smile. "Hi."

The boy glanced nervously toward the door. "Is Robert here?"

"No, he's not. Something I can do for you?"

The boy's composure dissolved upon a trembly sob, and Jess was immediately all awkward compassion. He caught one of the thin wrists and gave a compelling tug. "C'mere, kid." He supplied a shoulder and a bracing hug. "What's the problem?"

"I don't want to die."

Man, oh, man, how the hell do you answer that one? Jess's arms tightened fiercely about the quaking little figure. A kid this age shouldn't be talking about such things. He opened his mouth, meaning to issue some soothing spiel, but the words wouldn't come. The boy's pain was too real to be pushed aside with placating sympathy. He squeezed his eyes shut and mumbled, "Yeah, well, neither do I, kid. But then we don't have much to say about it, do we?"

Jess could feel the boy wiping his face on the shoulder of his quilted jacket. His chest plugged up solid at the sound of the fragile voice. "I guess not."

"Casey."

The boy pulled away from Jess in response to Robert's firm intrusion.

"Shelly's waiting for you down at the dock. Tell her I said you could help her row. I'll come by later on, and we'll take a walk. Okay?"

The boy gave a jerky nod and the weakest smile Jess had ever seen before scurrying off toward the lake. He followed with his gaze, his expression naked, shattered.

"You're not going to fall to pieces on me, are you, Jess?"

"I feel like I could very easily," he admitted without a trace of shame. He exhaled a heavy breath and scrubbed unsteady hands over his face. "I didn't know what to say to him."

"You did fine. Just fine. You didn't lie to him. That's the important thing. You never lie, and you never tell them everything's going to work out. Because it won't. He could very well live a normal life span but not a normal life. Tough stuff to face at that age, but he will."

"Tough stuff to face at this age. How do you deal with it, day after day?" Suddenly he remembered who he was speaking to and that Robert Carter had no other choice. But before he could apologize, Robert dropped down beside him on the step and slapped a hand on his shoulder.

"It's like walking a high wire. You're all right as long as you don't look down."

"I feel like I just took one hell of a fall."

"Then pick yourself back up. You're all right, McMasters. You have a real instinct when it comes to knowing what someone needs."

"Yeah," he drawled dryly. "I'm a real saint."

"Aren't we all." He pushed off Jess's shoulder to stand. "Come on. I've got to get over to the dining hall, or they'll mutiny and serve Oreos and Ding Dongs for the main course."

Casting a reluctant glance back at the house, Jess hopped up and fell in beside Charley's brother.

"The way I look at it, Jess, is that at least we know we're not perfect. Unlike Alan the Almighty who, I'm sure, still believes in the Divine Right of Scientists."

Jess gave a rusty laugh, and Robert slid him a look.

"How serious are you about Charley?"

The question took Jess like a rabbit punch. He

reeled and sidestepped. "What do you mean?"

"What do you mean?" Robert mimicked. "Hell, man, what do you think I mean? Are you looking for the quick roll, or are you interested in the long run?"

"You're not much for tact, are you?"

"No time for it. You didn't answer."

"Serious," he growled and started to walk again. His gait was stiff, as if he'd frostbitten his feet.

"Good. Just wanted to hear you say it. She's going to need someone, and I wanted to make sure you'd be there for her."

Jess dug in his heels. He didn't like the ominous overtone at all. "What are you getting at, Robert?"

The younger man faced him with a soul-gripping solemnness. "I might not be around forever, and I want to know she'll be taken care of. Not financially. Emotionally."

"Where you planning to go?"

He laughed. "That I won't speculate on. Can you take it on the chin?

"Try me."

"We don't know why some Type I diabetics deteriorate and some don't. You can better your chances at having a normal life span by regimenting and regulating. Controlling blood pressure, calorie intake, meal timing and portions, and exercising all help but they don't offer an ironclad guarantee. You can never take a wrong step, and it can hit you just like someone who never bothered with any precautions. I'm a time bomb, Jess. And I don't know how long the fuse is. Charley's convinced herself that I'm going to live forever, and I'm the last one in the world who'd want to disappoint her. But I might. You usually have about twenty years after onset, then everything goes to hell in a hurry—the kidneys, the eyesight, the nerve endings. It's usually kidney failure that pulls the plug, but it can be something as simple as diabetic foot. A cut can take a year to heal because of poor circulation. There's no sensation of pain. You can be walking around on raw sores until gangrene sets in, and the next thing you know, you're losing pieces of yourself. Then there's my personal favorite, impotence, which is why I intend to use it before I lose it. Pretty picture, huh?"

"I've seen worse."

Robert gave him a long scrutinizing look and saw the toughness in Jess McMasters. "I bet you have. Anyway, back to Charley. She's been setting aside money for years in an account she doesn't think I know about. Mom told me and I promised I wouldn't say anything. When the eyesight starts to go, the blood vessels rupture. Laser treatments can arrest the damage, but they're not cheap. Charley's been building me this nest egg. She's given up everything she's ever wanted to do to take care of me, and dammit, Jess, I don't like it one bit. But what am I supposed to tell her? To get a life? She's never had one of her own, and she's scared to death. That's why she latched on to good ol' Alan. She has some idea that he's going to save me. Maybe he will, but I know one thing for sure. He's not doing anything for her. And I don't like that, either. Now that she has this big windfall, he's going to suck her dry, and I like that even less. And I sure as hell don't want to be accused of doing the same thing."

"And what do you expect me to do about all this?" Jess asked cautiously.

"Nothing. I'm not asking you for anything. Just thought you ought to know." And with that he walked away.

Seven

"Food exchanges are food units that can be substituted for one another in your meal plan. There are six categories—starch and breads, meat and meat substitutes, vegetables, fruit, milk, and fats. Each item on your list has roughly the same carbohydrate, fat, protein, and calorie value, so you can trade them off to give your menu variety. Portion control will . . ."

Charley let her monologue trail off as she caught sight of a girl in the first row of the several circles of chairs doodling aimlessly on a scrap of paper. A flash of temper flared. Irritation made her words sharp.

"Karen, this is your life I'm talking about here. Think you could pay a little more attention?"

The teenager's big blue eyes jerked up, surprised then stricken by the harshness of the command. Charley let her frustrations out on a gusty breath. She came to smile down at the teenager and touched her fingertips to the girl's flushed cheek.

"I'm sorry, Karen. I don't know why I snapped at you. I'm not myself this evening for some reason."

"We know why," snickered one of the older girls in back. "And he sure is cute!"

That brought a host of giggles and a surge of color to Charley's face. She made herself smile and adopt a casual impatience. "All right, ladies and gentlemen. We were discussing food groups, not appetites of a baser nature. Can we get on with it, please?"

The group settled down with a smattering of chuckles and whispers, and Charley picked up on her lecture. But Karen wasn't the only one distracted from the topic of food-unit substitution. Charley's mind wasn't on measuring proteins. It was on finding an accurate means to measure the increasing chemical reaction between her and Jess McMasters. She was both relieved and reluctant when it came time to dismiss her group. Now she could think. But now she had no further excuse to avoid Jess.

He'd been in an oddly-restrained mood all evening, withdrawing behind a bland smile and limited conversation. Because of what she'd said? Or because of the night before? She wasn't good at guessing games, and Jess was harder to read than most. His words troubled her, but it was his kiss that scattered all logic. Logic didn't apply to Jess, and to a woman who relied on carefully plotted statistics before making any judgment, Charley was lost when it came to him. He appealed to something very different inside her, to emotions she'd shut off at an early age. Bringing them back to life was a frightening prospect. There were no known factors, no predictable outcomes. It was research in its rawest form, and while it scared her, the challenge was unbearable. She'd be experimenting with an intriguing set of controls. What would happen if those attractive constants were perturbed? If the chemically-altering drug of passion was introduced? She owed it to the scientist in her soul to explore the possibilities. She owed it to the woman in her to take the risk.

But how?

Jess was unapproachable. How was she going to broach the subject with him? She was a pathetic flirt. An eight-year-old prepubescent knew more about stirring hormones than she did. She was equally uncomfortable with the idea of seduction. There was nothing in her meager wardrobe or in her reserved demeanor that would stimulate a man's fantasies. What was she supposed to do? Walk up to him and say, "I want your body for research purposes"? "Kiss me so I can hypothesize about the effect of elevated blood pressure on the production of adrenal secretions"? How incredibly romantic. She knew science, not sexuality. She was out of her field and fumbling. Twice she'd turned down his overtures. How to communicate her change of mind?

He didn't make it easy.

All evening he was a permanent fixture at her brother's side. She couldn't very well come on to him in front of Robert! More than likely he would burst out laughing at her unskilled attempts and ruin everything. But Robert wouldn't be there to serve as a buffer forever. Sooner or later she and Jess would be alone in the cabin, and then she would make her move. Whatever that might be.

She pictured it so clearly in her mind. She and Jess. Words weren't necessary. A look would do it. She'd sway up against him, and he would be lost to desire. Her fingers would fly deftly over his shirt buttons, then revel in the texture of his bared chest. She'd thread through his unruly hair and whisper love words to drive him wild. That was the picture. The reality was much more cumbersome. Running fingers through his hair and managing shirt buttons was out of the question. She couldn't do that with her own, let alone conquer his with any degree of grace or comfort with her hands bandaged. As for love words . . . she hadn't the slightest idea. The only swaying she'd ever done was in her first pair of heels. She'd overcome that by switching to flats. Compromise for security's sake, that was her motto. Not conducive to flinging herself boldly into Jess's arms.

Finally the moment came. Charley was a knotted mass of nerves. She wished Robert and Shelly a strained goodnight and followed Jess into the cabin. The glare of track lighting shocked everything into blunt focus, and Charley started cringing. She stood in the center of the room in stricken paralysis while Jess stacked and stoked a fire. She devoured him hungrily with her eyes as he crouched before the hearth. Excitement and sheer terror quickened a flutter of sensation around her heart. Like massive fibrillations, she thought wildly. Either she was crazy about the man or she should call in a cardiologist.

He straightened in one smooth motion, and Charley suffered an acute anxiety attack. Now or never. She swallowed convulsively as he turned around. Oh, he was gorgeous! Her sensibilities staggered and collapsed. One look into his cool gray eyes and she lost the thread of her existence.

"Jess . . ." The sound of his name was engulfed by a shaky breath. He couldn't have heard it. Without any recognition of her distress, he crossed to the couch to plump up his pillow. Her frantic heart crowded up into her throat. She made herself try again, concentrating on those husky tones she'd heard on his answering machine.

"Jess." The word trembled with all the passion in her panicked soul.

He gave her a quick, distracted look and said, "Oh. Good night, Charley." Then he strode to the bathroom and shut the door.

She came unglued. He hadn't noticed. She heard the shower gush on full blast. What now? She could join him, came a salacious thought. One nervously dismissed. Her bandages would get soaked. The couch. She could stretch out on the couch and wait for him. That would be obvious, wouldn't it? Too obvious? She snuck over to it and sat down. It gave with a welcoming sigh. Maybe she should just sit here and let him assume . . . No. She'd been too forceful in her rejection. She had to make the first move. Cautiously she sank down onto the cushions, her spine as rigid as a back brace. With her head on his pillow Charley closed her eyes and commanded her pulse to quiet. She would be in control.

Then the water stopped, and she was off the couch and darting up the stairs to the loft before her mind registered a conscious decision. There she slunk back into the shadows and prayed for the miracle of calm thought. Over the hammering of her heartbeats she heard him leave the bathroom. Suddenly the room below was plunged into darkness through which the warm glow of the fire rose in a radiant arc. He was going to bed. If she crept quietly into hers, he would never know that she'd been plotting his seduction. She started toward it, eyeing the safety of its fluffy comforter. Then she stopped. She might save herself the risk of rejection, but she would never know the pleasures that lay beyond that kiss, either.

She wouldn't think about it. Or about the man on the couch below. Hanging desperately on to that decision, Charley maneuvered awkwardly out of her clothes and into an ankle-length flannel nightgown. Not exactly the sort of lingerie designed to turn a man's thoughts to passion, she realized with some chagrin. But the more she tried to push herself toward the climb into bed and the search for sleep, the stronger became the draw to the loft's rail. She paced restlessly for some minutes, each pass taking her closer and closer to the edge. Until finally she looked over.

It was very dark below. Uneven firelight fell short of revealing his features but played about the bare feet he stretched toward the warmth. Those incredibly sexy bare toes. With a groan of reckless surrender she headed for the stairs.

He was lying on his back with his forearm braced over his eyes so that only the top of his head and the sensuous curve of his mouth was showing. He'd changed into sweatpants and a loose T-shirt—no buttons, Charley thought giddily. Her senses were overwhelmed by the scent of soap and pine logs. Her knees were shaking so badly that it was with relief she bent them to crouch behind the back of the couch, resting her elbows on the tufted top. For a moment she studied him, absorbed by his masculine aura and aware of a needy urgency mounting as each second passed in silent survey. Her hand was trembling as her fingertips reached and lightly touched the back of his.

"Jess." It was a sigh of longing.

He jerked into wakefulness and lowered his arm. "Charley?" Even in the shadows he could define the anxiousness tightening her features. Her eyes glittered softly. "What's wrong, baby?" He sat up and her eyes seemed to swell to twice their size. He could see her frantic swallowing. "You okay? Another bad dream?"

Charley shook her head. Bad dream? Hardly. Her every dream was more like it. But how to tell him? Her lips parted to say the words, *I want you, Jess,* but the sound dammed up behind the thickness of emotion clogging her throat. She forced a painful swallow and tried again. *I need you, Jess.* The muscles in her face didn't want to work. She couldn't do this! With a small moan of frustration she began to stand.

"Charley?" The concern knitting his brow shifted in confusion. "What is it?"

And suddenly she couldn't run from him anymore. She came back down, meeting his outstretched hand, rubbing her cheek into the cup of his palm. Her eyes slid shut as a sensual shudder escaped her. Her lips moved eagerly against his thumb as it softly sketched the curve of her mouth. A breathy sigh of relief drove understanding home. An understanding that shook Jess to the soul.

"Why didn't you tell me, baby?" His voice was low, rough with feeling.

Charley ducked her head, trying to hide her hot face in the concave of his palm. "I'm not sure how to go about this, Jess," she mumbled with a heart-clutching honesty.

Tenderness welling in his chest until he could barely breathe, Jess stroked her heated cheek and murmured, "Haven't you ever been with a man before?"

She pulled out of his hand with an angry toss of her head. "Of course I have," she snapped testily, as if by questioning her experience, he'd offered some terrible insult. Then annoyance gave way to embarrassment. "I'm just not very good at making love. About as good as I am in the kitchen."

He took her teary confession with a soft laugh, easing the sting of his humor by teasing his fingers through her hair. "Well, I'm good at it. And if you haven't enjoyed it up till now, it's because he was doing it wrong."

Jess followed that arrogant claim by catching her under the arms and dragging her over the top of the couch to lie fully upon him. His kiss was a potent taste of raw desire. Charley responded to it with a wild need to sample more. He reached up, framing her face in gentleness as his tongue slipped along the part of her lips like a whisper of wet silk. When her breath expelled in a rapturous moan, he plunged deep to probe the moist recess of her mouth, plumbing the pathway to her unseasoned passions. When he'd mapped out every hard ridge and yielding valley, he withdrew and went on to seek new territories. He charted the sweet swell of her tender eyelids, the delicate plain of her cheeks, moving to ride the pounding rapids of want coursing down the arch of her slender throat. Exquisite sensation woke beneath his briefest touch, and to Charley, it was heaven.

She twisted on top of him and the pressure of her hips ground a growling need way down deep. He responded with a wordless, nearly mindless rumble of want that vibrated beneath the soft mass of Charley's breasts like angry thunder. His fingers skimmed back to mesh in her hair, angling her head ruthlessly to fit the eager slant of her lips to his. God, it was good! The storm of desperate passion blew up so suddenly, so fiercely, that he had no time to prepare for it. It seethed through him, goading him to a roughness far removed from his usual consideration. His kiss was bruising, demanding, drawing her up into his whirlwind of frenzied hunger. With his heart slamming against his ribs he dragged his mouth off hers to fasten hot kisses in a blazing trail down her neck. She didn't try to protect against his hurtful urgency. That was what finally reached him through the glaze of desire.

She wouldn't protest. She was used to everyone taking all that she could give without a thought to what was returned to her. He couldn't do that. He wouldn't do that even though he was so aroused that it was worse than death to pull back from the edge. He had to put Charley first. Someone had to.

His chest heaving with the effort of restraint, Jess clasped her by the back of the neck and pushed her face into his shoulder. He made himself wait out the shaking weakness of will, that craving to know the taste of her, the fit of her around him and the savage ecstasy of his own release. And as she shivered in his embrace, incredibly the urge eased. At least enough to allow for some control.

"How you doing?" he whispered huskily against her hair.

"Fine," came a return whisper that sounded anything but.

"Up for some more?"

Her laugh was ragged, unbearably erotic. "You obviously are."

"Forget about that," he panted, searching for the necessary resolve. He moved his hips in a contrary motion. God, she felt good against him. His voice deepened, sounding raw with emotion. "Let me take care of you, Charley."

She struggled to lift up, and he finally relieved the pressure of his hand on her neck. Propped on elbows resting on either side of his head, she let her fingertips toy with the damp hair clinging in rumpled, finger-combed waves to his temples. His eyes were bright, hot, absorbing, offering everything she wanted. And was afraid to ask for. "Jess, I don't know . . ."

"I know," he argued softly. She let him lure her down for a sweet, sweet kiss. "We'll take it slow. Trust me."

He waited for belief to darken her gaze, then turned on the wide, accommodating couch until he was on his side and Charley lay stretched out in his embrace. To keep her from sliding off the edge, he nudged up the hem of her gown with his knee to lock one leg over hers. Then he began his lingering lesson in love. He started with a kiss, slower, more sensual than any they'd shared thus far. Caresses followed, long, leisurely strokes that outlined the contour of her body. Charley made a low, impatient sound in her throat, her lips opening wider, her body rocking insistently, but he wouldn't be rushed. And he wouldn't let her miss one iota of the pleasure he meant to give her.

By the time his hand found its way to the hem of her hiked gown, Charley was a quivering mass of anxious nerve endings. Just the brush of his fingertips along the inside of her thigh brought a groan of anticipation. He could feel the labored rhythm of her breathing intensify as each tantalizing movement brought him closer to the core of her passions. Then he was there, and he paused as her body jerked and trembled.

"All right?" he asked, voice low and strained as hell. Her face jerked an affirmative in the cove of his shoulder, and she started to breathe again.

"Jess . . . oh, Jess."

The way she said his name was a wild aphrodisiac. He almost lost it. Then, clinging to his intentions the way she was clinging to the woven couch cushions, he began to move his hand. Slow, sure revolutions, tempting excited little breaths from her, bringing back the twitch and tremble to the legs entwined with his.

"Jess."

The sound caught in a soft sob.

"That's it, baby. Let go."

Her face was jammed against the side of his neck. The hot little jets of air upon his skin had him gritting his teeth in an agony of control. God, if she didn't go over the brink soon, he was afraid he would.

"Jess . . ."

"Hey, Jess!"

His mind registered the different voice, but his concentration was trapped on the woman coming apart beneath his knowing caress. He thrust his fingers hard, deep into the heat of her, and Charley cried out, her body snapping rigid, then dissolving into a series of wonderfully violent tremors.

"Oh . . . Jess."

"Jess! The door's locked. Are you there?"

As the spasms quieted to a nerveless shaking, Charley lifted her head. At first her gaze was dull, desire-drugged, then her focus sharpened upon a thought, upon a word.

"Robert!"

Jess slipped both arms around her in a fierce embrace, but she was twisting against it.

"I can't let him see me. He'll know."

Jess was about to growl, "What the hell does it matter if Robert knows?" when she wriggled off the edge of the couch and out of his grasp. She started up on wobbly legs, then, almost as an afterthought, came down on one knee to kiss him so hard it knocked the breath from his lungs. And she was gone, stumbling through the shadows and staggering up the stairs.

"Oh God . . ." Jess groaned with feeling. He scrubbed his hands over his face and exhaled on an unsteady sigh. Everything inside him was wired tight and tensed to the limit. As he forced his muscles to relax, he heard the doorknob rattle impatiently.

"Jess? Come on, man. I know you're there."

Muttering every dire curse he could think of, Jess crawled off the couch and tottered to the door. Even before he'd jerked it all the way open, Robert was pushing inside. His gaze swept the room suspiciously, then turned upon the man leaning against the door.

"Man, you look like a truck hit you," he

stated with typical bluntness.

Don't punch him, Jess. Charley would never forgive you.

Voice gritty, he said, "You woke me out of a very pleasant dream."

"Sorry." Robert brushed off his new friend's mood with an airy gesture. "Where's Charley?"

"Upstairs, asleep unless all your bellowing woke her up, too."

Robert smiled in oblivious good humor, then gave Jess's arm a fond slap. "I'll just get what I need and get out of your way."

"Too late for that," Jess muttered under his breath.

In spite of his promise it took Robert a half hour to actually leave. By then Jess was grinding his molars and debating seriously on whether to break the man's neck or just toss him bodily out the front door. Part of him wondered cynically if her playful brother knew exactly what he'd interrupted and was just trying to give them hell. Jess was unraveling, seam by seam. The pressure building was too big, too powerful, too intensely personal. He knew he couldn't hold it in much longer, but neither could he let his pent-up emotions rip loose in front of Charley's brother. *Goodbye, Robert. Go on. Get going. Get out—get out—get out!* The image of Charley pushed into his mind, and he tightened his jaw.

"Well, g'night, Jess."

No words had ever sounded so sweet with

promise. Jess's breath slid through his teeth in an uneven hiss. He resisted the urge to shove Robert toward the door to hurry him along.

"You okay, man? You're really on edge. Better cut back on the coffee." And he smiled with such annoying devilry, as if to say, *I'm no fool, buddy. A man's got to watch out for his sister.*

"Keeps my heart going," he replied with a narrow smile. Wouldn't old Robert love to know what had his pulse hammering away like a pneumatic drill. His mouth widened into a wry grin.

Then, finally, the door was shut and secured. For a moment Jess leaned against it, clawing for the control it took not to bolt for the stairs. If Charley had seen the lean, ravenous look sharpening all the angles of his face, she would never again doubt what it was Jess McMasters felt for her. It was a look of raw need. Slowly he pushed away from the door and started across the room in a stiff, unnatural gait. His quicksilver gaze was on the darkened loft above. He took the first step, then the second. By the time Jess reached the top, his breathing was harsh and ragged. His chest hurt from the strain of it.

"Charley?"

There was no answering sound from the shadows cloaking the bed.

Nerves stretched to the limit and trembling tautly, Jess advanced. He could make out the outline of her figure beneath a pile of covers. It seemed hardly bigger than a child's. And added to the intolerable pain of want, a throat-aching tenderness rose. A protectiveness so savage, so deep, it wrung his spirit dry.

She was asleep. He realized it the second he leaned over the bed. He'd intended to kiss her but he paused with his face inches from hers, his rapid breath feathering back her hair. She was so peaceful. So beautiful. Longing clamped around his windpipe like a vise.

"Charley?"

She murmured in contentment. She might as well have reached inside him and yanked out his heart. His features contorted in a spasm of emotion. And he knew he couldn't wake her. Not to satisfy his desperate need for fulfillment. Though it cost him, and cost him dear, Jess backed off the edge of the bed.

"Sleep tight, baby."

Eight

Leaving was always hard on Charley. But this time it wasn't only Robert and the sense of helping one-on-one she was leaving behind. It was the unexpected intimacy she'd found with Jess. She didn't try to fool herself into thinking they would experience that again once they returned home. She had Alan and Jess would have a bevy of husky-voiced messages from ladies waiting on his machine. And then, there was the unavoidable fact that he hadn't come upstairs to finish what they'd started.

Charley wasn't exactly sure when she'd begun falling in love with Jess. The way he'd soaped her face, sleeping with him in the big recliner, that first soul-searing kiss. It really didn't matter. What mattered was what now? He'd given and given and given to her; of his time, of his tenderness, of his heart-stopping talent in the love making department. But he hadn't asked anything of her. When he saw her need, he filled it.

Wasn't there anything he wanted from her? She'd hoped when he kissed her . . . but those kisses weren't pursued. Was it because of Alan? Or because she wasn't the kind of woman Jess wanted for himself?

It had taken every scrap of her inner courage to go to him the night before. But it had been well worth it. There was no way to describe the sensations he'd caused to shatter through her. They were like nothing she'd ever experienced. She'd tried to stay awake while he and Robert were talking downstairs but the seeping lethargy had stolen her will. When she woke, it was morning and the realization that Jess hadn't come to her was a crippling disappointment. Apparently what had been an intensely moving moment for her hadn't meant as much to him. But she wouldn't hold it against him. He'd given her paradise. It wasn't his fault she had nothing he wanted in return. It wasn't his fault he couldn't love her. She should be used to her gifts of affection not being enough. But still, she ached for more.

Charley cast a troubled look toward Jess. He'd said little since getting behind the wheel except concern about her hands. Nothing about the state of her heart. He'd been so terribly remote this morning. There'd been no time to discuss what had happened on the couch, what might have happened had Robert not intruded. And now that she and Jess had time aplenty, he was disinclined to explore that unfinished business.

Perhaps to him, it was finished. What could she say that wouldn't sound like she was whining for his attention? Like the insecurities of an immature girl? Better to stay silent and retain her dignity then to reveal the confusion in her heart. At least this way she was giving him the choice. No pressure, no weight of obligation. It would be up to him. And Charley trembled, at his mercy.

As they turned into the parking lot of her complex, there was no feeling of homecoming. Only a mounting sense of impending separation. When he pulled into a space and cut the engine, Charley felt as though part of her shut down as well; the part of her that beat warm and fast, that knew excitement and joy, that understood how painful it was to yearn for a love returned. Moistness welled in her eyes and she blinked it back determinedly when Jess asked, "Ready?" She managed a brisk nod and got out while he reached around into the back seat for her bag.

"Hey! There she is! Miss Carter, can I have a moment for a few questions?"

The young reporter charged across the parking lot trailing cables and a camera man. He came to a stop before her, out of breath and flushed with eagerness. He talked so fast, she didn't have a chance to interrupt.

"You're one hard lady to get a hold of! Miss Carter, I'd like to say how much I admire you for what you did and it would mean a lot to those who've followed the story to see you in person. The papers have you built up like some kind of legend. I'd like to show my viewers that you're just an average woman who reacted to an extreme circumstance. I'd like them to feel that any one of them could be in your shoes. What do you say, Miss Carter? Do you have the time?"

Charley stood stiff and still, waiting for the attack of nerves. But it was just the one earnest-faced reporter and a bored fellow with his mini-cam. She took a deep, careful breath. And felt fine. What he said made sense. If she talked to him, perhaps the others would leave her alone. She'd be, as Jess put it, old news. She shot a quick glance across the car but he was burrowing in the back seat. She swallowed and turned toward the anxious newsman. Her first reaction was to touch her hair.

"I look awful."

The reporter grinned. "You look great! How about standing over here where the light is better."

"Just a few questions?"

"Promise."

She forced the tension from her shoulders and offered a faint smile. "All right."

After a brief introducing lead in, the questions were brief and general. There was no threat and Charley responded easily.

"How are your hands, Miss Carter? I understand you were severely burned when you attempted to reach the Osgoods."

"Starting to itch." Yes, she was healing, she

realized with some relief. She could get her life back on course.

"Have you had any contact with the Osgood family?"

"Not since the hospital. Though I have called several times to find out how Chris is getting along."

"Chris? The little boy, Chris Osgood. And how is he?"

"Better," she said with a genuine smile toward the camera. "Much better."

"Will you be seeing the Osgoods again?"

"I believe they'll be at the ceremony next Monday."

"Have you decided what to do with the reward money?"

"No," she answered honestly.

"You've become quite the media star since all this happened. I've heard that cable television wants to option your story. Is that true?"

"I really don't know. This is the first I've heard of it."

"What about print features? Does *Metro Magazine* have an exclusive or are you holding out for offers?"

"Metro?" Charley began to frown.

"That's enough." Jess cut in brusquely. He put one hand over the reporter's microphone and the other over the lens of the camera. "You have your story. Miss Carter is tired."

The reporter switched off the mike. He eyed Jess thoughtfully. "Yep. Got my story and my answer. Thank you, Miss Carter. This should air on the evening news."

Jess's fingers pinched her upper arm as he guided her away from them. She was a bit surprised by the vehemence darkening his expression, but that couldn't overshadow the way his protectiveness lightened her heart. He fished her keys from his coat pocket and held the door for her. But with every step on each of the three flights up, Charley's mood began to falter. Then he was swinging open the door to her apartment, issuing her inside the familiar clutter. He strode straight to her bedroom and tossed her bag onto the bed. He was out again before she could even think to suggest he linger a moment longer than the time it took to pitch her dirty laundry.

"Are you all set here? Is there anything you need me to do?"

Yes, she wanted to cry out. *I want you to hold me, to kiss me, to tell me you care. I don't want you to go.* But there was an impatience in his face, a restlessness that spoke of his desire to get away and back to the things he had waiting. So Charley choked down the massive lump in her throat and said, as if it weren't tearing the heart from her, "No, thanks, Jess. I can handle things."

He hesitated, toeing her carpet, canting a look at her from under a downcast brow. It was a small thing, just a quick glance up at her and then away. But in that fleeting second she got an impression of dragging reluctance so strong it was almost physical. As if there was no place on earth he'd rather be than here with her. That was ridiculous, of course. Probably wishful thinking on her part. But it brought a sudden fullness to her throat. She inhaled a tortured breath as his stare came up once more, slowly, affixing hers in a way that was intense, absorbing.

"Jess—"

The shrill sound of the phone startled her, shattering the taut mood. Without taking her eyes from his, she reached for the phone and muttered a hasty hello.

"Charlene, where have you been? I've been trying all weekend."

The petulant tones were like a dash of ice water. "Alan."

Jess blinked and just like that erased everything she hoped she'd seen there in his gaze.

"Well?" Alan insisted.

Charley struggled for a way to answer Alan and hold Jess. But Jess was fading back, easing toward the door, his expression impossibly distant. "I was with my brother at the camp," she said woodenly into the receiver as Jess stepped into the hall. She took a quick pace forward, but he raised his hand and mouthed, "Bye," then shut the door. For a moment she couldn't move. She could hear Alan's voice but not his words as his tone grew more demanding. She hauled the phone across the room with her, the dragging cord tipping over stacks of journals and magazines she never had time to read. They made a glossy spill across her rug. From the window she could see him striding to his car, settling his sunglasses on the bridge of his nose. He didn't look back. Exhaust plumed and vaporized as the car backed abruptly through it, then sped from the lot. Aware only of the resounding emptiness around the region of her heart, Charley hung up the receiver.

What was she going to do without Jess in her life? Was it possible that she had known him less than a week? It seemed a lifetime already. Everything about that week since the accident was intense, filled with concentrated emotion. He'd slipped so comfortably into her day-to-day existence that his absence left a gaping hole. How dull her routine was without the promise of his wide smile or just the simple expectation of seeing him at her kitchen counter. She found herself wondering how his lasagna tasted. She found herself dreaming of how it would have been had he come to her in the loft at her brother's cabin. And it took two painkillers to forget.

The next day she called a cab to keep an appointment with her doctor. He examined the burns and pronounced them free of infection and healing nicely. The scarring would be slight and full range of movement probable. After applying cortisone ointment, he redressed them with a lighter wrap and advised her to cut back to aspirin to relieve pain. She smiled and thanked him, knowing full well that aspirin wouldn't dull the hurt she suffered.

Glumly she returned to her messy apartment, kicked the day's stack of letters in next to the rest of them that lay piled and unopened inside her door, and went to pop the last of her microwave dinners in the oven. She could eat with relatively little distress now and, if she took her time, even manage buttons. There was scant satisfaction in these small successes. Faced with a lump of what might have been chicken and with her own swelling loneliness, Charley realized she had to do something fast if she was going to survive the loss of Jess McMasters.

She never expected rescue to come in the form of Alan Peters. When she answered the buzz of her intercom, she was ridiculously grateful to hear Alan's voice after the initial well of disappointment faded. And when she opened her door and found him standing there behind a bouquet of fresh spring flowers, she nearly burst into tears.

"Thought you might like some company," he murmured as his lips brushed past her cheek. Never had she cared for him as much as in that needy moment. She dragged him in out of the hall and, after some hunting, found an empty instant coffee jar to stick the flowers in. They drooped haphazardly, but she was pleased with the result. She was never any good at arranging flowers. She set them on her table and smiled at Alan, touched that he had made the gesture. That he would even think of it!

"I was worried about you, Charlene," he began in a crooning voice as she made them both coffee. "I was just about out of my mind when I couldn't get you on the phone." *When I got him instead,* was what he wanted to say, but he had to be careful. He wasn't fool enough not to see the threat of Charlene's handsome new friend. A friend who would answer her phone in the morning hours. Though she might be physically attracted to the rather arrogant fellow, he didn't for a minute fear he would lose her. He and Charlene had a kindred purpose. And so he would remind her.

"I'm sorry if you were concerned. I had to get away. The newspeople wouldn't leave me alone, and I knew I'd be no good to you unable to finish a day's work."

"Forget about work, Charlene. There are more important things."

Her brows shot heavenward. That was news to her! It was the only thing that ever seemed to motivate him. First the unplanned visit, then the flowers, now this. She stared at him, agog.

"We need to talk, Charlene. About the future. Our future." He reached out to take her hand, not seeming to notice how she winced when he pressed the bandages. "I know this hasn't been easy for you. It hasn't been easy for me, either. I don't want you to think that I was placing you second to my position. Everything I've been working for has been for us."

She continued to listen, but in the back of her mind a seditious whisper began. *For us or for you, Alan?* Their whole relationship could be reduced to work in the lab and hurried, heavy-breathing moments stolen as if in shame. She remembered using her hoarded savings to follow him to the annual American Diabetes Association's scientific sessions. While he enjoyed the bounty of a nice hotel and dinners with the other MDs, she was trapped in a squalid motel, forced to feed herself at the free buffet tables at the nightly hospitality receptions. When he came to her room, it was late, and he was tipsy from the effects of socializing glass for glass with his peers. His fumbling passion made her feel as cheap as the room rate, but she said nothing, assuming it would get better. Now he was telling her it was about to. Why didn't she believe him?

His sudden move took her by surprise. And so did his kiss. He hauled her from her seat opposite him. His lips were thin, moist, and hurtful. With one arm locking her against his chest, his free hand sought her breast. Charley twisted free and scrambled back into her chair, dazed and panting. What on earth . . . ? He didn't relent but, instead, went down on one knee before her chair.

"Charlene, I want to be with you. Not just a snatch at a time but really be with you, like a true partnership. We can be. With your help we can be."

Charley blinked, totally confused by his intensity, by his direction. "Alan, I—"

"Don't you see, my darling?" he gushed as he took her hands. She gritted her teeth against the pain of that dramatic gesture. Perhaps it was that stab of hurt that cleared her mind and for the first time let her really look at Alan. "The obstacles to our happiness will be gone. We won't need to worry about securing grants to move up in our research. We can go forward in our study of the auto-immune process. There might even be a Lily Award in it."

His eyes glittered as he spoke of the outstanding young researcher honor. It was a rapturous gaze. It was the way Jess had looked at her when she'd come to him on the couch. But it was prestige that moved Alan to a glaze of excitement, not passion.

"Don't you see, Charlene," he went on to explain as if she were a dense child. And she felt as though she had been one. "We don't have to apply for grants and pinch pennies. With your money we can make progress that will have the entire field taking notice. We can publish new quality findings. We can forget about scraping by on a university salary. With that kind of backing I can step into a position with a pharmaceutical house and jump right up into the one-hundred-thousand-dollar-plus bracket. I'll have my own lab, my own name on publications, without having to give unearned credit to a bunch of overseers. Think of it, Charlene."

She was thinking.

The money.

That's what this was about. The flowers, the unexpected visit. He was romancing her the way their superiors did the big drug companies to lure their financial support. Was any of that brightness in his gaze because of her, or was it all focused on what she could now give him?

"I don't know, Alan," she began coolly, withdrawing her throbbing hands from his as she spoke. "I've been thinking of investing the funds in my brother's camp."

"What?" It was a roar of sheer outrage. "Charlene, you can't mean that! I'm talking about the development of our theories. Our future!"

"I'm talking about the future, too. A future that involves a lot more people than just you and me. You know how I feel about Robert's work. Or do you?"

He sighed and assumed an air of weary patience. "We've been over this, Charlene. We agreed that research will be of greater benefit. Can't you see the money would be used to the best advantage if put toward my project?"

She saw that he'd begun to say "my" instead of "our." And she also wondered whose benefit he was concerned with—people like Robert or his own. "I'm not totally convinced of that, Alan," she told him quietly, and she could see his surprise. She was surprised, too. But she didn't want to back down. She didn't want to give in to his pressure. Not this time. Not when she had the means to make a difference for a lot of people.

"Convinced? About our future?" He gave her that boyish smile meant to sway her from her purpose. Not this time.

"What you mean by our future has never been clearly defined," she pointed out.

Alan studied her for a moment. His eyes narrowed the way they always did when he was perplexed by a complex cell structure. He was angry, but for once she felt no urge to soothe it away. Let him be angry. He had to see that she was serious. Serious about having a voice in how the money was spent. Serious in her bewilderment over their relationship. But he was typically myopic.

"You need convincing, Charlene? All right."

He shoved his hands up under her sweater. Her cry of objection was canceled by his wide, wet kiss. And everything inside her went stone cold. Everything about it felt wrong. His reason for pushing intimacy. Her reaction to it—a surprisingly vehement rejection of his touch. She wrenched her head to one side and braced herself against him with her forearms.

"No!"

Alan rocked back on his heels, panting, plainly furious. "No? It's because of him, isn't it?"

She was so startled that her mind went as blank as her expression.

"It is! Why else would he be answering your phone for you. Did you really go away for the weekend, or have you been holed up in here with him doing God knows what?"

Only parts of what he was accusing her of clicked right away. "When did you talk to Jess on my phone?"

He sneered and stood, brushing at his pant legs as if contact with her had left him soiled. "Friday morning. While you were . . . busy. Busy doing what, Charlene?"

"But I wasn't even here. I was at—" She broke off. She was at Jess's. She clamped her lips shut. Alan would never understand that particular explanation in his frame of mind. Why hadn't Jess told her he'd talked to Alan? If he had, she would have been prepared for Alan's rage. Prepared with a convenient lie to cover up what she and Jess had been flirting with so dangerously? No. She'd never lied to Alan before and wouldn't start now. But neither did she feel capable of explaining away Jess McMasters to her jealous fiancé. Was that what Alan was? She wasn't sure of that anymore.

"Alan, I think you should leave."

"But, Charlene, what about the money?"

"I have to think about it. I have to think about a lot of things. Now, please go."

He didn't like it, but he didn't argue.

And when he was gone, for all the confusion,

Charley felt a wonderful sense of control coming into her life.

The cursor blinked impatiently against a bright field of blue. An empty field of blue. It beckoned for input, seeming to say, "Come on, Jess, put me to work." For the hundredth time that morning he placed his fingers on the keys and willed the words to come. Usually his problem was not in how to start but when to stop. But this wasn't a usual story. It was about Charley Carter.

He'd seen her on the news. That's what did it. He'd been fine until then—well, almost fine. Then he'd found himself mesmerized by her shy smile, by the modest lowering of her eyes that was seductive without being coy. He studied her mannerisms the way an art lover worshiped a Picasso and let the soft tones of her voice tease his senses into a restless frenzy. Worse, a sign of how far off the deep end he'd fallen, he'd recorded the interview. He lost track of how many times he played and replayed it from the comfort of his recliner, a beer in one hand, a roll of antacids in the other. He munched and swallowed into the late hours of the night with Charley's image playing before him. Finally he turned off the sound and just watched her. From a wallow of remorse almost too deep to climb from, he dragged himself out of the chair and to bed. Not to his own bed but to the one in the spare room, on the sheets where she'd slept. God, he was pathetic. He would have laughed if he hadn't felt so intensely miserable.

A vivid dream plagued his sleep, of Charley and the accident. Only in this tormenting version he hadn't reached her in time. He woke with the image of a fireball braised upon his eyelids and a film of sweat clinging to him. By daybreak he was a ragged mass of nerves, with every nerve ending feeling exposed. Showering didn't help. Breakfast wasn't even remotely appealing. So with coffee gnawing away in his belly and a fresh pack of Rolaids in his pocket to quiet the ulcer that was threatening to growl back to life, he gathered his notes and went to work. That's what he needed. Work. He was a journalist. He would purge Charley Carter from his system in front of a keyboard. Only not at home. Not where the memories of her were fresh and painful. He'd go to his university office, and he'd do his job.

Only he couldn't.

For hours he'd sat in front of the blank screen. He'd gone over his notes. He'd listened to the recording from the restaurant, trying to block out the bittersweet sensations of longing the sound of her voice evoked. He had all the information he needed to write one hell of a story. All the elements were there—he just couldn't seem to settle them to his satisfaction.

Because the focus was wrong.

He'd plunged into it looking for a harsh angle

against which to contrast Charley Carter's heroic deed. Only there wasn't one. If anyone was guilty of selling out honor in the name of greed, it was him, Jess McMasters. He'd done it a long time ago when he'd turned from the kind of writing he wanted to do into the business of making money off lurid words. And he'd done very well. He could blame Sue for pushing him in that direction, but after their divorce he'd had no excuse to continue down that lucrative road. Except that the passion of words was dead inside him. He worked from skill alone, not heart. And it took a sweet soul like Charley's to show him the difference.

Now what the hell was he going to do?

He picked up the phone on the table beside him and started dialing. He asked for the proper extension and waited, watching the cursor wink.

"Matthew Bane."

"Matt, it's Jess."

"Did you fall off the edge of the earth or something? Did you see that piece on the news last night?"

"Yeah."

"What have you got for me? I need it now."

"Matt . . . I've been thinking about the slant of the story."

"What about it?" That was asked warily. Matthew Bane knew his best feature man well enough to know big trouble was coming.

"The hardball angle just isn't working out. I want to try something different, more of a human-interest piece."

There was silence. Then the line vibrated with the force of his editor's reply. "Fluff? You want to do bleeding-heart crap? Jess, Jess, no one reads J.T. Masters to get in touch with their inner feelings. They love you because you shove the truth down their throats like the barrel of a loaded gun. You're a hand grenade, Jess, and you're asking me to settle for a water pistol? No way, man. You write the story the way we discussed it. You do it the way you always do it. Or I can get someone else to cover it. Are you listening to me, Jess?"

Silence, then a soft, "I'm listening."

"All right, then. Give me something my readers can sink their teeth into. I want pure Masters gold. Or should I say brass." He laughed at that, and when the other end of the line was too quiet, he asked in some concern, "Jess, are you all right with this one? This isn't like you. You want me to pull you off? Say the word. You could give Harris your notes—"

"No. It's my assignment, Matt. I'll do it."

"Attaboy, Jess. When can I expect it on my desk?"

"By press time," came the grim promise.

Jess hung up the phone, took a deep breath, and began to type.

Nine

Charley couldn't bring herself to watch herself on the news, but apparently she was the only one who hadn't seen it. Interest hadn't abated. If anything, it increased fivefold. The calls started again. A disgruntled postman left a terse message in her box that her mail would be waiting at the main post office—there was too much of it to deliver. She was overwhelmed and she didn't want to be. She wanted control back. What she needed was a plan.

First things first. There wasn't so much as an ice cube in her refrigerator. She caught herself smiling at the thought of Jess's scorn. Even the master chef himself couldn't put together a meal with what she had on her shelves. Time to gird herself for a trip to the closest supermarket. Her doctor had given her the okay to drive, so she had no excuse to put it off. Oral surgery was the only thing that ranked higher on her list of things she hated than pushing a shopping cart.

All those endless canyons of make-from-scratch items made her palms sweat. She aimed straight for the microwavable epicenter in the frozen-food section. Feeling a little more competent, she began loading up on prepared breakfasts, lunches, and dinners. Then the glossy representation of an Italian entree caused her to pause. It was probably a crazy idea. But just in case she turned over the box and scanned the table of ingredients. She wrinkled her nose.

"Excuse me," she said suddenly to a woman pushing a cart past her. She had one child in the basket and one hanging on her coattail and a figure suggesting she knew a thing or two about cooking.

"Yes?"

Charley blushed but was determined. "Do you know what ingredients go into lasagna?"

Later, when she was putting the noodles, herbs, and cheeses away, she was certain she'd lost her mind. Just in case, she told herself again. If not, she could always throw it all away when it got fuzzy. And the wine wouldn't go to waste. She'd been extravagant there, and it had felt good, knowing she'd gotten the best. As tempted as she was to pop the cork now, she made herself store it on its side the way the wine merchant suggested. Then she went to see about the next step on her agenda. The answering machine.

It installed easily, and after she recorded a

timid-sounding message, she flipped it on. The whir and flash of red lights was reassuring. Better than a dead bolt for keeping the world at bay. She turned off the telephone ringer and set to her next task. A harder one—the mail.

There was an incredible amount. With what she'd picked up at the post office added to what she already had, she felt like Santa at the North Pole on December 23. But if there was one thing she could do well, it was organize. It took several hours, but she finally had the mail sorted into categories: well-wisher cards, bills, charitable institution requests—she hadn't known so many existed!—wacko letters asking her to invest in wild schemes or proposing marriage, and bona fide offers. The latter she listed on a separate sheet of paper, then all the stacks went into individual boxes and were prioritized.

Then, the last and hardest. With a clean sheet of note paper in front of her and a calculator to her right, she wrote a big number five at the top of the page and followed it with all those zeroes. She divided the page in half. On one side she listed the practical things she could do with the bounty she'd received. Then, thinking wistfully of Jess's goading smile, on the other side she wrote down the things she wanted, dreamed of having. It was hard to get started. After fifteen minutes all she had written was "a nice pair of low-heeled shoes" and "a new raincoat." She stared at those two painfully practical items and suddenly began to laugh. How typically Charley Carter. She hadn't the slightest idea how to focus on her own wants. Even her dreams were dull. What did she want? What would she have if she could have anything her heart desired? She found herself frowning and laughed again. She was taking this far too seriously. In fact, she took everything in her life too seriously.

Grinning rather foolishly, she wrote "a week on an exotic island beach nude sunbathing with Jess McMasters." Now *that* was a dream. After thoroughly stirring up her libido imaging it, she wrote beneath it "diamond earrings." Now that was just as impractical. Where would she wear diamonds? Except she'd always admired them. No, she'd always wanted them. Yes, she had. And a matched set of real leather luggage. She cringed when she thought of picking up her old battered bags at the airport. "Luggage," she wrote. "Silk underthings." She blushed at that. She'd gotten a dainty set as a gift, and they'd felt so delicious against her skin. What did it matter if no one else saw them? She'd feel good wearing them.

Once she got started, it was fun. Like Christmas, only better. She let her imagination go and let greed run rampant through her soul. It felt wonderful. After an hour of hedonistic pleasure, she had listed everything from a spa beauty treatment to cooking lessons. She ran the tip of her index finger across that last, smiling to herself.

And though she didn't write it down on her list of heart's desires, mentally she added a final item.

A man with whom to share her good fortune.

If she truly could have anything she wanted, she realized with a guilty heart, that man would not be Alan Peters.

The woman's face, her pleading eyes, her silent scream.

Charley's own cry woke her as she jerked upright and covered her face with shaky hands. It took several taut seconds for her orientation to return. She'd been lying on the couch, watching the start of an old movie. It was playing out its final minutes now, so she placed the time at about eleven o'clock.

The woman's face. When would the horror of it let her go? Her heart chugging as frantically as it had during that terrible slice of time when all their lives were altered, Charley reached for the phone. If she spent another minute surrounded by the terror of that morning, she would go completely mad. Desperately she flipped through the pages of the phone book, then dialed. Everything inside her had shut down except for the need to reach out, to connect with a saving reality.

"Please be there. Oh, please be there," she panted softly, clinging to the receiver as if it were a life preserver for her sanity.

The ringing stopped and she heard a brusque masculine voice.

"McMasters."

"Oh, Jess—"

"I can't take your call right now. Leave a message and I'll get back to you."

Charley expelled her breath jaggedly. He wasn't home. She closed her eyes against the sudden blinding start of tears. "Oh, Jess, I need you." She forced herself to replace the receiver in its cradle, severing the link, unaware that she'd spoken the words aloud. Impulsively she grabbed it up again and hit the redial button. She had to hear his voice. Just one more time. And the low tones repeated, soothing the raw state of her nerves. Then the beep sounded and carefully she hung up.

Jess.

Huddling back upon the couch cushions, Charley summoned his image to mind and held to it like a charm against the stark memories.

Two A.M. Jess was yawning as he dropped his keys into his coat pocket and hung it by the door. Next he kicked off his shoes and shuffled in his socks into the living room.

It was done. And it was damn good. Now for

a cold beer, a hot shower, and a dreamless night's sleep. But the minute he opened the refrigerator, a snarl from his stomach reminded him of its empty state. Oh, well, he needed something to go with the beer anyway. He took a steak out of the freezer and chucked it into the microwave to thaw. On the corner of his counter the strobelike blink on his answering machine demanded his attention. After grouping mushrooms and an onion on a cutting board, he flicked it on and set to slicing.

Patty, Matt, Matt again, Jerri, Matt a third time. He listened idly as butter sizzled in his sauté pan. Then after the next click came a barely-audible whisper.

"Oh, Jess, I need you."

"Oww! Son of a—" He stuck his thumb in his mouth, sucking fiercely to stem the flow of blood.

The whispery plea was followed by an empty click and then two more messages, so it must have come in earlier in the evening.

Oh, Jess, I need you.

Charley.

Still nursing his throbbing thumb, Jess reached for the phone and punched in the numbers he had scrawled on a notepad. Two rings and then her voice. "I'm sorry, I can't come to the phone right now, but if you'll leave your name and a short—"

Jess hung up. His pulse was laboring. Behind

him the butter began to smoke. What was he going to do about Charley? What the hell was he going to do?

Somberly he stabbed his forefinger down on the erase button and went to scrape the vegetables into the pan, trying to put Charley Carter out of his mind. *Let it go, Jess. Let her go.* But by the time the meal was prepared to his liking, Jess found he had no appetite. Gaze touching upon the neatly-typed, double-spaced article lying on the table, he carried his uneaten meal to the garbage can and dumped it. Then he picked up his beer and headed for the recliner. The long night was just beginning.

She needed to talk to somebody before making her final decisions. Her conscience insisted that she make that person Alan. Though she was still annoyed with him for his behavior the night before, Charley attempted to forgive him. She touched the droopy flowers on her tabletop. Of course, he would expect her to channel the bulk of her funds into their project. It was what they'd been working toward, together, as a team. Before the accident, before Jess, she'd known no dissatisfaction with their plans. She'd been content to let him lead their lives. He had such clear vision, such single devotion. It was easy to get swept up in it.

But she couldn't avoid the change in their relationship. Suddenly she was more than an assistant in his grand plan. If they were a team, she was the more equal partner. She controlled the direction of their future and was somewhat disturbed that their directions weren't quite the same. She fought down the urge to give him control. It suddenly became very important for those decisions to be hers. But she needed to know what he thought. She owed him that.

So, with her briefcase stuffed full of lucrative offers and her head spinning with half-formulated dreams, Charley headed to her car. She stopped briefly to talk with an awkward openness to the reporters lying in wait. They didn't intimidate her as they once had. She was beginning to see what a useful tool the press could be. If only she could find the courage to utilize it.

There was a sense of relief in returning to the lab, almost as if the familiar smells and familiar chaos could convince her things could go back to normal. Alan was studying slides, and for a moment she just stood, watching him, examining her feelings as carefully as he did those muscle tissues. There was a sense of fondness, of respect, of irritation, as well. But no warming surges of want. Not the complex longings she'd come to identify as love. This was the man she'd agreed to marry. Hadn't she ever loved him?

He glanced up at her then and smiled excitedly. "Charlene, take a look at this." No greeting, no indication of shame or anger after their last meeting. Work. Always work. That was his one clear purpose.

Obligingly she set down her case and purse and went to peer into the microscope. A twist of a knob brought the small dot of light into focus. And she was aware of her own enthusiasm rising.

"When was this taken?"

"I did it this morning. I'd like you to prepare another one. I'll need a cleaner example for my findings, and you're much better at it than I ever could be. If you would."

Alan asking? That was different. But before she had a chance to evaluate the change, he'd put his hands upon her shoulders and was massaging them lightly.

"Charlene, about yesterday . . ."

She straightened to look him in the eye. And waited. She wasn't about to make it easy for him to apologize by going halfway. He would have to come to her this time.

"I realize how upsetting all this must be to you—the accident, the burns on your hands, the sudden burden of all that money. I want to help you, Charlene. Maybe I didn't make that clear enough before. I'm sure you've had time to reconsider what we discussed and have come to the sensible, reasonable conclusion."

Charley's brows lifted slightly as she drawled, "Which is?"

"That I know what's best." He continued to rub her upper arms convincingly. "You've been under a tremendous amount of strain. You're confused. Trust me to know what's in your best interest."

"My best interest," she repeated quietly. Indeed. His condescending words twisted the knobs in her head until everything was in perfect focus. And she didn't like the picture at all. It was the picture of their entire relationship in one revealing image. She and Alan never had discussions. He decided and she went along. Did he even know what her interests were? Or was he too absorbed in his own to see or care that she held opinions other than his?

"That's very kind of you," she began in a neutral tone. "But I have some ideas of my own that I want to explore."

His expression froze immediately. "Such as?"

Her sudden reluctance surprised her. Why should she be afraid to ask Alan for his support? This was the man she'd been ready to wed. She took a breath.

"I've been thinking that this whole situation could be used to promote awareness of what we're working toward. Now that I've got the public eye, I could use it to—"

"Wait a minute," he cut in curtly. "What are you talking about, Charlene? Are you thinking of becoming some kind of media crusader? You?" He looked her over in a manner of cool evaluation, and for the first time she felt unattractive in his eyes. Was that how he saw her? The pain of it lanced through her. "Don't waste your time pretending to be some glamorous spokesperson. It will only distract you from what you are good at. Put your talents and your money to work where they can be of some benefit. Behind me. Don't confuse good intentions with good sense. Now, let's not hear any more of this nonsense."

That was it. In his mind all was settled. She should back down and meekly accept his final decree. Well, it wasn't settled. If anything, he'd just upset the whole foundation of their future. If he wouldn't listen or let her have any say in the decisions of today, what chance was there that he'd be any more inclined to let her have a share in their life together? A life that suddenly looked very unappealing.

She was frowning as she turned away and ran squarely into an immovable wall. Her head jerked up. She gasped and every bone in her body melted. If not for the palms lending support beneath her elbows, Charley would have gone right down the drain set in the floor tiles between her feet. *Jess*. She couldn't speak. Her heart bobbed up to clog her throat. She didn't need words. Everything was plainly spoken in her dark, liquid gaze. For one insane second she wanted to fling her arms around his neck and kiss him wildly. But there was something about him that made her hold back that impassioned display. A guarded something shadowing his stare. And there was Alan boring a hole in her back with his furious glare.

"Am I interrupting something?"

How much had he heard? Charley's face flamed hot. She forced a jerky swallow. "No. I was about to . . . I was about to prepare a slide. Was there something you wanted? Could you wait? It will only take a minute or two." She was stammering like a flustered teenager. Her fingers clutched at the sleeves of his leather jacket. It was still cool from the morning air. As cool as his mood.

"I want to talk to you about something, Charley. I'll wait."

She took a calming breath. Her pulse was fluttering madly, distracting her from rational thought. He'd wait. *Oh, Jess.* She hadn't realized how badly she'd needed to see him until this moment. Avidly her gaze flew over him, hungry for every little detail, from his battered loafers and snug denim to the enticing texture of his nubbly wool sweater. Stretchy yarns did marvelous things to a well-developed upper body. Funny, she'd never noticed that so exquisitely before now. And leather . . . there was something about a man in a leather jacket that was primally exciting. The way a girdle of fur would have been on his prehistoric ancestors. Jess McMasters stirred everything primitive within her.

Then she looked up at his face. At the wind-rumpled hair that she longed to comb back with her fingers. At the strong jaw that could have used a shave. At those piercing gray eyes that saw so easily inside her soul. There were smudge-like crescents beneath them and a tightness at their corners and about his mouth that spoke of weariness and worry. A protectiveness of surprising force surged at those signs of self-abuse. And she had to wonder what weighed so heavily on his mind. Did it have to do with her? She needed to take him aside, somewhere separate, out of Alan's domain.

"You look as though you could use some coffee."

"About a gallon or so," he admitted.

"Come on. You can drink it in my office while I finish up . . . if I can find a chair."

He smiled faintly. And that ghost of his usual humor was what provoked her alarm. Why had Jess come to see her? She steered him back to her cubbyhole under Alan's disapproving glare, dumped a heap of journals on the floor so he'd have a place to sit, and shoved over a stack of files to clear a spot for his coffee cup. She smiled an apology.

"It only looks like clutter to the untrained eye. It's a case of too much volume, too little space. There's an elaborate filing system . . . really."

He didn't seem to mind. In fact, he didn't seem too interested in anything outside the contents of his cup. What was wrong?

Repressing an uneasy frown, Charley grabbed her lab coat. "Be done in a minute."

Jess gave an absent nod and stared vaguely at her back wall while warming his hands on the coffee cup.

"What's he doing here?"

Charley breezed by her disgruntled boss. "He won't get in the way. I'll have your slide in a second."

But that didn't satisfy him. Alan followed her around the counter and made himself an unavoidable nuisance at her elbow. "Why is he here?"

Charley stopped what she was doing and turned, placing arms akimbo. "Ask him if you're so curious. Now please move so I can get on with this."

Scowling, Alan shifted to one side. He watched her face, distrusting the flush of color and the keen nervousness that had quickened her movements the moment the other man appeared. Unfamiliar emotional turbulence provoked the demand, "Have you been sleeping with him?"

The utensils clattered noisily to the countertop from Charley's awkward wrapped hands. She inhaled sharply, then spun on the glowering scientist. "Are you asking if we've been having sex?" Alan blinked at her directness, and she felt dangerously close to striking him. "No. No, we have not."

"Charlene, I'm—"

"Sorry? I don't think you are, Alan. Now, please let me finish so I can see to my guest. And might I remind you that I am doing this as a favor, not as an obligation."

Jess came to his feet, startled from thought by the abrupt intrusion of her voice and by the violent jerk of his pulse. It settled into an agitated rhythm as he resumed his seat. Here, in her element, she had a different look about her, a kind of remote, all-business intelligence that couldn't quite best the softness underneath. It had knocked his equilibrium crooked the second he saw her, and he had yet to recover it. It wasn't supposed to be like this, with her all calm and collected and him so jittery inside that he couldn't keep his thoughts together. His professional air had deserted him along with his detachment. He was desperate to distract himself from the want to pull her down onto his lap when she moved around him.

"What are you working on?"

Charley gave him that shy, half smile that put his heart rate into double time. "Oh, you don't really want the details, do you?"

"Sure I do."

"Well, you asked for it." She sat on the edge of her messy desk and smiled down at him, pityingly, as if she knew she was about to bore him silly. What she didn't realize was that anything to do with her held his undivided interest. He was as greedy to learn as a child taking its first steps. And just as anxious to preserve the comfortable mood between them.

"There's a lot of research being done in our field. We've narrowed ours down to the intervention of the auto-immune process." She smiled apologetically. "I told you you'd regret asking."

"I don't. Maybe you could put it into English, though. I understand that very well."

"Okay. When Type I sets in, the individual is at extreme risk, very ill. Then suddenly there's a change, and for about two years—what we call the Honeymoon Phase—the body seems to recover. Then after that two years the metabolic disorder reinstates. We don't know why, but with treatment at the time of diagnosis with steroids and other compounds, we've been able to intervene and delay that resurgence of the disease. If we could delay it indefinitely until we could discover the cause and cure . . ." She shrugged meaningfully.

"Then what you're doing is very important."

"Yes, it is." And her pride was evident.

"And Alan, he knows what he's doing then?"

Charley smiled again. "He may not have the greatest personality, but he does have the finest mind I've ever known."

"Like yours?"

She laughed modestly. "Oh, not quite. I'm skilled in the technical end of it. Brilliance is his department."

"So what were you arguing about when I came in?"

Charley's good humor fled. Her gaze dropped and her lips tightened into uncommunicative roadblocks. Silently cursing Alan Peters for having the prior claim, he amended quietly, "If it's personal, just tell me to butt out."

"It's not. Not really." Her gaze flickered up beseechingly, and her color heightened. "It was a difference of opinion. Nothing you want to hear about. Shop talk."

The more uncomfortable she grew, the more he wanted to know why. "You look like you could use a good friend about now," he coaxed softly. "Aren't we friends?"

Friends? The idea startled her for a moment because she was used to thinking of him on a more visceral level. Friends? Yes. Yes, they were. From the beginning she'd known instinctively that she could confide anything without fear of being judged. He was her friend, and right now she needed him in that capacity a lot more than she needed the sexual tension between them. She sighed and looked chagrined.

"Yes, we are friends, Jess, and I do need a good listener."

His hands cupped either ear. "Try me. What's the problem?"

"The money."

"Ah." He said it all with that one short sound.

"Alan wants it to go into his—our research. He thinks spending it in a practical application is a waste."

"That's because he has the sensitivity of a snail. I'm sorry. Go on."

He didn't look sorry. And he was right. So she continued.

"There's more. I didn't show these to him. We were having enough trouble without moving decimal points even further." She passed him the stack of letters, and he went through them one by one in silence. Finally he exhaled in a gust.

"My God, Charley. You've got a fortune here. This cable movie thing, alone, could bid up to twenty, thirty thousand, easy. News and women's magazines, a spot on that emergency rescue show, the late-night and daytime talk-show circuit." He glanced up and was arrested by the distraught pull of her features. He put a hand on her knee, rubbing gently. "What's the matter, baby? This stuff's great."

Her cheeks grew even warmer, and he didn't understand her contrary reply. "I know. It's a wonderful opportunity. I had this idea about using all the attention to educate the public."

Jess laughed warmly. "I could just see Robert in front of a camera. What a natural."

"Yes, he is." She was looking down at her bandaged hands, a frown furrowing her brow. "And we could certainly use the extra funds."

"So?" he prompted. When she didn't respond,

he tipped her chin up with his forefinger. She wouldn't meet his eyes. "Still camera-shy, is that it?"

Charley grabbed a quick, unsteady breath. Alan's words still burned in her memory. "I just don't know if I could carry it off. What kind of representative would I be? I live in a world of lab coats and crepe-soled shoes. I'm more comfortable with lab rats than most people. It would be like having a bag lady pitch in a cosmetic ad."

"Whoa! Who told you that?" She didn't have to say it. Fury ground through him. "Charley, baby, he's wrong. You can reach out and touch the hearts of millions of people. I know you can. You touched mine and I'm one tough audience." She looked up at him then, listening, paying very close attention. "Can't you see what he's doing? He wants to keep you here, working for him. He's telling you you can't do good out there. He's lying to you, baby. You know it and I know it. Stop thinking about Alan Peters and what he wants. What do you want to do?"

"I want to do this, Jess. I really do. I just don't know . . ."

He smiled, warmly, convincingly. "You'll do fine. And you'll have Robert in your corner."

"And you?" she asked in naked need. "Will you be there, Jess?"

For a instant she thought she saw something stark and despairing in his expression. Then it was gone. He took up one of her hands very carefully. “If you want me to be, I will.”

Charley clutched his hand briefly and gave a tentative sigh. “I don’t know, Jess. Magazines are one thing, but television . . .”

“Baby, you’re beautiful. The cameras will love you.”

She blushed. “You don’t have to be nice.”

“I am not nice.” He said that so sternly that he almost convinced her of it. Then she smiled softly, disbelievingly, and lifted his knuckles to her cheek.

“You’ll have to do more than growl to convince me of that.”

And Jess McMasters’s conscience went straight to hell.

Ten

This is crazy, Jess. What are you doing?

He couldn't answer any more than he could draw a breath that didn't ache all the way down to his toes. He'd come to see her with one purpose only—to tell her the truth. She'd hear it sooner or later. Better from him, straight out. It would be easier for her that way. Then he could explain—Explain, hell. It was going to rip her heart out, and he was feeling just bad enough to want to suffer and bleed along with her. Some nice guy! Well, he'd show her the real Jess McMasters, wouldn't he? Not a pretty picture. Not one he was proud of at this minute. She'd know that all that stuff he was pitching at her about following dreams and trusting was a lot of bull. Who should know better, right?

But she'd smiled at him, she'd touched him, she'd reached inside and dragged him by the tender heartstrings to a state of total madness. Because it was madness. He knew that, too. Madness to believe the way she believed—completely, blindly. Madness because even though he knew better, one sweet smile from her turned him into tapioca. He'd set out to prove she was a ruthless, greedy monster and had found that monster was inside himself. He'd rushed into this project to convince himself that she was no different, nothing special, not worth the cost of his emotions, and now he was on his knees, writhing for mercy. Because she was all of those things. And he was going to hurt her. That knowledge was crippling. She was going to hate him. That was devastating. And there was nothing he could do to prevent those things.

So he'd come to sever the ties cleanly, honorably. He was going to tell her who he was and show her the article he'd written. Part of him was eager to get it over with, to feel the scourge of her disappointment and the affirmation of his own jaded beliefs. And part of him was cringing, terrified of hurting her, of losing her. Of cutting loose the only good thing he'd ever had. The only promise of any happiness he'd ever known.

"So, what did you come to talk to me about?"

Jess couldn't look up. He knew if he did, she'd be able to see right down into the depths of his tormented soul.

"Jess?"

He tensed at the inquiring graze of her fingertips along his jaw. Dear God, how could he build her confidence and then knock it out from under her? Especially now, when she was vulnerable and reaching for the first time toward the accomplishment of her dreams. Who was he to knock them down? It was bad enough that he was going to break her heart. He owed her. He owed her for proving basic goodness still existed. He owed her for grabbing on to things inside he thought long dead and buried. And for a moment, he'd wanted to dream again, too.

"Jess?"

"Nothing, Charley. Nothing important." He looked up and smiled. His cheekbones ached with the strain of holding it. She peered at him suspiciously, then abruptly smiled back. God, she was easy to fool. The good ones always were. The sudden need to protect her closed around his heart like a vise. Just for a while. Just until she got her feet firmly under her. Until she was strong enough not to need him or anyone else.

Who was he fooling?

Just until Monday.

Then she'd know everything.

He had until then to give her everything he could, to be everything she thought she saw in him. It wasn't a totally noble decision. It gave him three more days. . . .

"Let's get out of here." He stood and stripped the lab coat from her shoulders. Charley blinked in surprise but didn't protest as he flung the coat aside. She couldn't help smiling at his burst of contagious enthusiasm. "I know just what you need. There isn't a woman alive who can resist the charm of the Magnificent Mile and not feel like a million bucks."

Her smile grew bewildered.

"Chicago," he explained in a word. "We'll drive down for the day, and you can go shopping. We can be there by lunch and home in time for a late dinner."

Charley hesitated. She did her shopping out of home catalogs.

Seeing her balk, Jess grinned wider. "Come on, baby, where's your adventurous spirit?"

She was about to say she didn't have one.

"It'll be fun," he coerced with that beguiling smile.

Fun? When had she ever had fun? When had she ever had time? Buying clothes was like buying groceries. A painful necessity the sooner done, the sooner forgotten. But Jess intrigued her into seeing the possibility for more. And then there was the undeniable appeal of her personal guide . . .

Sensing she was weakening, he pulled out all the stops. "You want confidence? I know where you can get it. And with money as no object, you can't miss. We'll put together a package that'll knock their socks off. What do you say?"

"Jess, I don't know anything about shopping and clothes and stuff," she trailed off lamely.

"Trust me," he crooned. Her gaze lifted and warmed in an instant. It was as if she'd smacked him in the gut with a nine iron. It was all Jess could do not to wince. "What kind of limit do you have on your cards?"

"Cards?"

He laughed. "Lord, you are a babe in the woods, aren't you? Credit cards. You can't go carrying around cash."

She thought a moment, then told him, "I have twenty-five hundred on my bank card."

He laughed again at her naïveté. "That'll get you in the parking lot. Never mind. We'll dust off mine, and you can pay me back. I have tickets to all the best places in town. My ex used to wear the numbers off regularly. She carried them in a Rolodex clipped to her belt. I used to get Christmas cards just like I was a major stockholder. When we divorced and I took her name off them, I got condolence calls from every credit department on Michigan Avenue."

Charley was staring up in rapt amazement. Then she blinked and laughed at him. "Jess, you are such a liar."

He grinned wryly. "That's right, baby. You can't believe a word I say." He took her by the elbow. "Let's blow on out of here."

With Charley walking tamely at his side, Jess strolled through the lab. Alan Peters stopped what he was doing to glare in well-founded fury. As Jess was about to settle his dark glasses on his nose, he let loose a wide, cheeky grin in the other man's direction. *You lose, sucker.* He pushed up the sunglasses and ushered Charley out the door.

As they left the building, Jess stopped short at

a mailbox flanking the walk. Before he could give it much thought, he drew an insulated mailer out of the inside of his jacket, opened the chute, and let it slide. Then with Charley Carter on his arm, he strode away without looking back.

Charley was aware of excitement mounting, mile by mile. The closest she'd ever come to shopping in Chicago was buying a magazine at a gift shop in O'Hare International Airport during a layover. An adventure, Jess called it. An adventure. She'd never had one of those before. She liked safe, predictable things, yet here she was, tossing off her inhibitions, fleeing responsibility in a westbound car with a man of mercurial moods. And oh, it was exciting.

She spent the first hours rationalizing her behavior. She did need clothes. If she was going to be in the public eye, she needed something a little more glitzy than oxfords and the sensible twills and cottons she had hanging staunchly in her closet. There would be publicity pictures, cameras, parties, and fund-raisers, if everything went as she was beginning to anticipate. And those things required a certain amount of on-the-back flash. She could, of course, have gone to any number of the department stores in Ann Arbor or Detroit. But Chicago had one distinctive allure. Jess McMasters. She couldn't shake the feeling that he wanted to take her to his home ground. And at that moment she would have boarded a shuttle to the moon to spend the day with Jess.

They left Michigan and began the curve around the lake, through the rolling Indiana countryside and past the acrid stench of Gary, finally looping up into Illinois. The closer they got, the thicker the traffic, and the more edgy and animated Jess became.

"Right up there, through that next break of trees. That's my favorite view of the skyline."

From out of the mists of an overcast day, it was like a mythical kingdom set in the clouds.

"That tall one's Sears Tower. The one with the antennas is the Hancock Building. They're built to give with the wind off the lake. I remember the first time I went up in the tower. I was just a little kid. The ride up in the express elevator had my stomach bobbing around under my Adam's apple. My brother talked me into pressing up to one of the glass windows to look down, and about that time you could feel the whole building moving. I threw up in front of about forty people. It's one of those golden moments from childhood you don't ever forget." Jess laughed with a trace of embarrassment that endeared him to her.

"Is your family still here?"

"No. I have a brother in L.A., one in St. Louis, and one that kind of blows around out west like a tumbleweed. My sister's in Philly."

"Your parents?"

"Mom remarried a couple of years ago. She's got a condo down in St. Pete's. My Dad died my last year in college."

She touched his shoulder. "I'm sorry."

Jess glanced her way, smiling faintly. "Yeah, me, too." He was still wearing the dark glasses, but when he looked back to the road, she caught a shimmer along the ridge of his lower lashes that turned her heart inside out. "He was a great guy. Wanted me to be a pro ball player in the worst way. He was in the minors until his arm gave out, and I guess he wanted me to carry on the tradition. The whole family practically lived at Wrigley Field in the summertime. I think all those hot dogs are probably what tore my stomach up, even though the doctor said it's stress-related. Ulcers. Occupational hazard."

Of teaching? Charley wondered but didn't comment.

"Anyway, I was a pretty good third baseman, good enough to get me a scholarship. Had a couple of scouts feeling me out in my junior year, but I really wanted to finish school. I don't think Dad ever forgave me for that. And the next year he died."

Jess made it sound as if the two things were connected. As if he'd been responsible, and that Charley wouldn't stand for.

"I'm sure he'd be proud of how you turned out," she stated with conviction.

Jess shot her a quick look. His mouth quirked up in a brittle smile. "Yeah. Sure." He was silent for a moment then said, "I thought we'd have lunch at Berghoff's. I had my first legal glass of beer in the basement there." Subject of family closed. Charley got the message.

"Sounds fine, Jess," she replied softly, blinking away the evidence of a too-tender heart.

It was drizzling by the time they reached the city. Charley stared up in awe at the buildings that rose on all sides like a mountain range with peaks buried in the clouds. The wet street bisected them like a dark canyon stream. She'd never been to the Rockies but this was how she imagined them—majestic, soaring spaces of breathtaking splendor that reduced humanity to the size of a flyspeck.

"Oh my God! Look at that! I don't believe it!"

Jess hauled on the steering wheel, cutting two lanes and earning an angry blare of horns from the motorists around them. Charley grabbed for the dash, her heart lurching up into her throat as she looked about in alarm for a sign of some threat. The car squealed to a stop, slammed into reverse, and cozied up snugly to the curb. Jess shifted into park and leaned back, grinning as if he'd just experienced some very self-satisfying victory. Then he glanced at her and frowned at her pallor.

"What's wrong?"

"You tell me. What were you yelling about?"

"Oh. A parking spot," he explained triumphantly as if that should make some kind of sense to her. She mouthed the two words, trying to slow the panic of her pulse rate. "You have no idea how hard it is to find a place to park downtown."

"Parking? I thought we were going to be killed!"

"Believe me, people have been known to kill for a space this good. Damn! This is great!"

Charley glared at him. He was laughing and she'd almost had a coronary! She was about to scold him fiercely when he leaned across the seat to erase her frown with the quick, conquering press of his mouth on hers. Every thought in her head blanked completely. She was still sitting, as stunned as a stump, when he came around to open the door for her. He had to practically drag her up to the sidewalk. By then he was sweet-faced and contrite.

"I'm sorry if I scared you. Parking is like a religious experience to us city folk. We forget outsiders don't understand."

She smiled somewhat wanly and he laughed again, curling his arm around her waist for a good-natured squeeze.

"Let's eat."

The Berghoff was a comfortably noisy Old World-type restaurant with a bold black-and-white tiled floor and huge brass fans humming overhead. The scent of hearty German food and yeasty beer brought a sigh of appreciation from Jess McMasters. He ordered Berghoff beer from the tap for both of them, spicy brats and spätzle for himself, and a more conservative Dover sole for Charley from their tuxedoed waiter. When their steaming platter arrived, Jess inhaled and closed his eyes.

"God, I love good food! I may be on a liquid diet of Maalox for a week, but some things are just worth it, don't you think?" And he dug in with gusto. Watching him, her chest thickening with emotion, she had to agree. Yes, some risks were worth everything. He finally slowed halfway through his second beer and looked across at Charley with an expression of incredible contentment. "Almost better than sex," he sighed, then grinned at her blush and goaded, "How was it for you?"

She didn't back down from the smoldering insinuation of his stare. "It was fantastic," she returned in a tone so breathy his grin faltered and dwindled down into a strained smile. His gaze dropped to his beer. He reached out and began to lightly buff the pad of his thumb across her fingernails.

To keep from blurting out, *I want you, Jess McMasters!*, Charley grasped for something safe to say. "So, where are you from in Chicago?"

The fire eased in his eyes, but he continued the lazy caress of her hand. "The west side. Big Irish neighborhood. Right around the corner from Mayor Daly."

"Do you see very much of your family?"

His hand stilled as he shook his head. "No," he admitted softly and her fingertips became the aggressors, gently massaging over his. "After my divorce Mom got all puffed up with Catholic indignation. She thought I should have tried harder and told me Hell was going to swallow me whole." He gave a sad, self-deprecating smile. "She was right."

"What happened, Jess?"

"What happened? I don't know. Whatever happens when two people fall out of love. She wanted lots of things and I wasn't one of them." He smiled crookedly down at his empty glass.

"Jess . . ."

He glanced up cautiously.

"She was a fool."

He gave a soft little laugh, but his eyes were flat and his lips unsmiling. "The whole thing really, really hurt me, and I just don't want to talk about it anymore, okay?"

"Okay," she agreed quietly.

He pulled in a sharp breath and attempted a grin. "Are you still taking any medication?"

"No. Why?"

"You're going to need a tranquilizer if you're going to be my copilot while I drive down Michigan Avenue." He signalled for the waiter and ordered her a Mr. Bs. When the drink came, Charley eyed it warily and took a sip.

"Oh, my! What's in this?"

"About six liqueurs, cream, dark chocolate, espresso, and coffee."

"Oh, my," she murmured again, then obediently drank down every drop of her medicine.

And as soon as he pulled out into traffic, she was grateful for the anesthesia. While a sane and fairly careful driver in Michigan, something about the streets of his hometown turned Jess McMasters into a fierce, type-A aggressor. He drove as if he had an irrevocable right-of-way and the car was armor-plated to see he got it. He zigzagged across lanes, dodging buses and cursing at the cabbies who were about the only ones ruder behind the wheel than he was as the Els, the elevated rapid transit trains, rumbled overhead. Charley held on tight and prayed to Chicago's God of Parking that they wouldn't have to go around too many blocks.

He turned onto Michigan Avenue and Charley forced herself to study the scenery rather than their proximity to the other cars. Block after block of galleries and small shops existed behind old weathered brick and Victorian facades, standing shoulder to shoulder with soaring walls of reflective glass-fronted office spaces. Police officers in checkerboard caps gestured to the traffic and maroon liveried hotel staffers held umbrellas to assist guests from limos to canopied walk. Bridge construction forced vehicles to funnel into one lane, and Jess maneuvered for a spot with deft skill and colorful adjectives.

"Welcome to the Mile," he told her with the flash of his grin. He seemed to be enjoying the chaos of bumper-to-bumper traffic. She returned his smile faintly.

"Are we having fun yet?"

He laughed and swerved to avoid a bold jaywalker. He pounded on the horn. The pedestrian responded with a provoking hand gesture that had Jess cranking his window down.

"Jess! For heaven's sake!"

He took in the alarm-widened eyes and smiled sheepishly. "Habit," he explained. "I was just going to suggest that he and his mother—Oh, never mind."

She sat grumpily in the passenger seat, forcing him to behave himself. Finally he turned off on a side street, and within a few blocks they'd reached the lake. It was a rough, slate gray fading hazily into the horizon. Charley shivered instinctively as a group of skimpily-clad joggers trotted along the side of Lake Shore Drive. Jess went down several blocks and made a turn, angling sharply into a public parking structure. He found a rare space and cut the engine.

"You can open your eyes now."

Charley expelled her breath audibly.

"What do you want to hit first? Saks, Neiman-Marcus, Bloomingdale's, Cartier, Marshall Field?" At her rather dazed expression, he took up her hand, entwining just their fingertips. "Come on. Let's spend some serious cash."

As soon as they stepped out of the shelter of the parking garage, Charley discovered it wasn't called the Windy City for nothing. Cold, damp air sliced right through her old raincoat, making her think more of a lingering winter than the approach of spring. Snug in his leather, Jess didn't notice her discomfort. He was too busy soaking up the familiar scents and sounds of the city. Grimly she squared her shoulders and vowed to be a happy camper if it killed her.

"Warm enough?"

Huddled down inside the thin folds of her coat, Charley nodded bravely.

"Now who's a liar. Let's walk. The pace of the city will warm you up quick enough."

She didn't understand what he meant just then, but after several blocks she began to notice a different cadence, a faster heartbeat to the streets around her. It was noisy. It was hurried. It was crowded. It was exhilarating. Shoppers rushed by in their bright nylon jogging suits with umbrellas tilted into the wind. A vivid blue tarp flapped about the edges of the corner newsstand it covered. They were the only sources of color on the drab, rain-splattered walks. The streets were lined with evenly-spaced trees and wrought-iron fenced flower plots that were still barren. She could see why Jess would have thought that concrete was the natural order of things.

"We'll start at Water Tower Place," Jess was saying as they reached a corner. The walk sign was on, so Charley stepped off the curb. He casually reached out to snag her about the waist, hauling her up just in time to keep a cab from hitting her. She pressed back against him, startled by the brush with disaster. And it felt so good that he kept her there, tucked close. She must have thought so, too, because she didn't pull away.

If first impressions meant anything, Charley knew she was going to be awed by the cluster of shops anchored by Marshall Field and Lord & Taylor. From the street side lobby, escalators rose through a verdant jungle complete with waterfalls and emptied out into a soaring cylinder of exclusive shopping. She stared, overwhelmed.

Jess bumped her impatiently. "Don't just stand there gawking like a tourist. Let's start at the top and work our way down." He towed her toward twin glass elevators, and she assumed he meant to start at the top floor. But he didn't push seven. Seeing her confusion, he murmured, "Trust me," and followed it with a smile that would have charmed her into anything.

Almost anything.

She dug in her heels. "What are we doing here?" She glanced nervously at the Vidal Sassoon logo repeated in stark black on white throughout the interior of the salon and at the woman in spiked orange hair filing her inch-long nails at the counter.

"Start at the top," he reminded her with a smile as he dragged her inside. He showed a lot of white teeth to the receptionist, and she was instantly alert. "We need the works," he confided in a husky tone. "Who's your best available?"

"No appointment?" She arched a penciled brow.

Jess smiled wider. "No. Sorry. Can you work something out?"

She looked him over and smiled back. "Let me see what I can do." She clicked back into the monochromatic depths of the salon.

"Jess," Charley whispered uneasily. "This place has got to cost a fortune. I don't need a cut."

He reached up and let his fingers sink into her fine, unstyled hair. His gaze caressed her face with a discomforting intensity. "You have no idea how beautiful you are, Charley. You will."

And at that moment, if he'd suggested she shave her head bald and paint stripes on it, she would have numbly agreed.

The receptionist returned and her bright smile foiled any hope Charley had that they couldn't take her. "You're in luck. Our creative director had a last-minute cancellation."

Charley's restless gaze caught on a black-enameled plaque listing the salon services, priced by the experience of the stylist. The creative director was the top of the hierarchy. A cut was seventy-five dollars. Everything else was extra. Her jaw dropped. Her last haircut had been done by beauty academy trainees. The works had cost eight dollars.

"If you'll come back with me, we'll get started by testing the tensile strength of your hair."

Charley cast a desperate glance in Jess's direction, but he smiled and waved, letting the woman lead her off like a reluctant lamb to the fleecing room.

Several hours later she found Jess lounging on the black leather sofa. A mutilated Styrofoam cup was on the glass tabletop in front of him next to a half-consumed roll of Tums.

"What do you think?"

He looked up from the issue of *GQ* he'd been thumbing through, and his gaze was arrested. After a couple of very long seconds he said, "Yeah. Oh, yeah," in a hushed voice.

Charley flushed. She knew it looked nice. For more than two hundred dollars it ought to look nice! "The works" had consisted of a rinse to burnish in soft highlights, a body perm to add lift, and a cut that was feathered and full and flattered the delicate structure of her face. At the warming approval in Jess's eyes she turned and drew from her supply of cash, paying without a thread of regret. Some things were just worth it.

Jess was right. Her credit-card limit wouldn't have allowed her to survive beyond the first level of shops. She never would have guessed a man would be fun to shop with. Alan hated to be bothered with anything even faintly resembling the female domain. But Jess looked comfortably, confidently male among the silks and sequins, and his grin and sense of style made him popular with the clerks who waited on them. He knew exactly what he liked and coaxed her to express her opinions. He made it a sensual game, grabbing something off display, holding it up in front of her, making her close her eyes and feel the fabric against her skin. Then he'd create an image of her wearing it, some of his stories silly, like wearing a twenty-five-hundred-dollar beaded evening gown barefoot down a beach, some steamily suggestive, like walking down Michigan Avenue in a particularly supple suede coat with nothing on underneath it. He made her laugh and relax, and sometimes just the way he ran his hands over a garment was enough to encourage her to buy it. Because she could imagine, too. Imagine how it would feel to have his touch on the outside when she was on the inside. After she almost went into shock upon seeing the cost of a simple blouse she liked, he made a habit of keeping his thumb firmly over the price tag until after she made her choice. Then he'd obligingly lay out the appropriate piece of plastic and hoist the package.

Then Charley caught sight of Victoria's Secret. She started toward it eagerly, then the thought of looking through lingerie with Jess stopped her cold.

"You want to look in there?"

"Not with you."

He studied the window display with interest. "Are you sure? I'd be more than happy to have you model some of those things for me."

"No!"

He made a noise of weary disappointment. "I'll wait."

She gave him a grateful smile and dashed inside.

Jess paced. Graphic images of garters and scraps of black lace knotted him up into a dry-mouthed frenzy. When she came out of the store, his gaze was riveted to the parcel she carried.

"What did you buy?" Was that him speaking? He sounded as if he were talking through gravel.

"Silk," she said with maddening brevity.

Jess stood, paralyzed for a long second. Then he reached for the bag. "Can I see?"

Charley placed it out of reach behind her. "Have you some unhealthy fondness for ladies' underwear, Mr. McMasters?"

"Only when the ladies are still in it, Miss Carter."

"Then there's nothing in this sack that should interest you."

He studied the forbidden package and released a slow, wide smile. "You can show me later." Shifting the shopping bags to one hand, he put his arm in an easy loop about Charley's shoulders. And was devilishly pleased to feel her trembling beneath it.

Eleven

Her feet throbbed. Her head ached from the intense lighting and vivid colors. She was hot and drooping. And never had the first level looked so appealing.

"You fading on me, baby?" Jess followed that soft question with the brush of his forefinger along her cheek. She tried to rally an energetic smile but failed miserably. He made a sympathetic sound. "We have time for two more stops. Think you can make it?"

"Oh, Jess," she moaned wretchedly, slumping against his shoulder. "I don't want to see another dressing room for as long as I live."

"Poor baby," he soothed. "How about I get you a little reward for being such a trooper?"

"Does it involve sitting down?"

"If you show me what's in that sack." He nudged the lingerie bag with his knee.

"No."

He groaned in resignation, then steered her toward the up escalator. That made her groan.

"Back up?"

"It'll be painless."

When they reached the proper floor, Jess blocked her view and said, "Close your eyes and take a deep breath. What do you smell?"

She did. "Chocolate?"

He put a hand dramatically over his heart. "Oh, don't say it like that! We're talking chocolate of the gods here. Just the thing to perk you up."

Charley was disbelieving until, seated at a small café table, she had her first taste of Godiva chocolate and knew heaven. They sat silent, sipping foamy cappuccinos, sampling the rich chocolate, watching the crowd of shoppers pass outside the store's window. Everyone from teased-haired old women in high heels carrying fancy shopping bags to a group of rowdy sailors still in uniform. Charley sighed, reveling in the moment, in the man at her side.

Jess canted a look up at her profile. She was so damn beautiful it made everything swell shut inside his chest. She looked happy, relaxed, and weary. Her smile was just a slight curve, but it wrapped itself around his heart and squeezed big. And there was nothing he wanted more in that moment than to snatch her up and drag her off to the closest private corner to make fast and furious love to her until he'd exhausted what little strength she had left. But that would be one big mistake. Because come Monday she was never going to want to see him again. Why give her more reason to hate him by taking advantage of her blissful ignorance? Charley Carter wouldn't want to make love to a man who'd lied to her from the moment he met her. How clearly he could still recall Robert Carter's words. *Don't ever lie.* He was trying—trying so hard it hurt!—to give her some good things to remember when she thought of him. But it was a precarious balance. He'd never been very good at living up to what people thought he should be. Especially those he'd loved. And Charley wanted so much!

It was his fault. He'd encouraged her to want, to dream. When she'd looked up at him first thing this morning, it hit him squarely. All her dreams were wrapped up around him and what she thought she saw. A nice guy. A man she could trust. A man she could depend on. And he'd criticized Alan Peters for using her. At least all she had invested in Alan was time. She'd sunk a hell of a lot more into him. Why was he even trying to make amends for something that was going to devastate her? Did he really think a little charm and a guided tour of Chicago's couturiers would make up for breaking her faith and possibly her heart? What he was doing was wrong. There could be no crossing the line between professional and personal, and he was so disoriented that he didn't even know what side of it he was standing on. What was he doing? Begging for her forgiveness before she even understood why he needed to ask for it? Trying to convince her, or himself, that there was some good in him?

The sudden scrape of his chair drew Charley's attention.

"Let's go."

He saw her puzzled recoil at his harsh tone. How to explain it? He didn't try. He grabbed up the various shopping bags and began to stalk toward the glass elevators. He could hear Charley hustling after him, but he didn't slow his pace until she called out his name, softly, in confusion. Then if he didn't feel bad enough, she ground the guilt deeper.

"I'm sorry, Jess. I guess I'm just not very good at this. But I really have had a good time, and I want to thank you—"

He turned on her, expression hard and angry. "Why are you apologizing to me? I'm the one who's being a jerk, and you're telling me you're sorry. Well, it's not your fault, Charley. Goddammit, stop letting people wipe their feet on you!"

She stared up at him, her eyes showing surprise and agitation. He couldn't stand it. Cursing under his breath, he whirled away and then ran the last few feet to catch the empty elevator just as the doors were beginning to close. He held them open for her and stared straight up so he wouldn't have to see her wounded face.

"Jess, whatever I did—"

His gaze dropped, leveling a fierce glare. "It wasn't you. It was me. Okay? Why do you always assume it's you? You're not responsible for me being a son of a bitch, so why don't you just come out and say, 'Jess, you're acting like a son of a bitch. Knock it off.' "

The door shushed closed and the floor began to drop. Charley braced, then met his glower unswervingly.

"Jess McMasters, you're acting like a son of a—"

He grasped the back of her neck, digging his fingers into her hair as he dragged her up against him. His kiss was hard and demanding, wild with the want bottled up inside since she'd told him the underwear in her secret bag was silk. His tongue slashed along the crease of her lips and then plunged between them when they yielded with an unguarded softness. She tasted of coffee and rich chocolate and his control fractured. His knee jammed between hers so that she rode his thigh. Her back was pressed to the glass as he moved against her, rocking, rubbing with the whole length of his body until she moaned his name in helpless abandon.

"Jess . . ." The world was falling out from under her. Whether it was the drop of the elevator or the soaring intensity of his kiss, she wasn't sure. But for a second Charley was flying. She was vaguely aware of the blur of storefronts as they sped downward from floor to floor and of everything shuddering to a stop as they reached the first level and Jess eased away. His mouth brushed by her temple, and she could hear the whispered words, "Thanks. I needed that."

Then the doors opened, and strangers crushed in all around them. Jess struggled with the bags, catching the door with his foot and angling Charley out. Neither of them looked at the other or spoke of what had just happened. He started walking and she followed. She would have followed him into the fires of hell.

Jess stopped at the top of the escalator that led down through dense greenery to the street below. He looked everywhere but down at her. It was as if he didn't trust himself to. "Well, do you want to go home or stick it out for a couple more?"

"Let's go the distance."

She saw him inhale slowly, then he smiled at her, that weak, wide flash of a smile she'd come to recognize as a mask for things that had nothing to do with smiling. "Attagirl. I think I have a few more cards in here just dying to be abused."

He touched her elbow and almost withdrew his hand before taking a firm hold. The nervous uncertainty of the gesture bewildered her. Charley wished she understood men better. She wished just as fervently that she understood what was going on inside herself. Then maybe she could interpret his mixed signals and her mixed emotions. But this was a day of fun and fantasy. It wasn't made for deep thought. She had to remember that as they ran across the street, hunching against the cold drizzle, through the revolving door of I. Magnin. Jess directed her past the jewelry-counter maze to a bank of elevators. Charley stared behind them, amazed.

"I think there's a clerk and a security guard for every two customers."

"I think you're right." He steered her inside the elevator and pressed the button for their floor. He stood with toes against the door, breathing so loud and fast she'd have thought he was running up the steps. When she shifted her weight, he nearly jumped out of his water-spotted loafers.

He's scared.

That notion came to her all at once. At first she wanted to dismiss it. Jess McMasters? Scared? Of what? Of her? How ridiculous. But then she watched him as the elevator crept upward. His chest labored. His hands twitched uneasily on the handles of her shopping bags. He looked edgy enough to claw his way out through the door. Why? Because he'd been moved to kiss her in a glass elevator in full view of hundreds of shoppers?

The doors opened and Jess all but bolted out. Scared? Yes, he was, and Charley wanted to know the reason why.

The overwhelming elegance of I. Magnin was hard to resist. It was sleek. It was sophisticated. The salesclerks looked as though they could be modeling in the international fashion magazines. Charley felt woefully underdressed in comparison to the other shoppers but followed Jess into what he probably would call "designer sportswear of the gods." He flashed his worth-a-million-dollars smile at the stunning black saleswoman and drawled, "Spoil us with the best you have."

They were shown to a chic grouping of chairs, and while Charley looked puzzled, Jess reached for the flip-book of drawings set out on the coffee table. He thumbed through several pages and pointed to an exquisitely-tailored pantsuit. "Let's see this." He turned a few more. "And this one . . . and this. Baby, what do you think? Like this long or short?" His gaze slid along her legs. "Short," he decided for them.

By the time he went to the second book, she'd caught on and leaned into his shoulder to make some selections of her own. Purposely she kept her eyesight limited to the item and description, not the price. That would ruin the mood of delicious excess. Her bargain-basement morality had a hard time dealing with a four-hundred-twenty-five-dollar jacket and one-hundred-seventy-five-dollar trousers. So she just didn't look. Not this time when everything else was so perfect. Perfect. Her senses filled with Jess McMasters: the damp leather scent of his coat—sexier than any cologne—the rough unshaven shadow darkening his cheek and jaw, the feel of hard, strong man beneath the denim where her fingertips rested casually on the curve of his thigh, the jagged sound of his gasp when he turned his head to find her kissably close. Their gazes mingled and she got a jolt of something sizzly, as if she'd scuffed the rug and been zapped by the first thing she touched. The delicate hairs on her arms tingled. Her skin tightened. The sensation was sharp, electric. She knew he felt it, too, because the pupils of his eyes swelled in size until black nearly engulfed the cool gray. Then he jerked his head away, his concentration reaching, scrambling desperately, for another distraction. He gave the approaching saleslady a big, grateful smile as she toted an armful of garments and motioned for Charley to follow her into the dressing area.

Under Jess's smoldering scrutiny, she paraded out to make a runway turn in front of him, waiting for his hand signal of thumbs-up or neutral wave, then was helped into the next outfit like a turn-of-the-century socialite. She couldn't recall ever feeling quite so pampered and important as an individual. With three outfits—one long, one short, one pants, boxed and bagged—Jess led her back to the elevator and pushed two. The tension was back, thickly sensual and disturbing.

"Last stop for clothes, I promise," he told her with a fleeting grin. "You need something with flash and dazzle."

"Flash and dazzle," she repeated. "If you say so."

The doors opened onto the eveningwear and fur salon. Charley's first instinct was to shrink back inside the elevator and press for the next floor, but Jess nudged her out with an insistent elbow.

"Tough it out, Charley. This is the best of the best."

"Where am I going to wear the best of the best?" she challenged sensibly.

His smug reply was, "You never know."

The fact that the gowns hung four to a rack and were all individual designs clued her not to look at the ticket price. Instead, she allowed herself the fantasy of pretending she would have use for clothes like these. Intricate beading made some as heavy as suits of armor. Sequins winked against others like a front-window display at Christmas.

"There's no back on this dress," she exclaimed in conservative amazement. Then she blushed. "And no front on this one!"

"Try them both," was Jess's suggestion. She passed. If she was going to pay more than two thousand dollars, she wanted more than a half yard of fabric for her money.

She moved practically from the full-length to

cocktail dresses, while Jess fingered a sheath that would defy gravity, looking thoughtfully at her. She tried to ignore him. She wasn't the beaded, sequined, backless, frontless type and couldn't pretend otherwise. As Jess speculated over a slip of tissue-thin gauzy stuff with strategically placed bands of feathers, she grabbed the first sensible black dress she found in her size and announced she was trying it on. Once she'd stripped out of her clothes in the dressing room, she was dismayed to find that her little black dress was held together by what seemed a zillion tiny buttons from neck to waist down the back. The bad news was, she loved it. The fit was perfect, snug and supple. Its understated elegance was a compliment to her petite form. She had to know what it looked like done up.

Peeking out of the dressing room, she gestured to Jess. "Where's the salesclerk?"

"With someone else. Why? What do you need?"

She tried to wave him off, but he was approaching with a "let me help you" smile. "Buttons in the back," she mumbled. "I can't get them."

"Turn around." It sounded simple enough. Until she felt his hands at her waist, his fingers working up the row of fastenings. She was intensely aware of him standing close. She could hear the soft, quick pull of his breathing. And she held hers. Finally his palms soothed along her shoulders and he rasped, "All done."

It was hard to look at the dress in the mirror when his reflection was there behind hers.

"What do you think, Jess?"

He'd already started back down the tease of buttons, watching with fascination as fabric gave way to an increasing amount of fair skin. "I love this dress. Get this dress." His voice was low and raw, and she nodded in numb accord.

On the first floor she found them. Diamonds. Gorgeous half-carat studs in the precious-gems collection where iron security bars and armed guards clashed with velvet and mirrored elegance.

"May I see these?" she asked the woman almost reverently.

Jess watched her hold them up to the light to admire the flash and fire of the stones. He gave a half smile. "You didn't strike me as the expensive-jewelry type," he commented mildly.

"Oh, I'm not." She laughed with a touch of embarrassment. "Just these. I've always wanted some just like these."

"Then get them."

Carefully Charley positioned the earrings back on their tray. "Not this time. I don't want to buy up all my dreams. I won't have anything to look forward to." She thanked the clerk and smiled at Jess's mystified expression. "What's next?"

He shook off the paralyzing tenderness. "Neiman's. Then home."

And she was almost reluctant to nod. This was a day she didn't want to see come to an end. A day when dreams came true. But not all of them. Not yet.

Neiman-Marcus was like a cathedral of prismatic brilliance. The moment the doors opened, the scent of sophistication took hold and drew her in. She could have easily gotten lost in the miles of lighted glass counters backed by mirrors into an optical illusion of infinity. She was staring dazedly up the central bank of escalators when Jess steered her to a cosmetic counter.

"Improve on this," he told the artfully-painted clerk. Then his thumb brushed Charley's cheek and he added, "If you can."

Before she could protest, Charley was seated on a high stool and bibbed. Enough colors and brushes were spread out around her to touch up the Sistine Chapel ceiling. She swallowed uncomfortably, then looked to Jess who was leaning indolently against the counter on an elbow, watching the proceedings like some intriguing foreign ritual.

"You don't have to hang around," she said hopefully. "This will probably bore you to death."

She wanted to groan in aggravation when he smiled and said, "I'm not bored." Then he tapped restlessly on the glass top with his knuckles. "But I do have something to take care of. I'll only be a minute."

"Take your time," she suggested, trying not to sound too relieved.

By the time he returned, smelling of rain and cold and city exhaust, the consultant was applying the finishing touches to Charley's new face.

"How's it going?"

"Just trying to decide what color of curtains to hang," she replied dryly. Bravely she tipped her head back to let him review the final product. Which he did with considerable attention. She was dazzling. Color and shading accentuated all the best of Charley Carter. Her eyes seemed to have doubled in size and dewy softness. The delicate angles of her face were sculpted perfection. What he saw was the final step in a transformation he'd been watching all day. Oh, not the physical one enhanced by clothes and cuts and cosmetics but the inner one. A metamorphosis of shy moth to confident butterfly. It was as if each outward layer had reinforced the inner. Hadn't anyone ever told her how strikingly lovely she was? How animation deepened her eyes into pools a man could drown in? How happiness could bring a sensual bend to her mouth that wrung a man's heart dry? Before speaking, he plucked a tissue from the counter and rubbed it gently over her lips.

"Too dark," he pronounced huskily. "Something lighter. Softer."

It was back to the brushes until Jess nodded his approval.

"Great. Wrap it all up."

Then it was back out into the rain with the noise of the city to consume the silence between them as they went back the way they'd come.

Charley fell into the front seat of Jess's car with a sigh and closed her eyes, listening to him wrestling the packages into the trunk. Part of her was glad to put an end to this adventure, and the other was already mourning the fact that it was over.

"Have fun?" he asked as he settled in behind the wheel.

She smiled and answered without opening her eyes. "Yes. But Cinderella is going to turn into a pumpkin if she doesn't get back home soon."

"Gotcha."

The engine growled to life.

She was too tired to even take note of Jess's driving. Leave it to him, she thought limply as she watched the soaring skyline ebb to the squalor of the suburbs. The energy of the city became the depressive grime of low-income housing, with scrawls of graffiti replacing storefront signs and the roar of trains traveling next to the highway sucking up the noise of traffic. They were swallowed in a tunnel where the yellow overhead light flickered eerily, then the cinder block apartments and crowded rowlike houses gave way to the monotony of the interstate. And she could feel Jess relax at the wheel.

"A little R + B?" he asked.

"Fine," she murmured, her eyes slipping shut

once more. And to the sultry, soulful sound of Smokey Robinson and rhythmic slap of the windshield wipers, she must have fallen right to sleep. The next thing she knew, Jess was slowing on the exit ramp. She stretched, and as she gave her shoulders a limbering roll, Charley felt his arm slip from behind her, and he assumed a neutral position with hands on the wheel.

"Hi. Almost there."

"Good."

He was silent for a moment, then darted a quick glance in her direction. "Want to stop someplace for dinner? It's going on nine. I didn't want to wake you."

"No. I've seen enough people for one day."

"Okay. I'll just take you home."

He said that rather stiffly, and she hoped he didn't think she included him in that statement. On the contrary. The day didn't have enough hours to sate her need to be with Jess McMasters. But all too soon he was pulling into her complex and parking the car. He didn't say anything as he came around to open her door, then gathered her treasure trove from the trunk. She led the way to the stairs and soon was flipping on the lights in her apartment.

"Where do you want this stuff?"

"The bedroom's fine." That thought lingered lustily as she devoured the sight of leather and denim when he crossed to the short hall. Then he was back, skirting her awkwardly on his way to the door. That's when the knowledge that he was leaving sank deep.

"Take it easy, Charley. I'll—I'll catch you later."

"Jess . . ."

He drew up and waited, tense, expectant. There was a wariness in his eyes that almost held her at bay.

Almost.

She crossed the space between them, spanning his rigid shoulders with her arms, pressing her face into the soft leather of his coat. "Thank you, Jess. I will never, ever forget how much you've done for me. It was a wonderful day. Like a dream come true." She should have stepped back then, but she couldn't. Her fingers clutched the back of his jacket. Need was a flood inside her. Finally she felt him take a breath, and then his arms came up to encircle her in a cautious embrace, as if she were something he feared he could crush too easily.

"Don't go."

That slipped out before she could catch it. She felt a tremor run through his arms. Floundering for a way to back down from the obvious interpretation of those quiet words, she rambled, "I hear you make a great lasagna."

"You hear? Where did you hear that?"

"It was written on the ladies' rest room wall on campus."

He chuckled and the rumbling vibration shook

the very fibers of her soul. "I'm flattered. And it's true." He leaned back to see her more clearly. "Are you saying you have the ingredients for lasagna in that bacterial no-man's-land of a refrigerator?"

She smiled smugly in the face of his doubt. "So happens I do. At least I think so. I have the noodles and the cheeses, and tomatoes and herbs for the sauce and—"

"Stop it! Stop it! You're killing me. This I have to see."

Spurred by basic appetite, he accompanied her to the galley kitchen and made a hasty inventory of what she'd bought—just in case. He was instantly at ease, in his element rummaging about for the proper-sized pots.

"Oh, yeah. This will do." He examined the wine and his brows shot up. "Nice."

Charley leaned on the counter, thoroughly enjoying the sight of him taking charge of her cooking space. "Can I do something to help?" she asked timidly, expecting him to say, "Yeah, stay out of the kitchen."

But he didn't. He cast a swift, too casual look at her and remarked with a smooth nonchalance, "You could put on that black dress."

She lit up inside like a pinball machine at full tilt. "Okay," was all she could manage in a breathless little voice. He smiled thinly and began to chop the fresh herbs with a vengeance.

When she emerged from the bedroom, the

smell of savory sauce permeated the air. Jess paused with the tasting spoon halfway to his lips to stare at her. Blushing, she turned to present him with the row of gaping buttons.

"Could you do me up?"

She heard the clatter of the spoon and a muttered curse, then a husky, "I sure can."

By the time he reached the top button, she was nearly in a state of sensory shock. Her knees rattled together, and her mind was so dazed with anticipation she could barely remember how to function. His fingers stretched along the slender column of her neck from collarbone to earlobe, stroking softly as if to quell the frantic pulse thundering beneath them. Her head lolled back languidly, and she felt the stir of his breath at her temple. The waiting was sheer agony.

Then the kitchen timer began buzzing.

Jess ignored it for as long as he could, and then he stepped away from her, muttering something that sounded like a fervent wish that he'd shoved dinner in the microwave.

The food was marvelous, the wine superb, and the company strained to the nervous limit. For the fourth time Charley complimented Jess on the meal and he thanked her, using the same words each time as if he didn't remember uttering them moments before. Their table talk was not in cumbersome words but in a delicate conversation of glances and flirtatious half smiles.

When their anticipations had simmered and steeped to a restless boil and the pressure of want had built to an intolerable level, neither of them could pretend to enjoy another mouthful. They both stood at the same time and reached for the same dish to clear the table. Fingers brushed and gazes collided in a recognition of need. For a moment neither one of them breathed. Then bodies leaned one toward the other, eyes slowly closing and lips touching—once briefly; twice softly; three times slowly. Charley made a low, contented sound. This was the perfect end to the day, this sweet mingling of breath in a surrender to the inevitable. The money, the shopping, the spending had all been fun, a frivolous adventure for the spirit. But this . . . this was a reality for the heart and soul. One she'd longed for since that first unplanned kiss. The one dream her riches couldn't buy. Then abruptly he broke away and grabbed a handful of her plates. Silverware rattled noisily.

"I'll just clean up here and get going. I'm sure you're tired and you want to—"

"No." She was panting, hanging on to the edge of the table for balance.

"What?"

"You can't leave, Jess."

He stared at her, plates clattering dangerously in his hands.

"Not until you undo my dress."

Her logic was simple. But there was nothing

simple about the invitation in her dark, liquid gaze.

The plates were dropped to the countertop and forgotten. And it took the span of a heartbeat for them to come together in a galvanizing kiss. With one long stride he was close enough to catch her face between his hands, to take her lips with a frantic roughness. Even after the bountiful meal, Jess's mouth was hungry, ravaging, as if he'd been starving for the taste of her. Hers parted for the thrust of his tongue as he feasted on the moistness inside her mouth. He reached for the buttons, moving down them, popping them free with the deft movement of thumb and forefinger. His other hand skimmed along her ribs, over her hip where his fingers began to gather the fabric, moving it up higher and higher. Until he could feel the smooth stocking covering her thigh. Even higher until he came to a band of elastic and nudged beneath it. And came in contact with an unmistakable sleekness.

Silk.

And Jess McMasters caved in completely.

Twelve

Jess, back down. Walk away. Don't do this. Don't do this. You're going to hurt her. Don't hurt her.

Jess retrieved both hands, using them to mold her tightly to him. He broke from the kiss, and when she tried to recapture it, he clasped the back of her head, forcing it into his shoulder. Securing her there, firmly, gently, while his mind raced out of control. His teeth bit together, jaw aching from the strain of it. Tension gripped his muscles, making them tighten to the point of trembling. Want washed over him, pooling hot and heavy in his groin. He couldn't hold out much longer.

"Stop me, Charley." It was almost a plea.

Her head moved within the cove of his shoulder. Her voice was muffled. "I don't want to stop you, Jess."

Oh, God. Do something. Think of something. You're a smart guy. A resourceful guy. Get out of this. Now!

"We have to. I—I don't have anything with me. Guess I'm not a very good Boy Scout. This caught me unprepared." He laughed nervously and tried to push her away. But this time she hung on, refusing to give, refusing his delay tactics.

"I am," she whispered huskily. "Don't worry about it."

Worry? God, he was coming unglued. He took a stumbling step backward, colliding with a bank of kitchen cabinets, leaning against them while his legs shook fiercely. Then he felt her hand nudge beneath the bottom of his sweater, lightly rubbing the body-warmed cotton of his T-shirt, purposefully tugged it up and out of the band of his jeans.

Goddammit, Jess, don't let this happen! Stop it now. Push her away. Think, man. Think of Charley.

It was impossible not to when the soft pads of her fingers reached bare skin. His flesh jerked taut across his ribs and quivered beneath that skimming caress. Her hand rose higher, her fingers threading through the mat of hair on his abdomen, following it up to where it spread in a V over his chest, until her thumb stroked over one of his nipples, rousing it into a hard nub of attention. Jess's head smacked back against the cupboards, and his eyes squeezed shut. His big, unsteady hands clutched at her bottom through the fabric of the black dress, dragging her hips across his in a restless seduction of the senses. His breath labored, coming in short, jerky gasps that never quite brought an adequate supply of air down into his burning chest.

There was a second of respite when her hand drew out from under his shirt. He should have taken the opportunity to run. But he couldn't move for the life of him. Then he felt the tormenting trace of her fingers against denim where it was strained to the limit. His whole system short-circuited.

"Don't . . ." Was that him? His throat closed up around the sound, strangling back the protest as he heard the rasp of a zipper and experienced the relieving give of encasing material. A short-lived relief.

"God . . ."

Her mouth pressed hot and wet just below his furred navel. He raised his arms over his head in an unconscious pose of surrender. The backs of his hands fluttered and knuckles thrummed against the wood of the cabinet as sensations of surprise and intensity ripped through him. He pushed down with his heels, digging them into the floor tiles, struggling to lock his knees. He couldn't breathe. He couldn't stand it. . . .

With fingers clenching in her tousled hair, Jess dragged her up to meet the urgency of his mouth. Hers opened, wide and wild for him. At the same time he wrestled the hem of her dress up to her waist and skimmed down the barriers of nylon and silk. An impatient sweep of his arm sent dishes crashing into the sink. With fingers hooking behind the curve of her thighs, he lifted her, turned and set her down quickly on the kitchen counter. He heard the sound of her soft, panting cries through the roar of blood in his head. He felt the backs of her knees convulse over the tops of his shoulders and her heels beat frantically against his back as he used his mouth to drive her to an explosive release.

"Jess . . . oh God. Jess . . ."

And then it was very quiet, the calm after the storm, with only the ragged saw of their breathing. Jess was sitting on the kitchen floor, dazed beyond thought, slumped back against the lower cabinets with Charley's bare feet dangling over either shoulder. His heart was racing like a stock car engine. He ran his tongue over his lower lip and tried to speak.

"God—what was that? What happened?"

"Earthquake, I think," came her hoarse voice from above him.

He managed a smile and a raw, croaking laugh. He caught one slender ankle and turned his face against her smooth calf. His lips traced the soft curve and she began trembling again. "Oh, baby . . . what are we going to do?"

Her other foot twisted. Her big toe rubbed along the angle of his jaw and tickled his ear. "You're going to do my dishes, and I'm going to work on taking a shower."

"Okay."

Her toes grazed his neck. "You're easy, Mc-Masters."

"I know."

She came down off the counter, straddling his outflung legs. He glanced up drowsily and got an eyeful of lush, rounded bottom. He reached up and caught the edge of her hem, coaxing the wrinkled fabric down with a gentle tug.

"I love this dress," he muttered.

"I love you," she replied.

It took Jess a moment to grasp that, but by then she'd already gone. He moaned wretchedly and let his head roll against the front of the cupboard. He tried to get up, but nothing wanted to work right. His every sinew had gone as limp as the cold lasagna noodles. Finally, cursing himself under his breath, he rolled to hands and knees and hauled himself up by clinging to the sink. It took a full minute for the shaking to stop, and by then his mind was beginning to function. Sort of. He looked vaguely into the sink. Hell, most of the dishes were broken anyway. He began distractedly to pick out the pieces and throw them into the garbage bag under the basin. *Don't think. Don't feel.* He moved in a staggering reel to the table and gathered up the remaining dishes, scraping what he could and putting the rest to soak in hot, sudsy water. *Oh God.* His stomach muscles tightened around a familiar ache, and his heart pounded with one that was frighteningly new. *Help me, God. Help me find the strength from someplace. I don't want to hurt her. Give me some Hail Marys, some Our Fathers, and get me the hell out of here before it goes any further.* He rested his forehead upon soapy forearms and swayed like a drunk.

With the sink drained and wiped out and the pots and dishes drying, Jess walked with a numb calm into the living room. He paused, listening to the spray start up in the bathroom. He licked his lips and forced a dry, dragging swallow that hurt all the way down to the burning pit of his belly. And he reached for his jacket.

Oh my . . . oh my . . . oh my . . .

Charley stared at her reflection in the mirror, seeing a wide-eyed, bruise-lipped stranger with subtly made-up features and a tangle of expensively coiffed hair. What had happened? The shivering started up again, nerveless, tingling, exhilarating. She'd never wanted anything in her life the way she wanted Jess. She closed her eyes, unable to face her image with the memory. Of what they'd done . . . of what she'd done to him. And he, to her. She'd never . . . never wanted to . . . But Jess . . . She'd just gone crazy. Wanting to touch, to taste, to give and take in ways that left modesty, even sanity, behind. Knowing there was more to discover had her breathless.

Stop daydreaming about the man, she chided herself, *and get down to business.* The awkward business of showering with her hands still swaddled and sore. She wanted to be all clean and soft and sweet smelling for Jess. For when they would come together as man and woman for the first time. Hurriedly she scrubbed her face free of the cosmetics, wondering as she did if she could ever master the same clever tricks of highlighting, contouring and, shadowing. She should have gotten a paint-by-number chart to follow. Then she brushed her teeth, smiling as she remembered Jess's offer to do that for her. As if he didn't already do enough. For her. To her.

But she was digressing again. Thinking of Jess was much more pleasant than pondering the shower predicament. She shimmied out of what she now considered her favorite dress and shook out the lesser wrinkles before hanging it on the door. In just her slip and silky bra—her pantyhose and underpants were someplace in the kitchen—she stretched out to turn on the water, testing it with her fingertips to get the right temperature before switching to overhead spray. She was working the clasp of her bra when there came a soft tap on the door.

"Charley? Can I come in?"

In a second of panic she looked about and started to grab for a towel. Oh, for heaven's sakes, she laughed at herself. Hadn't they gone beyond the stage of shyness with each other?

"Sure."

He peeked around the edge of the door, his eyes darting up and down. He looked nervous and that made her relax completely.

"Hi."

"Hi." He edged in and leaned against the sink. He'd taken off his sweater and his shoes and looked heart-stoppingly wonderful in his white T-shirt and jeans. And bare feet. "How you doing?"

Her hands shook with the want to touch him, but they were still fencing cautiously with their emotions, so she held back. Physically, at least. "I'm fine. Better than fine. I never realized I could enjoy myself so much in the kitchen."

He grinned fleetingly at that. "Yeah, well, I know my way around a countertop." His toes brushed over hers. "And you're not so bad, yourself."

"I was inspired."

"Give me your hands."

Perplexed, she stuck them out and frowned slightly when he slipped sandwich bags over them, securing them at the wrist with rubber bands.

"Watertight," he explained and she looked down at them, marveling.

"You're a helpful guy to have around, McMasters."

"Right now I'm a guy who needs a shower bad. I can wait—or I can scrub your back."

Charley hesitated all of half a second before handing him a washcloth. "I'm all for conserving natural resources."

"I was hoping you would be," he admitted gruffly. He reached for her, his big, powerful hands sliding over silk-clad breasts, then skimming around to release the hook in back. Without pause, without dropping his gaze from her eyes, he let his hands stroke down the curve of her spine, catching his thumbs in the band of her half-slip to ease it down over her hips. When he let it go, it pooled around her feet.

"Get wet," he told her huskily. *Get ready,* his gaze concluded hotly. Then he nudged her toward the shower.

Charley was trembling beneath the warm spray. She heard the jingle of the curtain and tensed in expectation. She couldn't make herself turn around. After a second she felt the bar of soap move up and down her back in slow, unhurried strokes. The breath she'd been holding expelled noisily when he moved closer, letting the friction of skin on skin work up the lather. He rubbed against her, his chest to her shoulders, his thighs to her buttocks, the hard swell of his groin to the small of her back. Then he chafed the soap vigorously between his palms and began on the front. He started with her arms, his palms gliding up and down them before easing over to her taut-tipped breasts. His hands kneaded slowly, sensually, until she was arching against him. Then they slipped downward, gliding on wet skin, circling over her flat belly before converging in a sleek, plunging V between her thighs. Her body bucked and quivered in the circle of his arms.

"Easy, baby. It's just a shower."

She revolved abruptly, her arms sliding over his shoulders to curl about his neck, pulling him down so she could kiss him deeply, with desire-drugging thrusts of her tongue. His hands kept moving, building the lather, building the intensity of passion to its extreme. Charley broke away from his eager mouth, gasping frantically against his wet neck.

"Jess." She twisted in his embrace as he tasted her earlobe, her throat, the slope of her shoulder. "Jess, I want us to make love."

"Rinse first." He reached for the shower head and angled it up and down. Then, reluctantly, he stepped away from her and turned them both to face the spray.

"Your back," she murmured.

"Who cares about my backside?" he muttered, finding her lips again.

"I do. It's the first part of you I fell in love with."

He turned, kissing her, caressing her with a mounting impatience as the water beat upon his back. After a minute he claimed, "All clean," and she wasn't about to argue. Plastic bags were stripped off her hands and left where they fell in the bottom of the tub.

While they dripped and shivered standing toe to toe on the bath mat, Jess wrapped a towel around Charley's shoulders and began to buff slowly. She closed her eyes, arching, leaning back into it, until she heard his low groan. Then there was the exquisite feel of his mouth at her breast. First one, then the other, and his tongue lapping at the beads of moisture that trickled between. Jess patted the towel down the curve of her back, over her buttocks and trim legs as he lowered to his knees on the rug. He rested his damp head against her hip while drying her legs with long, leisurely drags of terry. His rapid breathing scorched across her skin.

"There's more room for this sort of thing down the hall," she told him in an incredibly strained little voice.

"Let's go." He stood, keeping the close contact of flesh on flesh.

"But you're still wet."

His hand dipped down, plunging briefly. "So are you," he growled roughly. What could she say? He was right.

He started kissing her again, and when she was wound about his neck, he reached down to pull her legs up around his waist. She locked her ankles and held onto him for all she was worth.

"Where do you want to do this?" he asked

raspily

She was kissing his mouth, his cheeks, his eyelids, his temples, gasping in between, "The bed, the floor, the kitchen table. I don't care as long as it's soon. Make it soon, Jess."

He walked with her wrapped about him, carrying her down the hall to her bedroom. He bent her back at the edge of the bed, letting her down easy and coming down with knees on either side of her. With one hand anchored behind her head, the other flashed out, knocking the shopping bags and boxes to the floor in an expensive spill to clear the way as he dragged her in a fireman's carry up the quilted cover. Finally he settled on top of her, moving, shifting, so the fit would be just right. Then he lifted up on his elbows and smiled.

"God, you feel good."

Charley reached up to rub her fingertips along his scratchy jaw. "So do you."

He moved again, nestling between her uplifted knees. And he hesitated, more than a little concerned. She was so tiny and he was so aroused he feared he'd tear her apart. "Let's do this nice and easy."

"Jess."

"Umm?"

"Just shut up and do it."

"Okay."

He lowered his head slowly, touching her parted lips with his tongue, touching, feathering light little flickers until she moaned in an anguish of impatience and jerked his head downward to smash their mouths together. She thrashed beneath him, moving her legs restlessly on either side of his as yet motionless hips. She rocked hers, tempting him, begging him.

"Jess, please love me."

"I do, baby. I do."

She made a soft noise of anticipation as he pressed against her, unsuccessfully at first. Realizing the wait was almost over made her bold. She reached down, touching him, stroking him, finally guiding him while his kisses stole her breath away. Then she accepted him inside, sheathing him in tight, liquid fire until the sense of fullness was incredible. She wanted to weep with the joy of it, that sensation of complete and utter harmony. He was still, lodged deep, breathing in light, shallow pants, wanting to be sure, very sure, he wasn't causing her any discomfort. Then the low, purring rumble vibrating in her throat answered his concerns.

"Oh, Jess, quit stalling before you drive me out of my mind!"

She responded to his first tentative strokes with an urgent exuberance, clutching him about the neck, arching off the bed to receive more of him. Her little body trembled and twined around his, hips shifting, heels running up and down the backs of his calves and thighs. She made exquisite little moans as her face pressed into the side of his neck.

It was worth waiting for. It was worth dying for, she thought wildly, trying to cling to the moment, to sustain the taut edge of ecstasy even as he provoked her so far beyond that she wasn't sure she could ever find her way back. Then her tension burst into long, wracking shudders that seemed to go on and on forever. The violent pulls of her pleasure were enough to drag him with her over that last hurdle of sanity into pure sensory paradise. And his ragged sigh of satisfaction was the sweetest sound Charley Carter had ever heard.

It took a long time for them to regroup even a shred of their composure. There was no hurry. It was too much of an effort to do more than breathe. Finally Jess turned his head slightly and brushed a languorous kiss across her forehead. That's all it took to recharge her desire for him. She moved against him, charting the swells of his shoulders with her fingertips, tracing the cording of his throat with her lips. She felt him give a start of surprise.

"What's this?"

"Ummmm," she answered, licking along his jawline, letting her mouth drift over to find his. They shared a long, thorough sampling, then he tucked her in close and simply held her. For all of ten seconds. Then she was shifting impatiently, nibbling along his shoulder, rubbing her knee over the crisp hair of his thigh.

"What?" he demanded. "More?"

"And more and more and more."

That concept might have enticed him if she hadn't already sucked his energy level dry. He twitched away from the provocative forays she was starting along his hip. But she wouldn't be discouraged. She followed him as he rolled onto his back, straddling him, riding his hips with the encouraging movement of her own.

"Charley, come on. Give a man a minute." He tried to sound stern. It was hard to do when her hot little mouth was biting at his chest.

"Take all the time you like," she purred.

If he'd hoped she'd allow him to burrow into the embracing comfort of her covers, he was mistaken. She began to scoot down the length of him, nipping sharply along the taut curve of his rib cage while her hands moved lower. She was impatient with the gauze covering that kept her from reveling fully in the textures of his body, his wonderful, wonderful body.

"Jess." Her voice was thick with desire.

"Don't," he cautioned with a touch of aggravation. "Charley, come on. I'm not kidding."

"Do I act like I'm kidding?" She licked long and lasciviously down the flutter of his abdomen. He grabbed her shoulders and hauled her up. Her attention shifted immediately to his mouth.

"Charley, stop it." But she could feel him smiling. "Don't. I'm an old man. I'm tired."

Her thigh rubbed across his groin. "No, you're not," she argued huskily.

He groaned. The hands gripping her shoulders began to knead involuntarily. She felt his breathing alter, deepening, roughening, and she grinned.

"You're not going to give me a break, are you?" he grumbled as his hips started to rock with her insistent rhythm.

"No."

He closed his eyes and shuddered briefly. His gaze was smoky when it fixed on hers once more. His hands plied the smooth flesh of her back, working down to cup the firm curve of her seat. "I thought you scientists were a patient lot. Always sitting back to watch things grow at their own rate."

"This scientist likes to accelerate the process. I prefer hands-on research and lots of input."

"Input, huh?"

"Lots of it," she affirmed with a naughty wriggle of her hips.

"All right, goddammit," he growled. "You asked for it." He shoved her roughly on her back and thrust into her with a pile-driving force. She jerked, going rigid, her eyes squeezing shut, her breath suspended. And his heart stopped. "Charley? Baby?"

Her eyes opened, all dark and dazed and dewy. "Oh . . . Jess." Her arms curled around his neck, drawing him down to her.

Between her hot, gobbling kisses, Jess told her, "You are one greedy, demanding woman."

"Only where you're concerned," she murmured, moving with the hard strokes of his body. "Now stop complaining."

"Oh, baby. I've got no complaints."

Jess wouldn't have believed an atom bomb exploding at the foot of the bed could have roused him from sleep. But a mewling sound of panic did. He opened his eyes, blinking off the disorientation. Where—? Charley's bed. Hers was the balled form quaking beside him. Fully awake, he leaned over her, stroking her shoulder.

"Charley?"

She whimpered, tucking tighter into the wad of isolating terror. He could see the moisture rimming her closed eyes, spiking her lashes, and his heart turned inside out.

"Charley. Charley, baby, wake up."

She felt the strong hands pulling at her, drawing her away from the danger, from the horror, from the pain. But she fought him, wildly, glancing blows from her ineffective fists off his arms and chest and the side of his head.

"No," she wailed. "Let me go!"

"Charley. It's all right."

She struggled against his attempt to embrace her. The frantic race of her pulse quickened his own. The sight and sound of her tears and her terror twisted his emotions in brutal knots.

"No. I have to save them. I promised. I promised."

Jess dragged her to his chest, crushing her rebellion, absorbing the violence of her weeping. He could feel the wetness on his own face as he cradled her close. His voice was raw. "Don't. Charley, don't. Let it go. You couldn't have saved them. You did everything you could. Please, baby, don't cry. Don't cry."

He felt her jerk sharply, and then her arms went around his neck, chokingly tight, trembling fiercely.

"Jess?"

"That's right. It's Jess. Shhh. It's all right. Shhhh. I've got you. You're safe. Shhhh."

"Jess . . ." She suddenly went still. He could almost feel her confusion gathering. She touched him almost disbelievingly, running her hands along his shoulders, the back of his neck where it met with the wavy ends of his hair. "Jess . . ."

"Shhh."

"Oh my God," she whispered softly.

She pushed against him and he let her go. From a cautious distance she looked at him, wide-eyed and uncertain. As if she were seeing a ghost. Or the truth.

"I never saw your face," she whispered hoarsely, staring at it now as if for the first time. "It was you."

He didn't like the stark intensity of her expression. This was it, when the lies started surfacing. He tensed.

"Why didn't you tell me, Jess?"

"I . . ." What could he tell her? The truth? That would be a switch. Panic started swelling in his chest, clamping around his throat, but he struggled to speak. "I tried . . . You didn't know me at the hospital. I was afraid . . . Oh God, Charley, I'm sorry. I didn't want to hurt you. I didn't mean to hurt you."

But she continued to stare at him, not understanding anything beyond a basic fact. "You saved my life." And then an even scarier one. "You could have been killed." Her arms flew around him, hugging desperately. "Oh God, Jess. You could have been killed!"

He started shaking and couldn't seem to stop. All the vivid memories of that day resurfaced with a blinding stab of mortality. And the words poured out, tumbling over one another, almost a babble of fear too long suppressed. "Oh, Charley. I keep seeing it over and over and I keep thinking, 'what if I hadn't been in time? What if I'd waited just one more second?' I could have lost you. It makes me crazy to think about it."

She was stroking his rumpled hair gently, soothingly. "Then don't. Don't think about it. You should have told me. You're a hero, Jess. Part of the reward—"

He cut her off coldly, jerking back out of her embrace. "I didn't do it for the goddamn reward!"

Charley touched his cheek, feeling the muscles tense and tremble beneath her fingertips. Her voice was hushed. "Neither did I, Jess."

He blinked. Then he scooped her up, pressing her close to the thunder of his heartbeats. "God, I love you!"

Charley squeezed her eyes shut and smiled. Everything was perfect. A dream come true.

Thirteen

A shrill ringing. A low muttered curse. A chill of cool air as the covers were jerked from her.

"Get the goddamn phone."

Jess?

Jess.

Charley didn't have time to truly appreciate the fact. The phone kept ringing. Why hadn't she thought to put the machine on? And Jess had rolled onto his stomach, dragging all of the covers around him in a swaddling cocoon. A string of expletives grumbled up from under the pillow he'd pulled over his head.

The phone.

All she wanted to do was cuddle up to the man in her bed for another few hours of undisturbed rest. But the ringing wouldn't stop, and when she tried to wiggle under the blankets next to Jess, he snapped them selfishly about him and growled, "Leave me the hell alone!"

"Well, excuse me," she muttered at his mummified figure. "I have to get up to answer the phone anyway." And for leverage, she pushed off from the pillow, shoving his face hard into the mattress.

Aware of her own lack of clothing once she stepped into the brightness of her living room, Charley snatched up the first available covering. That happened to be Jess's jacket, which was draped over the couch. Then, she shuffled to the end table on the other side of the sofa, half hoping the phone would quit before she picked it up.

" 'Lo?"

"Charlene? Is that you?"

"Good morning, Alan. What time is it?"

"Almost eight. Where have you been? I've been calling since you left yesterday."

"Why didn't you leave a message?"

"You know I hate those things. Where were you?"

"Chicago."

"What? It sounded like you said Chicago."

"I did. I went shopping in Chicago."

"Shopping." He made it sound like some dubious unnatural habit.

"I needed some things." Why was she explaining? And why was he calling at this ungodly hour on the weekend? "What was it you wanted?"

"I *want*," and he stressed that, "to finish our

conversation. I'm sure you've had time to think over what we discussed and have made the right decision."

"Yes," she said. "Yes, I think I have."

"Good." He sounded positive and pleased. And Charley realized it had never occurred to the man that she might not have decided in his favor. "I think we have cause to celebrate. How about dinner tonight?"

"Aren't you afraid someone might see us together?" She couldn't help it. Nor could she ignore the bitterness edging those wry words. It was as if she were recognizing for the first time how his concealment of their relationship had hurt her.

He sounded smug and that made her teeth grind with unaccustomed fury. "I don't think we have to worry about opinion anymore."

"Does that include mine, too?"

There was a long silence, then he said tersely, "I'm not sure I understand what you mean."

"I'm sure you don't. As for dinner, I'm afraid I have plans." Or she was hoping she did.

"Cancel them."

"I don't want to cancel them, Alan."

He blew up. "What could be more important than what I have to say to you? I'll pick you up at six."

"Alan, no!"

"No? What are you trying to say?"

"I'm saying no, I don't want to go out to dinner with you. I have plans that are important to me. We can talk when I come in to work next week."

"If you still have a job," he drawled menacingly.

Charley drew a breath. Her temper hit a flash point. "Are you implying that if I don't go to dinner, I don't have a job?"

Silence. Then an exasperated, "No, of course, not."

"Good."

"What about my money?"

"*Your* money?"

"For our research," he clarified quickly.

"I'll be making a press announcement at the award ceremony on Monday. You might want to be there."

"Are you sure you're all right, Charlene? You just haven't been yourself lately."

"On the contrary," she murmured more to herself. Alan would never understand.

"Maybe I should come over."

"What? Now?" She gave a start as something warm blew against her ear. One of Jess's arms banded her middle beneath the bulky jacket, and the other gathered her hair away from the nape of her neck. And he began to nibble that sensitive skin.

"We need to talk, Charlene. I don't know what's going on with you, but I don't like it."

She was liking it. Very much. Jess was nuzzling her neck, his morning beard supplying a devastating friction. "Ooooh."

"What? What did you say?"

"I–I said I'm sorry, but I'm going to be busy. Ummmm."

"Charlene–"

Jess snatched the receiver. "She said no, you jerk. What's with you? They teach you to split an atom, and you can't understand a two-letter word? No. N-O. Get it? Or don't you know how to spell, either? Or how to put two and two together and come up with get lost!" He slammed the phone down, then looked at a startled Charley to see if he'd overstepped his bounds. Her gaze was unpromisingly cool.

"My, we are into some rather nasty chest-beating this morning, aren't we, Mr. McMasters."

He reached for the phone. "Want me to call him back?"

She caught his hand, redirecting it to her hip. "No. Do I have to spell it out?"

"I was an English major. I'm good at spelling. But I'm not too sure about chemistry." His look questioned without words. Where did he stand in this particular equation?

"The chemistry's fine, Jess. Just fine."

"Teach me something about chemical reaction."

"After last night? I don't think there's anything I could teach you."

"Don't be too sure. Let's experiment."

Jess lifted her up, letting his jacket fall to the floor, and he carried her back to bed.

Ten A.M.

Ten A.M.?

Charley repressed the moral outrage claiming the hour positively slothful. Everything she wanted was right here in bed, anyway. Smiling, she stretched out her hand. And met with cool sheets.

Jess. She bolted upright. Oh God . . . He wouldn't have gone without telling her. Would he?

"Jess?"

She scrambled from the tangled sheets, whipping a short terry robe from her closet and belting it on the run. As she rounded the hall corner, the first thing she saw was his leather jacket folded over the back of the couch. With a smile of relief she approached it, stroking the supple grain with her fingertips before turning toward the sound of singing in the kitchen. She paused at the breakfast bar, completely blown away by the sight of Jess cooking breakfast.

An unfamiliar boom box was angled on the corner of the counter playing a tape of something distinctly Motown. Accessorizing Jess's bare feet, jeans, and T-shirt was her lost pair of pantyhose, slung about his shoulders with ankles knotted loosely in front like a preppy sweater. She could smell sausage and he had something in a skillet, waving it across the burner in time to the swing of his shoulders and sassy shake of his hips. Bare feet shuffling and sliding, he continued to sing softly and not very well to the music.

"Hold on. I'm coming. Hold on. I'm—"

He executed a neat spin and almost dropped the frying pan when they came face-to-face. Then he grinned. "Gooood morning!" He set down the pan and did a nice James Brown glide to the refrigerator. "Breakfast is almost ready." He got out a bottle of orange juice and shook it on his way to the table in an interesting variation of the cha-cha.

"Pardon me, but I could have sworn you weren't a morning person."

Jess grabbed her around the waist and did a few fancy dips before returning to the stove. "Oh, yeah, I love the morning. After coffee. And after vigorous exercise." He gave her a quick wink. "After the first pot of java hits the bloodstream, I'm just a sweetheart of a guy."

"Remind me to give you an IV drip tomorrow about a half hour before you wake up."

He paused and frowned slightly. "Why? What did I do? I didn't kick you, did I?"

"You kick, too?"

"I've been told I am not a lot of fun to sleep with."

She smiled, a warm, contented smile. "Someone lied."

He slid her a wicked glance. "Why, Miss Carter, are you saying you like having me in your bed?"

She didn't even blush. "And in my kitchen and in the shower and on the couch and in elevators."

He raised an eyebrow, rather liking her answer. "Sit. It's ready."

When he leaned over to serve her breakfast, Charley caught the feet of her pantyhose. "What's this?"

"Found them hanging from the refrigerator door this morning. Why? Did you lose a pair? What do you say, Cinderella, shall we try them on and see if they fit?"

She pulled down on the nylon, bringing him close enough to make his tempting mouth easy prey. She kissed him with all the tenderness he stirred in her, and it was a long moment before he opened his eyes and began to straighten.

"Eggs are getting cold," he murmured as she reeled him in again.

"Too much cholesterol is bad for the body."

He indulged her for a time, then pulled away with a sly smile. "So is too much of other things I can think of. So be a good girl and eat your eggs and leave the poor old cook alone."

Charley marveled at him. Jess ate in time to the music, tapping his fork in the eggs, swinging his knee under the table, rocking in his chair to the rhythm. He caught her bemused look and grinned. "I like my blues with breakfast. You didn't have anything around, so I picked that number up when I went out for juice. Don't you have a stereo or CD player?" When she shook her head, he stared at her as if she'd told him she was from another planet. "What do you do to get your soul going every day? Share a peep at naughty slides with good ol' Alan?"

He scowled into his coffee cup, and Charley wondered delightedly if he could possibly be jealous. Of Alan and her. It was an interesting theory. One that warranted testing.

Last night he'd said he loved her.

"Jess, why didn't you tell me Alan called the morning we left for my brother's?"

He went very still. She could almost hear his mind working, feel his senses reaching out cautiously to chart her mood. "I must have forgotten." Then his tone tightened. "Why? Does it matter?"

Did it matter? "No," she told him softly. "But you should have told me."

"Sorry. I'll be a better messenger service between you and your boyfriend next time."

"There won't be a next time."

Jess lifted his head to look at her, his expression unreadable. "So that's it." His tone was barren.

"For me and Alan. That's over."

He chewed his lip for a moment, then asked, "Because of me?"

"For a lot of reasons, but you're among them."

He nodded, but that wasn't really a response. He'd turned inward again. It unsettled her, especially at this particular time, when they were discussing important matters. She was telling him she was severing all emotional ties to be free for him. And he was telling her nothing. Had he meant it when he said he loved her? Or was that just something a man said when he was in bed with a woman? She was so darn ignorant of such things. He'd mentioned Alan, so wouldn't this be a good time to bring up his past romantic interests to see if some were still lingering? And suddenly, looking at Jess, it didn't matter if there were a hundred before her. She didn't need to know the nasty details. Just as long as nobody came after her.

In an oddly hushed voice she said, "You can leave the tape player here if you want. That way you'll always have something to get you going in the morning."

He didn't smile. "Sure." He said that as if there wasn't a chance in the world that it would happen. And Charley was torn between two very vivid pictures—of Jess McMasters at her table in the morning, unshaven and teasing, and one of herself buttering her toast alone. A silence settled between them as they finished their meal, trying not to look beyond the moment to what would or would not be.

"Oh, before I forget." Jess nudged a small box toward her. "Here. This is for you. To make up for scaring you with my driving and growling at you this morning."

"Jess, you didn't have to—" She opened the box and gave a small gasp. "Oh . . . Jess." That's all she could manage through the sudden fullness in her throat. There, nestled in the I. Magnin box, was a pair of diamond ear studs.

He was watching her with a cautious reserve. "I know those aren't the ones you wanted, but I didn't have time to get a second mortgage on my house." He gave a wry smile that thinned with strain. He looked at the box where the diamonds glimmered brightly. They looked small. A lot smaller than they had in the store. And he tensed, waiting for her to mention that fact. "I guess it wasn't a great idea, considering you could buy their whole damn inventory. You can take them back if you want to trade up for something flashier."

"Take them back?" Charley looked up at him, her eyes glittering as brilliantly as the stones. "Why would I—"

Then she got a good look at his expression. It was shuttered against emotion. But just for an instant there was something in his eyes, a furtive shadow, a bleakness of inevitability.

With a throat-aching tenderness Charley realized he was expecting her to reject his gesture as not quite good enough. And she was suddenly furious with him. How could he think that? Didn't he know her well enough to trust her?

Then she could see with a crystal clarity that he didn't know anything beyond a past of painful inadequacy. And she knew what it cost him to make the gesture. He'd overcome an incredible barrier of self-protection to lay his fragile faith on the table along with the box. He was trusting her to see the worth, while bracing himself for the possibility that she would fail him. *I won't fail, Jess. I won't.* She would make him believe it.

It was hard to know exactly what to say. She was dangerously close to breaking down. She wanted to grab him and smother him with love and sympathy, to soothe the years of hurt away. But he'd hate that. His pride wouldn't stand for pity.

Carefully she chose her words, dragging them up from the heart. "I love them, Jess. Because they're from you. I don't care if they're a full carat or window glass. And if you try to take them back, I'll break your arm."

The first glint of humor touched his gaze. "Yeah?"

"Yeah." She came off her chair to hug him. "Thank you," she whispered against his ear. She heard his breath gush and felt the tension running out of him. And he was hugging her back. Tightly.

"That's nice to know. Next time I'll save myself some money and opt for glass."

Next time. Charley clutched at him and at the sweetness of that phrase. Then she pushed away. "I want to put them on."

He watched, smiling easily now, as she fastened the studs in her earlobes and turned her head for his inspection.

"How do they look?"

He reached out to tuck a strand of auburn hair behind one ear. "Beautiful."

Charley followed his hand, coming to him for a lingering kiss. When she traced his upper lip with the tip of her tongue, he ducked his head and laughed.

"None of that."

She wouldn't be discouraged. Her lips grazed along his stubbly cheek to sketch the whorl of his ear, eliciting a hard shudder.

"Cut it out," he warned direly. "I have no energy left for this, Charley. You're wasting your time."

"I don't think so," she purred throatily and let her tongue retrace the path her lips had taken.

"I'm telling you, there's no way I'm going to rise to the occasion."

She tipped his chin up, smiling down at him, then leaned in to lick across his lips in a slide as sensual as a hand running across silk. Her hand lowered to his lap, and she gave a feigned gasp of surprise. "Oh my! What's this?"

"A miracle," he claimed with a grin. "Let's not waste it."

It was dark. Charley squinted at the clock on her night table. Quarter past eleven. Sighing, she let her eyes drift shut and a contented smile curve her lips. She couldn't believe being with one person could fill the soul so full of satisfaction. Or be so fun, so sweet and sexy and silly. She'd never laughed so much or loved so much or been so wonderfully exhausted as during this day with Jess McMasters. He simply amazed her. One moment he'd be Marx Brother crazy, and the next as sultry as a Valentino. The not knowing what to expect left her giddily off balance. And it felt great.

Over the course of two short weeks he'd managed to coax her from a lifetime of reserve into an abandon that made her blush to think of it. He challenged her to speak her mind and chided her whenever she let him bulldoze her. He was full of new things and surprises. He liked to sample everything life put before him and prodded her to do the same. She discovered a fondness for soulful rhythm and blues, especially when it came to dancing with Jess in the living room with nothing on but a set of her new silk underwear. By dinnertime he'd managed to cajole her into modeling all of it for his appreciation. She was stunned by her own sense of freedom when around him. He gave her plenty of reasons to blush, but usually it was because of his outrageousness, not her own discomfort. And then there was the way she couldn't seem to keep her hands off him. It wasn't just because he had a wonderfully sexy body—which he did. He had a way of teasing with his eyes, of tempting with his smile, of fencing with his intellect to stimulate the mind. And a touch that excited the senses in ways she'd never imagined. She was crazy in love with him.

Thinking of him inspired a need to feel him close. She rolled over and then just stared for a moment at the empty sheets. She knew he hadn't gone home. Simply because she didn't think he had the strength to drag himself beyond the door. After eating one of her microwave dinners without complaint, he'd fallen asleep with his head on her lap as they watched television. It had taken some doing just to move him from couch to bed, and then he'd gone under like a drugged man.

Curiosity as much as the want of companionship drove her from the warm bed. With Jess's T-shirt brushing over her bare skin, she padded into the dark living room to find him sitting on the floor in front of the patio slider wearing just his jeans. His arms were wrapped about updrawn knees and an open bottle of Maalox dangled between them. He was rocking slightly to the quiet croon of the Temptations with head bowed and eyes closed. She knew he heard her approach. The flesh on his back tightened over muscle.

"Pretty hard-core, taking it right out of the bottle," she mused, bending to remove the Maalox from him and set it on the coffee table.

"We tough guys like it straight." He didn't open his eyes or lift his head.

She frowned, concerned. "Are you all right?"

"Just one big mess of stomach acid feeding on raw nerves."

"Ugh! Nice image."

He didn't smile. Now she was truly alarmed. She settled behind him, placing her knees on either side of his hips, and put her arms around him. She rubbed one palm lightly over his rigid middle. "What can I do?"

"This is kind of nice." He nudged his head against hers. "Probably not medicinally-sound, but it feels good."

She held him for a while, absorbing his tension, riding with the rock of his body. Something was wrong. And it wasn't indigestion. Though it may well have been the cause of his stomach distress. She couldn't guess what was bothering him, so finally she was forced to ask.

"What's on your mind, Jess?"

She felt him inhale mightily. For a moment he didn't answer. And when he did, her whole world caved in.

"I was just thinking about how much I've enjoyed these last couple of days with you." It wasn't what he said. It was how he said it.

He was saying goodbye.

Fourteen

"I've enjoyed them, too," Charley said softly, cautiously.

The tape player clicked off. The room was suddenly very still. Charley fought down the feeling of panic spreading like a sickening chill over every sense. Her heart refused to digest the truth her mind was telling her. She rubbed her cheek against the swell of Jess's shoulders, not wanting to acknowledge the prospect of losing him.

"I care about you, Charley. You know that."

Oh God. It was worse than she thought. A numbing paralysis cushioned the blow, enabling her to speak. "But?"

"What?"

"I'm waiting for the other shoe. Drop it, Jess."

It came out in a rush. "Charley, I'm sorry. I didn't want to hurt you. Honest to God. I shouldn't have let it happen. I should have stopped it that night at your brother's before things got—out of control."

A shiver started in her insides and built to a full-fledged quake. Even though he didn't move within the span of her arms, she could feel him pulling away. And the thought of that distance terrified her. "Are you saying you're sorry we made love?"

His voice was low, deadened somehow in a way that was very frightening. "No. No. That's the hell of it. I'm not sorry. Not one damn bit. But I gotta go."

She pressed her face against his shoulder blade, squeezing her eyes shut against the well of helpless tears. He sounded so sad, so sure. That's what undid her. He was still sitting here in her living room, but he was already gone. All the loving, all the laughter, they were over. Just like that. And suddenly one word surfaced with a fearsome force.

No!

No. She wouldn't let him go. Jess wasn't going to waltz out of her life after becoming as necessary as air to her existence. Not if she could help it. Not without one heck of a fight!

"Why?"

He stiffened at her combative tone. "Why?"

"Why are you doing this, Jess? I need a reason. Did you just get bored? Was it just the sex you wanted? Did you suddenly decide you couldn't spend another second with a woman who can't boil water? What?" That last word cracked and trembled.

"Charley . . ."

"You talk to me, Jess. You spell it out in big, clear letters so I won't misunderstand. I thought there was something wonderful, something special, going on here. Am I wrong? Tell me, am I wrong?"

She could see his knees shaking where he'd drawn them tight into his chest. She could feel his heart lurch to triple time and his breathing go haywire.

"You're making it harder," he told her hoarsely.

"Good. I want it hard. I'm not going to make it easy for you to leave. I'm going to hang on tight. You're going to have to drag me down three flights of stairs and all the way to your car, and then you'd better hope you have a crowbar to pry me loose. I love you, Jess."

"No." He bolted to his feet, jerking out of her embrace. One short step brought him to the patio door. He pressed his palms and forehead to the cold, damp pane, eyes closed, senses shattered. He could barely speak through the clog of emotion in his throat. "Don't say that. I don't want to hear it. Not tonight. Because you're not going to be able to tell me the same thing a week from now."

Shaken by his absolute certainty, Charley made her reply firm with an equal confidence. "You're wrong, Jess. I'll love you a week from now. I'll love you years from now. That's not going to change."

He rolled his head from side to side, discarding her vow. He didn't argue. He just gave up. And that put a deep panic in her heart. That fear made her say things that perhaps weren't the wisest under the circumstances, but she'd spent a lifetime holding her feelings inside and had been miserably alone. It was time to gamble on the straight, undiluted truth.

"I love you, Jess McMasters, and I'm going to spend the rest of my days and nights telling you that."

He shook his head again, and she wanted to scream at him in frustration. "It's not going to happen, baby. You don't know how impossible that is."

"I know all I need to know. I know you're a grouch in the morning. I know you drive like a maniac and curse like a sailor on leave. I know you like your coffee black and your loving hot. What else is there?"

He gave a low, raw laugh and rolled so his back leaned against the glass door. His features were stark with sorrow. His smile was a curl of cynicism. "Think you're so smart, don't you?"

She stood to face him. Her eyes glittered like the stones in her ears. "No. I'm not smart. I'm scared. I'm scared of losing the best thing I've ever had."

"Me?" He laughed again. It was a self-deprecating sound. "Oh, baby, that's a bad deal. What do you want with a dried-up would-be writer with a gutful of ground glass and a heart that's been broken too many times to heal? I'm nothing you want to mess with, Charley. You need someone who still has something to give. I'm all used up. Sure, it was fun pretending for a while. I even got to believing that maybe—" He sighed and gave that empty smile again. "I'm too old for fairy tales, and you're too naïve to see the truth. I'd just drag you down."

"That's crap, Jess, and you know it. I'm tougher than that. You were the one who showed me what I could be."

"But I'm not. I'm not tough. I'm an eggshell, baby, ready to crack. And I can't go through that again. I'm sorry. I can't. I won't."

She started to reach out to him, then gave an impatient curse. Jess frowned when she began tugging off the wrappings on her hands.

"Hey, don't do that. You're not supposed to do that."

"Shut up, Jess. Don't tell me what I can or can't do." She dropped the bandages to the floor and flexed her fingers. There was a slight itchiness and discomfort as the new pink skin pulled. The healing process was almost complete, and she was anxious to test the result. "I've wanted to do this for a long time."

He flinched as her fingertips touched his jaw,

then held himself rigid as her palms stroked over his face. His breathing had altered to a faint shiver.

"Don't push me away. I'm not going to hurt you. I'm not going to let you down."

He sighed raggedly and rolled his eyes toward the ceiling. "I know you wouldn't mean to, Charley. It's not you. It's me. I've spent my whole life not quite living up to what the people I loved wanted from me. I can't set myself up like that again. I couldn't stand seeing you disappointed. I can't wait around for that."

"But I don't want anything from you. I want you."

"You want something, Charley. You want me to be some saint, some super-nice guy. Don't lay that kind of load on me. I can't carry it off. You don't need me. Baby, you have it all, everything you've ever wanted. And you'll do fine. I know you will. I just got you on your feet. You don't need me to hold your hand anymore."

Her fingers slid up into his hair, gripping, forcing his head to tip down. But his gaze slid right by to study the floor.

"Thanks for the memory and see you around. Is that it?"

"Yeah."

"And I don't have anything to say about it?"

"No."

Let it go, Charley. Please. Jess was hanging on by his fingernails. There was an awful gnawing pain in his belly and a sharper one teething on his heart. If she didn't cut him loose, she was going to kill him. He didn't believe for one damn minute that she was going to stick by him once that article came out, but part of him wanted desperately to suck up every second from now until then, overdosing on the drugging sweetness of her love. As long as he didn't have to see the devastation in her eyes when it was over.

Crazily he wondered if it was possible to keep the article from her. She professed to not being worldly when it came to news. Maybe she would never see it. Maybe it would all blow over, and things could be good for them.

Yeah, right. Who are you fooling, Jess? Every minute you spend with her in a lie is going to grind her trust just that much farther into the ground. It's too late, buddy. You lost your chance. You lose, sucker.

"I gotta go."

He didn't look up, but he felt a tremor run clear through her. Slowly her hands lowered, trailing reluctantly along his jaw to his chin and then falling away. He'd almost started to breathe again when she winded him with the unexpected.

"Can I ask you just one thing before you go?"

Relief that all would be soon behind him made him sloppy. "Sure."

"Did you ever love me, Jess?"

"Oh God," he moaned. "Just cut my heart

out, why don't you."

"Is that a yes?"

He raised his head, his gaze just a tad slower until it fixed on hers with an intensity that stole her breath. So many things crowded that silvery stare that she couldn't begin to sort through them. But first and foremost was a lean, savage kind of wanting that gave her the strength to stand her ground. She knew his answer even before he spoke it, low and whiskey-warm.

"Yeah, I love you, Charley Carter. So damn much I'm going to spend the rest of my life trying to get over you."

She swallowed down the chest-crushing tenderness and asked simply, "Wouldn't it be easier if you just spent one day at a time trying to learn to trust me? I mean, if you're going to be miserable anyway, why not prolong the goodness of what we have for a while? A day or two. A week. A couple of months. Who knows, years could slip right on by. And someday you won't even remember a time when you didn't believe with all your heart that I would never hurt you."

A long second passed. Then a faint smile touched his lips. Charley smiled back, trying to ease the terrible tightness in her throat. Suddenly she needed to be close. Both palms fit flush to his chest and moved gradually upward. The sensation was more glorious than she'd imagined. And she swore to herself that she would never stop until she'd erased the uncertainty lingering behind his poignant smile. For today, she had. And the feeling of success was so sweet. She let one hand cup behind his head to coax him down to where their lips met, lightly, slowly, with a tentative hope.

"Day by day, huh?"

She nodded eagerly.

"I can try to live with that."

He hadn't let go of her even in sleep.

Charley woke feeling surrounded, protected, loved. And it filled her with such throat-aching wonder that she didn't move for the longest time. Not that she could with Jess wrapped around her in a tangle of arms and legs. They hadn't made love after she led him back into her bed, and somehow that made waking within his possessive embrace all the more precious in her heart. Because suddenly this chaste closeness had become as important as the intimate contact of the night before.

She absorbed the warmth radiating from the man beside her like a solar panel starved for energy. The more heat she drew, the more powerful she felt. The more sure she'd done the right thing. And it was right for her and Jess. All she had to do was hang on and love him out of his doubts. Because without him the rest of it—the money, the independence, the sudden confidence, the closet of designer labels, the new face and hair—was somehow an empty fantasy. He made it real. He made her believe things were possible. The outward things altered appearance, but Jess McMasters had altered her reality.

She studied the features turned toward her in sleep. Just looking at him made everything swell shut inside her. There was something so vulnerable about him in the unconscious state, quickening all her tender instincts. But she wasn't completely fooled. This sweet-faced man with his dark morning stubble was the most dangerous and disruptive influence her life had ever known. For him, she was taking risks the sane and sensible Charlene Carter of a month ago would have considered terrifying madness. She was building an entire future around his faith in her inner strength. He'd reached down into her timid soul to drag out that ability. He'd wrapped himself around her heart and made it beat with the potential of dreams. He'd stirred in her spirit an excitement and a sense of self that had been missing for long years of quiet dedication to the lives of others. And he had only himself to blame for her tenacity now. She may not have needed him to make her future plans a success, but she wanted him. With a fierceness that overpowered logic, with a desire that conquered fear. If he could breathe life back inside her, she could do the same for him. And if she had to endure the anxious uncertainty of taking it day by day, she would. She would heal the scars on his heart if she had to go minute by minute, second by second. Because Jess McMasters was worth it. Even if he didn't quite believe it. Yet.

Enough ruminating. She needed to start in on some positive fussing. She might not be up to a gourmet breakfast in bed, but she could supply coffee with a Maalox chaser. Now all she had to do was escape the sensual chains of his embrace.

Cautiously she began to withdraw her leg from beneath his. The image of pick-up sticks almost choked a laugh out of her, but she swallowed it down. Feet free, she started to ease his arm off the indentation of her waist. It was as if she'd tripped a trap. He jerked. His arms cinched around her convulsively. With a mutter that could have been endearment or curse, he burrowed his face just above her breasts, abrading her skin with his rough chin and her heart with his quiet sigh. She loved him so much at that moment that it was a physical pang. She gave in to the luxury of holding him, of playing gently with his rumpled hair, aware of her steeping fury for those who had conditioned him to be so hard on himself. No one would hurt him like that again. Not if she had any say in it.

She brushed her lips lightly across his brow. "Jess?"

"Ummmm."

"Turn over."

Obligingly he let her go and rolled to his other side, taking most of the covers with him. Charley smiled. He was a selfish son of a gun in his sleep. She gave him one last lingering look, then headed for the kitchen.

It was strange how his presence permeated her apartment. Bits and pieces of him were scattered all over with a casual intimacy that warmed her to the core: his leather jacket draped over the back of the couch, his sweater folded on the breakfast bar, the I. Magnin jewelry box still on the table, his loafers angled by the door, the tape player by the patio slider. It was a comfortable, comforting presence. One she wanted to be permanent. She refused to be intimidated by her inexperience or by the enormity of what she was trying to do. She'd brought something wild and wounded into her home, into her heart, and there was a definite possibility she could end up torn to shreds. But there was also a chance that she could have everything she desired and dreamed of. There was no way to fairly weigh the one against the other. Not when she considered the rewards.

It was like radar. The moment she knelt beside the bed, Jess's nose turned toward the cup of coffee in her hand and twitched at the rich, dark scent.

"Good morning, baby," Charley crooned. She let her fingers scrape along his bristly cheek while teasing him with the aroma wafting from the cup. With great pleasure she watched him struggle to consciousness. He pushed off the covers, freeing his arms for a limbering stretch, then rubbed his hands over his face to scatter the groggy dregs of sleep. His piercing eyes were dull as he blinked and finally focused on her face.

"Hi."

It was a low rumble so bedroom sexy it curled her toes.

"I brought coffee to tame the savage beast."

His mouth curved softly. "Thanks." As he dragged himself up to a half-sitting position against the headboard, Charley climbed onto the bed and straddled his denim-clad thighs. Interest piqued, he played with the hem of the T-shirt she was wearing.

"Isn't this mine?"

"All of it's yours." She let that linger, seeing him process it in the still-foggy banks of his brain. "What would you like first?"

Jess glanced longingly at the coffee, then he reached for the cup and the back of her neck at the same time. He drew her down for a leisurely kiss, one that was sleepily sensual. Just when it began to arouse all sorts of possibilities, Jess nudged her out of the way with a bump of his head so he could go for the coffee. He drank deeply and sighed deeply. "Ummm. Good coffee. Good kiss. Helluva way to start the day."

"Breakfast of champions," she returned with a saucy wiggle of her hips.

Jess took another sip, letting his thumb rub along the inside of her thigh in distracting circles. "Something on your mind, Charley?"

Yes, there had been, but at that moment his traveling hand ran out of smooth road and began to explore other byways. Coherent thought was impossible.

"No silk today?" he teased quietly.

"It's—it's all in the wash." She tried to pull together some degree of cognitive thinking around the surges of sensation making her legs tremble.

"And you weren't by any chance hoping that I liked to do laundry, were you? Because sorry to say, I don't do clothes. I pay dearly and willingly to stuff them in a bag, drop them off, and pick them up the next day all neatly folded. And I don't do floors or windows or the bathroom unless I absolutely have to."

"So much for keeping you on as a housekeeper," she gasped between quick rhythmic breaths.

"I have other good stuff on my resume."

"Ummm. You sure do." Sanity surfaced for a brief second. "Writing. You're a writer. I wanted to ask—to ask if you'd help me with my speech for tomorrow."

Jess went suddenly still. Left hanging by a sensory thread, Charley nearly collapsed on him. She wasn't so dazed that she couldn't recognize the purposeful distance in his gaze. And it brought her down to earth with brutal abruptness.

"I don't know, baby," he was saying. The words were evasive, the tone was not. "I've got to be going pretty soon."

"Going . . ."

He saw the anguished disbelief tighten her expression and was quick to allay it. He continued with his caressing seduction and forced an easy smile. "Home. You know, where I live, where I get my mail and water my plants. I need a shave and some clean clothes, even though I haven't spent all that much time in these this weekend. I have to check my machine and put some junk together for my Monday class. Just stuff. No big deal."

No big deal? She wasn't convinced. Something had jerked him off course a second ago, but she was afraid to ask outright. Afraid he would tell her he was having second thoughts about what they'd discussed last night. Then what would she do? Disgrace herself and embarrass him by falling to pieces?

"You can come along if you want." He said that very softly, so sensitive to her insecurities it made her want to weep. As much as she longed to accept, she didn't. She had to let him go and trust him to come back. After all, she was demanding a hell of a lot of faith from him. If he said it was no big thing, she owed it to him to believe.

"No. I have things to do, too. Even if they

aren't quite as appealing as spending time with you."

"Well, hey, I'm not gone yet." And he proved it by intensifying his touch. She moaned and let her head drop back as he taunted her toward an excruciating level of response, watching her with a look that was all too calm and smug. How dare he lean back sipping coffee and making conversation while driving her into a shattering frenzy.

Abruptly she shifted back, breaking the connection between his hand and her throbbing pleasure points. In answer to his questioning look, she said tartly, "You are entirely too relaxed, McMasters."

"What can I say? I'm a laid-back kind of guy." He gave a slow, provoking grin.

"Is that so?" She reached for the waistband of his jeans, never losing contact with his eyes. He maintained his mocking half-smile and the simmering suggestion of amusement in his stare even as she lifted up and settled down over him. He shut his eyes for an instant, breath catching, body tensing, then he was grinning at her again.

"Yeah, that's so." He was daring her to prove otherwise.

It grew to be an interesting point of challenge between them. Charley rocked against him with a slow, tormenting stroke, trying her darnedest to knock his confidence for a hard loop while holding out against the insistent forays of his touch. But the combined sensory assault was too much. Feeling the shivers of weakness building around him, Jess was wickedly pleased.

"Ready to say uncle?"

She was ready to say anything.

Except a sudden knocking on her front door interrupted.

"Alan."

Jess's choice of terms was all-inclusive. He was quick to grab on to her knees, holding her fast. "Does he have a key?"

"A key? No."

"Then let him knock."

There was the sound of a click and the front door opening.

"Hey, Charley. Still in bed?"

Jess gave her a look that would split atoms. She managed an apologetic smile. "My brother has a key."

"Your timing sucks, Robert," Jess bellowed out before she could stop him. There was a long silence from the living room. Charley cringed, picturing her younger sibling's shock. She couldn't quite see it as funny.

"Hi, Jess," Robert called back, then more quietly, "I'll be damned."

"I'll see to it personally if you come around that corner," was Jess's dire warning.

The absurdity of it finally struck home. Charley started to giggle, placing their position with each other in jeopardy. Jess clamped his palms down over her thighs to secure her in place.

"Don't you dare get up," he ordered softly with nothing akin to calm.

"Robert," she yelled gleefully. "There's coffee in the kitchen. Entertain yourself for a minute, and I'll be eternally grateful."

"Take your time."

"That was the plan," Jess growled in irritation. "Until some son of a bitch with a key decided to drop by."

"Geez, Charley. He sure is a crab in the morning. How do you put up with it?"

"Get your coffee, Robert, and keep your opinions to yourself." There was a blissful silence from the other room, and Charley turned back to matters at hand. "Where were we?"

"You were about to say uncle," Jess reminded her with a not-so-subtle shift of his hips.

"No, I wasn't," she argued with a smile.

"You liar!"

"I'll let you put your money where your mouth is later, McMasters. You haven't proven your point yet."

"Let me prove it now."

His husky growl incited all sorts of delicious sensations, but none of them could quite overcome the fact that her brother was out rummaging around in her kitchen. "Later."

"All right, all right. I give up." With a groan he sagged back against the pillows, gasping, grasping for a way to find some dignity in defeat. With a sudden grin he bowled her over and rolled off the bed. "Now that I consider it, I think I'm going to like losing better than winning. Give me my shirt."

When the two of them emerged from the bedroom, Robert smiled without offering comment. Jess headed straight for the coffeepot.

" 'Morning, Robert," he said with an endearing degree of warmth. "Had breakfast yet?"

Fifteen

"And he cooks, too." Robert cast an impressed glance toward the man in his sister's kitchen. "A match made in heaven if I recall your love for the culinary arts."

Charley nibbled on her toast, letting her eyes linger on Jess McMasters with a devouring pleasure. "But he doesn't do laundry or windows or bathrooms," she confided in a low undertone.

"Still think you ought to keep him."

The heat in her gaze intensified. "Me, too. I'm doing my darnedest."

Jess ambled to the table with a fresh pot of coffee. As he poured for the three of them, he grew aware of brother and sister's grinning study of him.

"What?" He gave a quick downward sweep. "Is my fly open or something? What's so funny?"

"Life, Jess," Robert replied. As Jess settled in his chair, he dropped a casual bombshell. "So when are you going to make an honest woman out of my sister?"

Jess choked on his coffee. Charley was apoplectic.

"Robert!" she gasped, going six shades of red.

Jess was more nonchalant. "Your sister is the most honest woman I know. And anything beyond that really isn't any of your business now, is it?"

Robert gave a full-bodied laugh. "I like you, McMasters. You don't pull a punch."

Charley had recovered enough by then to be indignant. "Really, Robert. You have some nerve poking around in my private life. You don't hear me pumping you full of questions about your little camp cheerleader."

"Ask anything you like." He was grinning in a very self-satisfied way. "In fact, that's one of the reasons I came down to talk to you. I've asked Shelly to marry me, and for some reason I'll never understand, she said yes."

"Oh! Oh, Rob, that's wonderful!" Charley instantly had her arms wrapped around his neck in a strangling hug. "I'm so happy for you!"

Over his sister's shoulder Robert gave Jess a long, steady look. Finally, when he needed his breath back, he gave Charley a push away. "So, now you don't have to fuss over me anymore."

"When have I ever minded fussing?" she argued happily, missing the point completely.

But Jess didn't. He understood Robert's meaning immediately. He was cutting his sister loose from her obligations. He was telling her it was time to get on with her own life. And he was assuming Jess McMasters would play a major part in that life. Jess's belly began to hurt.

"Enough about me," Robert claimed, smiling fondly at his sister. "What about you? Have you decided how to spend your fortune?" He touched a curled and colored twist of her hair. "I see you've been busy already. Nice."

Charley took a breath. She was surprised that she felt ready for this. In fact, she was remarkably calm. "I've done all the math, so I'll cut right to the bottom line. I'm putting half of it into the camp."

"Charley—"

"Shut up, Robert. You don't have a say in this."

His jaw snapped shut.

Okay, so far, so good. She approached the next bit of news a little more cautiously. "And I'm setting up a trust for you. Just in case."

"No."

"No arguments."

"No, Charley. I won't take it."

"Yes, you will. Consider it a wedding present."

"More like a going-away present."

She flinched and her eyes welled up with tears. "You have Shelly to think of now."

"And I'll take care of her. It's my life, Charley. You can't live it for me, and you can't make it last forever. I can take care of myself. I always have. I'm not going to let you do this. You've done enough. Tell her, Jess."

Jess froze as both pairs of angry dark eyes fixed on him. He looked at Robert, seeing his frustration. He looked at Charley, feeling her despair. He spoke softly, firmly, as if he had the power to settle everything. "Robert, you'll take the money and you'll be grateful, or I'll break both your legs." He heard Charley's breath expel in a rush, but he didn't glance at her. He was staring down her younger brother.

Robert seethed. He fumed. He looked ready to do some leg breaking of his own. Finally he ground out, "Thanks a helluva lot, Jess."

He smiled thinly. "No problem."

Charley's relief was short-lived. Now came the sticky part. "I'm putting fifty thousand toward Alan's research."

"What?" It was outrage in stereo.

"I believe in the work he's doing. And he's going to need the money to replace me."

That silenced both of them.

"I'm going to establish a family-education center. I want to teach classes through the hospital and the camp. I want to work with people again. I want to help them get through those first rocky months after they're diagnosed so they won't be as scared and hopeless as we were. I'm going to sign the cable deal and the one for television, and Robert, I want you to go on the talk-show circuit with me. We've got the ball, and we're going to run with it all the way. Okay?"

Robert nodded somewhat numbly.

"But first, as soon as possible, I'm going to buy myself an obscenely expensive set of luggage and fill it with nothing but sunblock and silk. I'm going to grab up the good-looking, consenting male of my choice, and I'm going to fly us down to the Caribbean where I'm going to spend a week or two working on an all-over strapless tan." Gathering her courage, Charley slid a look at Jess. He was staring at her, all stiff and stoic. There wasn't the slightest clue to his thoughts in his expression. Her optimism took a devastating plunge but she struggled not to show it.

"Well," Robert drawled. "You sound like a lady with a plan. It's about time."

Brother and sister talked until the coffeepot was empty, charting the course those plans would take. Charley was acutely aware of Jess's silence. He was watching her, his gaze shuttered, his mood remote. She didn't understand. Wasn't this what he wanted for her, what he'd been pushing her toward? She was taking her own steps forward. She was heeding her own needs, her own wants. So why did she feel with every step she took ahead that he was easing back, taking one away from her? She didn't know how to catch him, how to stop his retreat short of an all-out body tackle. The unexplained edginess increased, climbing up every nerve. She was so taut when Jess finally spoke that, she nearly snapped.

"I gotta get going." He pushed back from the table and extended a hand to her brother. "Good to see you again."

"Likewise." Robert's clasp was firm. "You going to be at the big to-do tomorrow to see Charley get her key to the city? I hear even the governor is planning an appearance."

Somber gray eyes cut to Charley. "If she wants me there."

"I do."

Jess nodded to her brusquely. "I'll be there, then."

She watched him gather his things, anxiety knotting up around her heart. He left the tape player. She clung to that like a life preserver. He was coming back. He was. But the thought of a minor separation was enough to lance her confidence with the poison of doubt. And his taciturn mood wasn't helping any. If only he'd show her a little of the playful Jess, the silly Jess, the passionate Jess. Then she could survive the parting. He was so withdrawn she couldn't help but tremble with the memory of his bleak expression.

Then he was slipping on his jacket, and the reality hit her hard. As if the past two days had been delirious fantasy and he was going back to the real world where he had his own home, his own work, his own life. Separate from hers. Pretend, he'd called their weekend together. Was it? Was that all it was? She refused to believe it. And she wouldn't let him believe it, either.

She followed him to the door, wishing he'd show some hesitation, some reluctance to leave, but he didn't. He looked eager for the escape, restless. He opened the door, and she stopped him with a hand on his cheek. When she would have stretched up to kiss him, he caught that hand in his and brushed her knuckles across his lips.

"I'll spare you my desperate need of a shave and a toothbrush."

"Don't do me any favors, McMasters," she told him huskily.

He grinned wryly and touched his fingertips to his mouth, then to hers. "You'll do just fine, Charlene Carter," he said softly. He took a step back and then abruptly turned and walked toward the stairs.

You'll do just fine. What had he meant by that? she wondered in a panic. *No, I won't, Jess. I need you. I need you to take care of me. I can't do it alone.* But that wasn't true anymore. She knew it. So did he. She didn't need him.

"The guy's crazy about you, you know."

Charley leaned gratefully into her brother's embrace, tears so close to the surface that she could taste them in her throat. "I've never, ever in my life asked for anything for myself. I've always thought about everyone else first."

"I know you have," he agreed quietly, not without a pang of guilt.

"But I want him. I want him so bad."

Robert stroked his sister's hair and looked thoughtfully down the stairwell. "We'll get him for you, Charley. God knows, you deserve to have whatever you want."

The light was blinking on his machine. One impatient flash. He slipped out of his coat and pressed play. Matthew Bane. He felt his gut contract.

"Jess, got your copy. What can I say? Great. It's great."

Jess opened the refrigerator, ignoring that it was 10:30 A.M. ignoring the acid burning in his belly as he reached for a cold beer. He wrenched off the top and leaned against the counter as his editor gushed on.

"No changes. I'm going to run it as is. And Jess . . . I was out of line the other day. What do you say? Give me a call and we'll crack a few beers."

Jess cocked the mouth of his longneck in the direction of the recorder and smiled narrowly. "Cheers, Matt." He drank deep and cramped up the minute the alcohol hit his stomach. "Oh God . . . geez." He curled against the counter, teeth gritted, bottle clenched in both hands. God, it hurt! He sucked air for a few seconds, and the searing eased enough for him to walk into his living room only slightly doubled over. He poked at a week's worth of mail without interest and wandered to the windows overlooking his backyard. It had started to rain, making everything look muddy and green. He loved this place—his house, his yard, his comfortable privacy. But today there was no sense of warmth or welcome, and that only deepened his brooding. He'd been alone in this big old place for a long time, and he liked it that way. Dammit, he liked it that way! He took another long drink and tensed like a fighter waiting for a blow. It ripped through his stomach mercilessly. A familiar pain. He could deal with that. It was clearer, more visceral than the lacerating rawness of losing Charley.

How was he going to get through tomorrow? The governor's presence demanded a full battery of press. Guys he'd worked with, colleagues who knew his byline. What was the chance of Charley not finding out who he was? Slim to none. And even if she overcame that little surprise, how was she going to accept her face on the cover of *Metro?* And his name under it?

He wished he could find it somewhere inside himself to believe her. Oh, it wasn't that he thought she was lying. No, Charley Carter was scrupulously honest. She just wouldn't be able to find it in her scrupulously honest heart to forgive him once the truth was known. And that would bring a swift end to her vow to love him forever. Romance over. Life moves on. Only he had a singular lack of enthusiasm about continuing without her.

She'd bewitched him, he decided philosophically as he downed the next swallow. Right from the first. All that marvelous courage packed in that tiny, lush body. Since he'd snatched her away from a martyr's death, he'd been consumed with a sense of responsibility for her. He'd nursed her, he'd catered to her, he'd dried her tears, he'd taught her about loving and about standing up for herself. He'd taught her too damn well! She was charging full steam ahead into all her grand and glorious plans, and where did that leave him? Left carrying luggage and serving as hired escort on her vacation. He'd made it easy for her to walk off without looking back. *Stupid, Jess. Always so cautious. So smart. So wary of all the angles and shy of commitment in any way, shape or form. And this innocent, big-eyed woman just steps in and scrambles your brain like an omelet. And know what? Now you're in love with her and too scared to spit. Great. Great planning.*

He did love her. It was crazy and yet it made perfect sense. That one unselfish act to save the lives of strangers opened up a deep well of hope in him. That maybe, just maybe, this woman could care for him enough to overlook everything else. And maybe he could be just what she needed, too. He hadn't been the big leaguer his father wanted. He hadn't had the strong moral fiber his mother demanded. He hadn't been the detached provider his ex could suck dry. And he hadn't managed to live up to any of his own expectations. But when he'd met Charley Carter, she'd touched some special key in him. She made him feel that he had something to give again. She had the wonderful quiet spirit of a healer and the gentle confusion of a needy soul. He'd seen a complement between the two of them that was just too perfect to ignore. And he'd dared to reach out. He'd dared to listen when she pledged, *I love you. I won't hurt you. I won't let you down.* She was the one person he might have believed.

How he wanted to believe in Charley's dreams.

Could she love him enough? There was no question that she had an incredible depth of compassion. There was no doubt in his mind that she was beguiled by all his clever charm and sexual energy. But did she love him enough to stand by him? Did she love him enough to honor her vow? God, he hoped so. He'd done everything he could to be everything she could want. And crazily enough, she even loved him for his eccentricities. But was it enough? Had he gotten deep enough into her heart to hold tight against the truth? Would she love him for who he really was?

He would know soon enough. Too soon.

Wouldn't it be better coming from him?

Miserably he dropped into the recliner and packed his knees tightly against him to squeeze out the aches of body and soul.

Charley, please love me enough.

It took her all afternoon to struggle through her speech. Charley knew research, everything black and white. Creativity was not her long suit, and she longed for Jess. But she couldn't ask for his help again. For some reason he'd resisted the idea, and she wouldn't pursue it. Not at the risk of bringing those shadows back to his eyes. She wouldn't push. She wanted to wrap herself around him to cushion all the hurts he'd known, to spoil him into submission and love him back to life. Now there was a life's ambition, she couldn't wait to get started.

Except that Jess wasn't here and she wasn't sure when she'd see him again. Tomorrow, he'd said. But that seemed so intangibly far away. After a weekend of being spoiled herself, with the luxury of having him within reach, the separation was an agony of restless waiting. She was poor company for Robert, but he merely smiled knowingly and encouraged her to recite her speech aloud again. He was a good audience, applauding vigorously, then quickly turning to the ball game on television.

She was ready. Her clothes were laid out for

tomorrow's ceremony and reception. Navy with gold that Jess claimed made her look like a cool million. She'd practiced with the collection of cosmetics until she felt reasonably confident and had learned to control the rebellious curl of her hair. All set. She would look polished and poised before the cameras and the crowd. They'd never guess she was a quivering disaster inside.

You'll do just fine, Charlene Carter.

Yes, Jess, I will, she vowed.

Tomorrow everything in her life would be different. The woman who appeared before the public would not be the retiring research assistant content to hide in her lab coat behind data sheets. She would be leaving her safe, responsible career to embark on—an adventure. She had the means to do whatever she wanted, to become whatever she wished. And what she wanted and wished for couldn't be bought, even with every last penny of her reward. She wanted Jess McMasters. At least worrying about him kept her from fretting about the ceremony the next day. One could only dwell on one terror at a time, and standing up before a crowd of strangers was a peripheral fear. A lifetime without Jess, now that was a consuming panic.

It was 9 P.M., pitch dark, and storming with a spring fury outside. Charley finally realized the futility of hanging around willing the phone to ring. She got Robert settled on her pull-out sofa; he'd decided to stay over rather than brave the weather, and she was grateful not to be alone. Then she took a long, hot shower, scrubbing as best she could with her tender hands before letting the beat of the water ease away her tension. Bundled in a thick, fleecy robe, she was about to try to seek sleep when a knock at her door was almost muffled by fearsome thunderclaps.

He was drenched. Water ran in rivulets over the leather of his jacket and plastered his hair down like slick, dark satin. From that rain-streaked face, his gaze was banked with a stormy intensity. Without a word he reached inside his coat and drew out his toothbrush, issuing her the most fragile smile she'd ever seen. Her heart melted. With the whisper of his name, she was in his arms, hugging his wet exterior, warming the bleak interior. And the only thing that mattered was getting him inside, inside her apartment, inside her body.

"Hey, Jess," Robert called cheerfully from the living room. "I was about to head out to pick up a movie and a couple of cold ones. Anything you guys want to see?" He looked from one to the other, noting that their sight seemed limited to each other. Then he frowned as they walked right by without a glance. "Well . . . don't mind me."

They didn't. And he was alternately grumbling and grinning as he plodded out into the rain, wondering how long it was supposed to take him to find a video. At least a good hour, he decided diplomatically.

Charley paused to snatch a towel out of the bathroom. Jess stood quietly in the shadows of her bedroom and let her pat his wet hair dry. Then allowed her to remove his damp clothes, piece by piece, never altering the intense, absorbing study of her face. The hurried rhythm of his breathing made her rush, cursing her clumsy fingers as she wrestled with buttons and his belt buckle. Then everything slid free and she stood, trembling with want. She went nearly limp when his hands tugged at the belt of her robe, sweeping it off her shoulders with the determined brush of his palms. Her eyes half shut as those big, gentle hands cupped her face. She leaned in for his kiss. But it didn't come. Instead, he used the piercing force of his stare to penetrate heart and soul.

"I couldn't stay away." His voice rumbled, as rough and volatile as the storm outside. She nodded, helpless in her understanding. "Make me believe, Charley."

With that he carried her to the bed.

Jess dropped down upon her without any teasing overtures, without any preparatory gestures. She had time for a small gasp as he grabbed her right knee and shoved it high, coming into her so hard and full that she was literally pinned to the mattress. No fancy stuff. No frills. Just hard, deep thrusts that ripped her passions raw and had her hanging on for dear life. If that time in the kitchen had been an earthquake, this was Armageddon. She arched off the bed, her fingers clawing the covers, clenching in his hair. She buried her face against the side of his neck, crying out in muffled tandem with the thunder of his pulse beats. Wave after wave of cataclysmic sensation spasmed through her. Thoughts of Jess, of existence itself, were lost in that surge of completely self-absorbing pleasure.

Finally a basic sort of functioning returned. She gathered awareness with a dreamy reluctance. Only the thought of seeing Jess made the struggle worthwhile.

His face was inches from hers. His eyes were tightly closed, his lips parted to accommodate the quick, gusty rattles of breath. She expected to find the harsh, lean lines gone from his expression, but they weren't. His features were rigid, screwed up into an agony of control. When he opened his eyes to look down into hers, the burning intensity was still there but steeped with something else so powerful it made her shiver. Then he lowered to kiss her, and she knew what it was. Yearning. Sweet, simple yearning and all the seams around her heart unraveled. *Oh, Jess,* her soul sighed, *I won't disappoint you.*

He held her for a long time, cradling her in his arms, touching her with little strokes that were as soft and searching as his kiss had been.

From the other room there was the quiet sound of Robert's return and the murmur of the television. Charley curled silently against Jess, trying to pretend he was shaking because of the explosive union they'd shared, trying to attribute the damp runnels on his face to the rain, trying to dismiss his taut quivers of breathing to exhaustion.

She was lying to herself.

"I love you, Jess," she said with a quiet conviction. She heard him inhale raggedly and felt hard tremors convulse down his arms. He said nothing.

She waited until she was sure he slept before easing out of his embrace. Once in the privacy of the bathroom, bathed in the cold light of reality from its single bulb over the sink, she let go and sobbed miserably into her hands.

First his sister's weeping, now this. Robert rolled irritably off the sofa bed, wishing he was sleeping anywhere other than with his head close to the bathroom wall. He scuffled around the corner and chose to omit the formality of knocking.

Jess was on his knees, hugging the toilet bowl. His face was hanging so dangerously low over the blue-tinted water that his labored breathing rippled the surface.

"Man, oh, man," Robert muttered as he ran

cold water on a washcloth. "Can't a guy get any sleep around here?"

With a colossal groan Jess lifted his head, letting it rest on one of his forearms. His haggard face was ashen, as pale as the porcelain bowl, and his hair was spiked darkly above it. He looked like hell. Slowly he forced open red-rimmed eyes to stare dully at Charley's brother.

"Kind of an odd time and place to be praying, don't you think?"

Jess would have sworn at him if he'd had the strength. Instead, he let his eyes sag shut and waited wretchedly for the pain to arc to its gut-tearing crescendo again.

"You all right?"

"Will be in a minute," he mumbled faintly. "Get outta here. This isn't a spectator sport."

"Hey, I've seen worse. Wouldn't want you to drown."

"Funny man. Robert, anyone ever tell you you're a real pain in the—oh God!" His head dropped back into the basin. He retched up sounds as if something industrial-strength were replumbing his insides, while Robert knelt, grabbing him by the back of the neck to keep him from falling in. They rode out the ravaging spasms together to their graphic end. Then Robert eased him over to slump limply against the tub.

"Man, Jess, that's one impressive ulcer. Looks like a gutful of coffee grounds."

"Spare me the details, please," Jess moaned weakly.

Robert flushed those details and dropped the lid, assuming a seat on it. "How long has it been bleeding like that?"

"Comes and goes." His legs shifted restlessly against the gnawing cramps. "You don't have to baby-sit me. I'm not going to die."

"Just feels like it, huh?" Ignoring the irritable grumbles, Robert blotted the cool washcloth over Jess's sweat-beaded features. "Charley know your insides are Swiss cheese?"

"No, and don't go telling her. She has enough to worry about."

"And what's got you worried enough to tear your gut open, Jess? Something I should know about?"

That inquiry almost got Jess to spill everything. At the last second a boring pain had him clamping his lips together with the truth inside. Robert watched him for a long minute, knowing something was very wrong with the whole situation but liking Jess McMasters too much to press it.

Sixteen

"What's this?"

Jess looked into the glass Charley handed him, suspicion creasing his brow.

"Milk," she told him crisply. "Drink it."

"Milk?" He looked at the other two cups brimming with steaming dark coffee and frowned. "I don't want this," he growled, setting down the glass and reaching for a mug. He looked at her in surprise when Charley rapped his knuckles.

"No coffee," she said in a tone of stern authority. "That's about the worst thing you could put in your stomach. I want you to eat at least every three hours all day today. I bet you didn't have anything after breakfast yesterday. You have to take better care of yourself."

Jess stared at her, disbelieving, then shot a severing look at her brother. "Thanks a lot, Robert," he ground out.

"No problem, Jess," he returned with an untroubled grin.

Surly as a bear with his aching gut and raw temper, Jess shoved back his chair and stalked to the kitchen sink. Charley gave a cry of warning.

"Jess McMasters, don't you dare pour that down the drain!"

He swung around on her, glass poised, expression taut. "Who the hell appointed you my mother? If I want a cup of coffee, I'm going to have a cup of coffee. If I want a whole goddamn gallon, I'll have a whole goddamn gallon. I don't need any lectures from you, Charley. Save your do-gooder crusades for the rest of the world." And with that he upended the glass.

Charley didn't say anything. Her eyes welled up in silent dismay, making him feel lower and infinitely more disgusting than what Robert had flushed down the toilet the night before. Without a word she rose from her chair and left the room. Robert shouldered by him on his way to the refrigerator.

"You're a real sweetheart, McMasters. Should have let you drown."

He was drowning now, in the churn of stomach acid, in the riptides of remorse. He muttered a foul suggestion at Robert's rigid back, then reached by him to jerk out the carton of milk. He refilled the glass and added enough coffee to give the illusion of something palatable. And he trod lightly into the living room after Charley. He didn't see Robert smirking behind his back.

She was standing at the sliders, arms wrapped about herself in an isolating gesture. When he brushed his cheek against her hair, she flinched away. When he nuzzled the side of her neck, she struck back with an elbow. She gave an ornery sniff and wiggled out of his attempted embrace.

"Look, Charley. See. Glass of milk. I'm drinking it." He took a tentative sip.

"I don't care what you do with it," she flung back at him, but the minute he took the glass from his lips, she added, "All of it."

"Yes, ma'am." He finished it and was aware of a twofold relief. His stomach quieted and Charley relaxed against him.

"I'm sorry I fussed at you," she muttered contritely. "I'm used to dealing with petulant children who won't do what's good for them. I had no right to scold you."

"Fuss all you like. I give you the right." He didn't mention that he had been acting like a bratty child. He rubbed his rough cheek against hers, letting the sense of contentment build and warm him. "I love you, Charley."

That was all it took. She revolved in his arms, twining hers about his neck to hang on tight. He held her easily, loving the feel of her, just loving her. She stepped back and placed her palms on either side of his jaw. Her dark-eyed stare was a simmer of sincerity.

"I just can't bear the thought of anything hurting you."

She saw the shift in his expression, the almost imperceptible softening of his mouth, the smoothing of the lines around his eyes. And for one glorious moment she saw trust there.

"You like French toast, Jess?" Robert hollered from the kitchen.

"Yeah," he called back distractedly. He lifted his thumb to trace the curve of her cheek.

"With confectioner's sugar?"

His interest was coaxed away from her by slow degrees. "And cinnamon. That's how I always make mine."

"Ummm. Sounds good."

Charley gave a snort and pushed off Jess's chest. "I feel like I'm caught between a pair of Julia Childs on steroids."

"We'd be starving if we depended on you, Charley," Robert declared sweetly.

"Maybe I'd better go give him a hand," Jess suggested, glancing toward the kitchen.

"Oh, by all means, you boys have fun playing in my appliances. I don't know what half of them are used for anyway."

Jess seized her by the shoulders, jerking her to his chest. His rumble was husky with promise. "I can show you all sorts of interesting things you can do with kitchen utensils. Later."

He kissed her hotly and she melted like the butter on her brother's skillet. And all through breakfast she was distracted, wondering what use they could come up with for her whisks and spatulas.

The civic award ceremony was set for 3 P.M. with a buffet reception to follow. Charley rode over with Jess. Robert followed in his car because Jess was afraid he'd have to leave early because of his class and didn't want them to be stranded. Charley couldn't help but smile at Jess's cautious, defensive driving. Nothing like the Chicago madman. He was quiet, having said little since they started getting ready. He'd brought over a change of clothes in his car and looked absolutely delicious in a jewel-toned sweater and dark slacks. She had a terrible time concentrating on the study of her speech when he was sitting beside her so neatly groomed and smelling good. He told her with a glance what he thought of her appearance. His eyes smoldered, probably envisioning silk beneath her crisp, tailored suit. She couldn't wait to get him back to her apartment. When he pulled up at the auditorium and came around to open her door, she realized how long a wait that would be.

"Jess," she called softly.

When he bent down to see what she wanted, she caught hold of his jacket and dragged him inside the car, sliding over to accommodate him on the passenger side.

"You're going to get all smudged," he muttered against the press of her mouth.

"Smudge me," she insisted.

Happy as he was to comply, he was still careful to put his hands where they would do no visible damage. He slid them under her jacket, cupping her breasts, using his thumbs to excite rigid little peaks of desire where they wouldn't show. He drew seductively on the impudent tongue she thrust into his mouth until she moaned with impatience.

There was a loud smack on the roof of the car. Jess jerked upright, smashing his head against the rearview mirror.

"Hey, you two, cut it out. For God's sake, save it for a motel."

"Are you sure you wouldn't want to be an only child?" Jess muttered as he backed out, hauling Charley with him. He made a display of brushing down her jacket and skirt, letting his hands linger over the curve of her bottom. He glanced at Robert and growled softly, "Get lost for a minute."

Robert grinned, unoffended. "I'll save you a seat inside."

When he'd ambled off, Charley leaned against Jess's chest, expecting more of the same, but he was no longer smoldering. He was very serious. He straightened her collar and pushed wisps of her hair back from her face, the gestures so tender that she could easily have dissolved on the spot. His thumbs brushed over the diamonds she wore in her earlobes, and he smiled slowly, somberly.

"Charley, I wanted to tell you how very proud I am of you."

"Oh, Jess," she sighed, wanting to reach up to kiss him. But he wasn't finished.

"I just wanted you to know and to try to understand that I'm showing it the best way I know how. I love you, baby. You mean the whole world to me."

He did kiss her then, softly with a delicate, chill-raising stroke of his tongue along her upper lip. Then he took her arm in his and drew a deep breath. "Ready?"

"If you are."

"Ready as I'll ever be," he replied with a strange melancholy. Then he escorted her inside.

The room was packed. As Jess predicted, a good portion of those in attendance sported press passes. As the crowd surged up around Charley, he felt her recoil, sinking into his side, and all his protective instincts went off like warning sirens. With a firm grip on her elbow, he used his own body as a buffer, clearing those in their path away with a sweep of his arm as if they were overgrown brush. He kept his head down, his face turned toward Charley, watching her as much as shielding himself, searching for any telltale signs of distress. But she wasn't that frightened little thing he'd shielded at the hospital. She may have been intimidated by the sheer press of bodies, but she didn't look scared. She was smiling, fielding questions with quick answers like a pro and hanging on to him as if her life depended on their not being separated. That he didn't mind at all.

"Miss Carter?" A tall, distinguished-looking gentleman approached through a part in the crowd. Jess recognized him. There weren't many who lived in and around the Detroit area who weren't familiar with Benjamin Osgood. When Charley responded with a smile, Osgood took her free hand. Cameras flashed and Jess shrank lower into the collar of his coat.

"It's good to see you again, Mr. Osgood," Charley was saying. Now she was pulling at Jess's arm, bringing him about to face the flare of bulbs. "And this is my—" She broke off awkwardly. Her what? How could she explain what Jess was to her? He was everything.

He filled in smoothly, extending his hand. "Jess McMasters, sir. I wanted to tell you how very sorry we were that we weren't able to save your son and his wife."

"Thank you. You were there, Mr. McMasters?"

"On the sidelines," he answered softly. "I wish I could have done more."

The older man nodded. "So do I, but that doesn't lessen how grateful we all are to Miss Carter. Young lady, I've someone here who is very anxious to meet you."

Osgood stepped aside, revealing a small, wheelchair-bound boy. Charley gave a soft cry and instantly knelt to the youngster's level. Her gaze flew over his wan features, touching the bandage on his forehead and the sling cradling his arm. Then the boy smiled timidly and Charley's eyes overflowed.

"Hello, Chris. You look wonderful!"

As she leaned forward to carefully embrace the boy, Jess had to turn away, blinking lest he be reduced to bawling like a kid himself. This was what it was all about for Charley. He knew that now. This one little boy and the chance to hug him. The evidence of her tender spirit choked him up so much that he couldn't swallow through the wad in his throat. She would save them all, one at a time, if she could, just as she saved his own jaded soul from its twist of cynicism. And he had never been so awed or so in love in his entire life.

"They're waiting for us, Miss Carter," Osgood said at last, and Charley straightened with reluctance. She hesitated and then said with difficulty to the boy the one thing that had preyed so mercilessly on her mind.

"I'm sorry I couldn't keep my promise. I tried. I really did."

Chris Osgood absolved her with a smile. "I know you did, and I'm not mad about it anymore. I know it's not your fault that they had to go live with God."

As the boy's grandfather wheeled him toward the speaker's platform, Charley turned to Jess in tears, her composure crumpling. He was quick to support her with reassurances and the circle of his arms.

"It's all right, baby. I think that's just what you needed to hear."

After a moment she nodded jerkily. "I think it's what we both needed to hear."

"Go on, Charley. They're ready for you." For the first time, as she stepped back, she looked worried, but Jess calmed her with the brush of his knuckles along her cheek. "You'll do fine."

Those words woke a fearful memory. She searched his expression for a long second, seeing only his devotion and admiration. "You'll be here?"

"Wouldn't miss it."

She did fine—more than fine. She captivated the audience and press alike with her gentle sincerity, and Jess felt himself caught up in that same spell. He was full to bursting with pride for the little lady with the big heart. He and Robert sat among strangers simply steeping in it. When she announced her plans for the reward, he watched the reaction of the crowd, ever the journalist. There was a positive effusion. He could feel it. He knew just when their rather guarded approach turned as they listened to her speak with determination and a tenacious passion. They were conquered just as he had been conquered, by the goodness of Charlene Carter.

"Hey, Jess," whispered someone close by. He slid a glance in that direction and froze. Already it was starting. The toothy cameraman nodded toward the woman on the stage. "Nice piece. Real nice."

Only Jess's quick reflexes kept Robert Carter from going down the man's throat with both fists. Jess had to wrestle him to hold him in his seat.

"Get a grip, Robert," he commanded the seething younger man. "That's not what he meant. Okay? Relax."

Robert shrugged him off, scowling doubtfully. But it was Jess who couldn't relax. He broke a sweat as a cramping pain rolled through his stomach. Tension built through his muscle groups, feeding the fire. He made short work of a handful of Tums and tried to focus on something else besides impending doom.

Charley. God, she looked good. She had the audience in the palm of her hand. There was no sign of the skittish girl who'd begged him to hide her from a few avid reporters. She'd come a long way since then. A lifetime. So had the two of them. He hung on to that thought while the rest of his world careened. He stood when the room rose in an ovation, swaying slightly, catching hold of the back of the chair in front of him.

"Jess? Hey, man, you all right?"

All right? What a joke. Anxiety was chopping away at his gut with a pickax. No, he wasn't all right. *Hang on, Jess. You can get through this. For Charley. Do it for Charley.*

Speeches made, presentations given, photos staged and snapped by the thousands, the focus of the celebration shifted from the formality of the auditorium to the casual milling of the banquet hall below. Jess pasted a smile on his face as he saw Charley winding toward him and Robert. She was in his arms, mindless of who observed it. And there was no way he could push her away just to stave off the curious. She didn't deserve that. He crushed her close.

"How was I? I was so nervous."

"Never would have guessed. You were great, baby." He squeezed his eyes shut so he could absorb her into all his senses. Once the shaking started, he couldn't control it. It flowed through him like a chill, rattling him to the soul. He clasped the precious woman in his arms in terror that he wouldn't get the chance to hold her again.

"Hey, save some of that for your brother."

Laughing, Charley let Jess go and hugged

Robert exuberantly. "It's going to happen, Robert. It's really going to happen."

"You did it, Charley."

She shook her head and pulled back. Her gaze went to Jess McMasters and lingered there with an enveloping warmth. "Not alone, I didn't." She looped her arms through theirs, hugging tight the two men she loved. "Come on, guys. I'm parched. Let's tap into some of that free champagne."

The trip across the room was a nightmare for Jess. He wasn't sure if he was walking on coals or carrying them in the pit of his belly. Everywhere he looked, it was into a familiar face. The minute he would see a light of recognition spark, he tamped it out with a rude, dismissing nod. He wasn't winning any friends, and he sure wasn't fooling himself into thinking the brusque tactics could hold all of them at bay.

"J.T." His hand was grabbed and pumped enthusiastically. "Just read it. Great work. No doubt, your best."

He should have known the man's name, but suddenly it seemed lost in the paralysis of his mind. He sensed Charley's puzzlement as she craned around him, but he jerked her away from a face-to-face meeting with an almost painful forcefulness.

"Jess, who was that?"

"Some guy I know," he muttered tautly. Then the bottom fell out. Matthew Bane. There was no way to dodge his approach, so Jess braced for it as best he could, affixing a thin smile and tensing his abdomen for the roar of distress to come.

"Jess, introduce me."

"Matthew Bane, Charlene Carter, and this is her brother, Robert."

Jess's editor nodded to Robert, then carefully took up Charley's hand. "I feel like I already know you through Jess. Hell of a thing you did. You must be quite the miracle worker, considering what you did to my boy, here. I didn't think anyone could wring a heart out of Jess McMasters."

Jess gripped his arm and gave him a compelling tug. "Come on, Matt, the lady doesn't want to hear this. Give me a break."

The lady obviously did because she was leaning toward them with an engrossed expression, but it was Jess who caught Matthew's attention. He allowed himself to be turned aside only to take hold of his featureman's shoulder and demand, "Jess, you look like the only survivor to walk away from a plane crash. Ulcer flaring up?"

"Can we do this later?"

"Just trying to make a few points with the lady for you."

"Don't need your help."

"Okay, Jess. Whatever you say. Jess . . . eat something."

He smiled grimly and turned back to Charley.

"Jess, who was that?"

"A friend."

"From the university?"

"No." The pain in his stomach was almost crippling. The distress building around his heart was nearly as bad. He made a quick decision, one he should have made long ago. "Charley, I have to talk to you."

Alarm surged in her uplifted gaze. *Don't look at me like that, Charley. Please.*

"Let's get out of here for a second."

"All right." She was staring at him, unsettled emotions plain on her face. He didn't have to tell her it was serious. She knew. And she looked as though she wanted to run from whatever it was he meant to say. But the last few weeks had taught Charlene Carter a lot of fortitude. She walked with him, but they didn't get far.

"Miss Carter, could I ask a few questions? Carl Parnell from On the Spot News. Hi, Jess. How you doing? Took a look at your cover. Impressive piece. Wish I'd done it."

His stomach went up like a volcano. It was make a run for it or heave on the spot, no pun intended. He peeled Charley's hand off his arm and mumbled hoarsely, "I'll wait for you out in the hall." Ignoring her startled look and trusting Parnell to hang on to her like a good newsman, Jess bolted. He didn't pause in the hallway but made for the nearest men's room, barely making it through a stall door before French toast and all came up with a vengeance. Weak, shaky but already feeling better, he wobbled to the sink to rinse off a film of cold sweat. He avoided the sight of his face in the mirror. What he could imagine was frightful enough.

After drying his face, he left the bathroom and sought relief from the closest drinking fountain. Swishing and spitting and swallowing, he started to feel almost human again when he heard his name called.

"McMasters."

Jess straightened. His mind had a chance to register the sight of Alan Peters before he took a hammerlike impact in the face. He crashed against the wall and slid down, clutching an eye. Hell of a punch for a scientist!

Peters squared off above him, fists balled and ready for more, but Jess had no inclination to move. Seeing his opponent meant to stay down, Alan snarled, "You scum-sucker. How could you do that to her? I ought to—" He left that threat empty, settling for kicking at the downed man's feet before striding off in a towering indignation.

"Wow," Robert exclaimed, looking after his sister's old beau. "Who'd have thought he'd get into macho posturing? Nailed you but good, didn't he?"

Jess nursed his eye, not saying anything. Robert put down his hand.

"Help you up." When Jess shook his head,

Robert shrugged and settled on the floor beside him. They sat silent for a minute, then the younger man finally relented. "All right, Jess, spill it. What's going on with you? And what does it have to do with Charley? You're going to hurt her, aren't you?"

One look at Jess's stricken features was answer enough. Robert pounded on his knee in frustration.

"I screwed up, Robert."

"How?"

"Bad."

"That's not telling me anything, man."

"You'll know soon enough." He was looking through the open doors into the banquet hall, following Alan as he bore down on Charley.

"She loves you, Jess. She'll forgive you anything if you're up front with her."

"Too late." He could feel all his hopes, all his expectations sinking, settling on the floor of his mangled stomach lining as Alan took Charley by the arm. He watched as she turned her head sharply to glare up at the sandy-haired scientist. He didn't have to be close to picture what would be burning in her eyes. Disbelief. Anger. A slow shift to uncertainty and dawning truth. Damning truth. He couldn't do this. He couldn't watch as everything he'd come to care about went straight to hell. The volcano in his belly started rumbling, warning of another eruption. His face hurt from Alan's punch. His chest hurt from the contracting squeeze of guilt and loss. So many things were tearing at him that he was numbed to the pain. To all but the thought of how disappointment would look on the face of Charlene Carter. That was the pain that crippled him.

Robert stood as Jess wobbled to his feet. He'd never seen a man look so bad. Jess had the worn-to-the-soul face of a man who'd come home from a five-day drunk to find that his family had left him, his house had burned down, a pink slip was in the mail, and his banker was in Mexico sipping umbrella drinks on his life savings.

"Jess . . . Don't do something stupid."

"I gotta go."

"That's stupid."

But he was already back-pedaling away from his own personal disaster. "Tell Charley something came up, that I couldn't stay."

"I won't lie to her, Jess."

He pulled a harsh, jagged breath. It was like inhaling undiluted acid. "Then you tell her I couldn't wait around for it. She'll understand." He smiled oddly. "That she'll understand."

"Jess . . . Dammit, Jess, don't you run out on her!"

But Jess was already striding toward the exit doors. He hit them with both palms, shoving hard, moving fast. The dying brightness of the day struck him, making him feel as if his eyeballs had incinerated. But even after he yanked out his dark glasses and settled them on the bridge of his nose, he couldn't see a damn thing. He had no idea how he ever found his way out of the parking lot.

Seventeen

"I don't believe you."

Alan stood his ground, his expression grim. But it was the surprising hint of compassion in his eyes that did Charley in. "It's true, Charlene. I'm sorry."

Fighting down the waves of rising panic, she shook her head stubbornly. "But he teaches at the university . . ."

"And he writes for *Metro Magazine.* I checked on him through Administration. Charlene, he's been using you. He's made you the cover story. That's what he was after. It wasn't you. It was never you."

She pushed blindly away from him. Jess. She had to find Jess. There had to be an explanation. There had to be. She was almost running when she spotted Robert in the hall. He didn't look surprised at her distraught state. He opened his arms and swept her in.

"He's gone, Charley. Just a minute ago, looking like he was expecting lightning to strike. What's going on?"

She had to get moving before the shaking settled in, before the doubts began to bloom. "Can you drive me to the university, Robert?"

"Sure, Charley . . ."

"Now. I have to go now."

She didn't speak during the drive. She couldn't. Her jaw was locked tight to keep her teeth from chattering in shock. *Jess, no. Jess, please. You have to tell me it isn't true. It can't be true.* Even as she thought those things, she was equally afraid it was. She tried not to think after that, just holding to the image of him standing outside her door dripping wet with a toothbrush in his hand, trying to ignore the sidelong glances of concern from her brother. It would be all right. It had to be!

She knew Jess had a class from six to eight on Monday nights but had no idea what building it was in. She was a foreigner to the academic side of the university. Alan and she rented the building space for study and research, but they weren't members of the university staff, so contact was minimal. Finally they found the English department and a parking spot, and Robert insisted on coming with her. It was only 5 P.M., too late for the press of midday classes, too early for the evening ones. A weary receptionist directed them to the third floor, to Jess's office. Charley didn't know if he'd stop there first before going to class, but she didn't know what else to do. She couldn't last until 8 P.M. without knowing. Robert tagged along behind her, a silent, somber shadow.

Jess's door was unlocked. Charley suffered only slight qualms about going inside. Robert mumbled something about finding a coffee machine, but she knew it was an excuse to give her time alone. She needed it. She needed those minutes alone among Jess's things.

The room had none of the comfortable charm of his house. This was where he worked. The furnishings were gleaming chrome and black lacquer. Hard, sleek, impersonal. But still Jess. She'd glimpsed that side of him before but hadn't understood. Here was her answer. Gingerly she sank down onto his swivel chair and studied the top of his desk. Everything was neatly stacked beside the coffee cups and antacids. She skipped over the stack of college compositions and picked up a glossy issue of last month's *Metro*. She wasn't much for reading about glitzy lives or crime dramas, so she'd never really looked beyond the cover before. And on this one she didn't even have to turn to the first page. There beneath a hard-hitting headline was the name J.T. Masters. She ran her thumb over the letters. He was a writer. Why hadn't he told her where his pieces were published?

There were a half-dozen issues in all, and she flipped through them one by one with mounting uneasiness. He was good. No doubt. His style was terse, crisp, provocative. And his slant was ruthless. She could see his wry smile between the lines and that cold, glittering study of the world through his eyes. His was a no-holds-barred journalism that stabbed straight to the truth regardless of consequence. She could see a pattern in his work, a want to take something with a shiny, pleasing surface and peel it down to its ugly core.

Why on earth had he wanted to write about her?

Unless he had a deep disgust for what she'd done.

Why did you take the money, Charley?

Her hands were shaking when she reached for the last file on his desk. It wasn't thick, but its contents were explosive. A single fact sheet and a cassette tape. On that piece of paper were the details of her life, listed succinctly in chronological order. Some of the information he could only have gotten from her. He'd written it down.

Perversely, she slipped the tape into the player he had on his window ledge and, after some trepidation, pushed the play button. Voices filled his office. His. Hers. The conversation was familiar. She frowned slightly, trying to remember when it had taken place. The restaurant, the one he'd taken her to for lunch the day after she was released from the hospital. When he'd been so nice, so solicitous. And she'd started to fall in love with him. He'd recorded it.

He's been using you to get a story. That's what he was after. It was never you.

And sitting in his chair, listening to the stolen conversation, Charley looked back through different eyes, disillusioned eyes, seeing a whole new slant on things. Jess at the hospital . . . no coincidence. He'd pulled her from the media pack, taken her under his wing, gained entrance into her home, into her trust, into her heart. She'd been so grateful for his buffer against the newshounds. She thought he was being wonderfully gallant. He was protecting his exclusivity to the story. She'd thought he was warm, sincere, interested in her views, her plans. He'd been pumping her for information. He'd taken her to the camp, for a respite from pressure, he'd said. But it had been to keep other reporters away and his identity a secret. Until he had his story.

Don't believe a word I say . . .

All the laughter. All the loving. How much of it was a lie?

I shouldn't have let it happen. He'd told her, hadn't he. *I should have stopped it that night at your brother's before things got—out of control.* Out of control? Was that what had happened? Her breath snagged in a sob.

Thanks for the memory and see you around.

A hand reached in front of her, punching down the off button on the tape player. For a long moment she couldn't look, afraid that he wouldn't seem any different to her now that she knew the truth. Terrified that he would. Slowly her eyes lifted.

If she'd had any doubts, his expression cleared them. It was shut down tight, detached from even the tiniest betraying flicker. For some reason that infuriated her. He didn't show remorse. He didn't show concern for her. He was wrapped up in his own defenses, guarding himself against hurt. And she wanted to strike out at him, to scream at him, to dent those staunch defenses. But she couldn't. She couldn't make herself hurt him.

"Why didn't you tell me?"

"I tried." No apology. Fact.

"You lied to me."

"No, I didn't. I told you I was a teacher. I teach. I told you I was a writer. I write."

"You didn't tell me you were writing about me! Was 'lie' the wrong word? You're the English expert. You tell me. Perhaps 'oversight' would explain it better. Did you just forget to mention that you were following me to get a story? Like you forgot to mention it was you who pulled me from that car? Like you forgot to tell me Alan called? That you were recording our conversations? You seem to have a very selective memory. Is that a prerequisite for your job?" Her voice fractured, and for a second Charley feared she was doomed to a flood of tears. Jess hadn't moved. He didn't try to touch her. He didn't try to speak. He was watching her through shuttered eyes, his posture so stiff and taut that a sharp blow would shatter him into a billion irreparable pieces. She hated it that he was so removed, so controlled, when she felt herself unraveling at every seam.

But he'd been expecting this.

He'd been preparing for it since their first kiss.

"Why didn't you tell me?" she moaned softly, unable to get beyond that one fact. It hurt so much that nothing else registered. "How could you? How could you let me think—" She clamped down hard on that as dampness swelled in her eyes. She lifted one of the copies of *Metro* and pushed it at him. Her tone was raw. "I could understand it from him, from J.T. Masters, but not from you."

Jess looked blankly down at the glossy magazine, his fingers brushing over the cover, over his byline. Then with a convulsive movement he crumpled it in his hand and flung it hard across the room. The pent-up violence released in the gesture startled her, but it wasn't an answer.

"Charley," he began in a low, strained-to-the-limit voice.

"Don't tell me that you're sorry," she warned fiercely. "Don't you dare say that. Sorry doesn't cut it, Jess."

In a flat, frighteningly emotionless way he said, "I told you it was impossible."

"So this is all my fault? Because I was naïve?" She gave a laugh that was as sharp as broken glass. "I guess you're right. It is. Because you told me and I wouldn't listen. I wanted to see something good, and I made myself believe it was real. Well, thank you for the lesson, Mr. McMasters. You taught me something very important, something I won't ever forget. There are no such things as fairy tales. And you—you—" She pushed herself out of the chair, groping blindly for a way to describe the hurt and humiliation she was feeling. She concluded with a spill of tears. "You aren't a nice guy."

She wrenched the diamonds from her earlobes and threw them at him. Jess rocked back as they struck him in the chest, reeling as if she'd smacked him with the desk chair. There, in his face, was a glimpse into his soul, a dulled anguish of inevitability, a twist of tragic resignation. And for an instant there was the faintest spark. He reached out, grazing her wet cheek with his fingertips. Very softly he asked, "What about your promise?"

Charley knocked his arm away. So embroiled in her own misery, she had no idea what he was talking about. "Some promises can't be kept."

He let her go. There was nothing he could say to take away her hurt at his betrayal. There was no way he could change what he had done. He was going to have to learn to live with the hole Charley Carter had left in his heart. In a way it would be harder to bear than the ulcer, because nothing was going to ease that pain. *Don't think. Don't feel. Just get on with it.*

What were you expecting? A miracle?

With a tense, controlled motion he reached for the papers on the edge of his desk. He had two hours of class time. Okay, he could get through those two hours. That was two hours down and the rest of his life to go. He'd call Matt and take him up on the beers. No way could he go home tonight. That would be suicidal. He was going to fall apart the minute he closed the front door and he knew it.

Class. Beers. Come on, Jess, hang on. You've gotten through worse things.

No. That was a lie. Nothing could compare to losing Charlene Carter. And he wasn't at all sure he could survive it.

The knocking on the door wouldn't stop. Robert had picked a fine time to go out for bucket chicken.

Hauling herself off the couch, Charley dragged the sleeve of her robe across her eyes and shuffled to send away whoever was disrupting her gloomy stupor. She hadn't slept, she hadn't eaten, she hadn't showered. She'd hardly stirred off the couch for the past fifteen hours, except to get more tissues. And now she could barely move through the film of exhaustion hanging over her. Maybe Robert had forgotten his key. Tears burned against the red of her eyes when she thought of her brother. He'd been so wonderful, never saying a word, letting her sob into his shirtfront until the crack of dawn. How could she have managed without him?

For a moment she stared blearily at the man in the hall. He seemed vaguely familiar, but there was too much effort involved in searching for a name to match the face. He helped her out most graciously.

"Miss Carter, I'm Matthew Bane. We met yesterday."

She blinked owlishly. "Oh . . . yes, of course. Would you like to come in, Mr. Bane?"

His smile was twisted. She really looked like hell. He was glad. "No, thanks. I left a friend of mine hanging over my toilet, so I can't stay long."

She took a tiny breath. Jess. She couldn't say his name. "Is he all right?"

Matthew gave her a hard look. "Sure, he's fine. We spent most of the night in the rest rooms of every bar in the suburbs while he chucked his guts out and moaned about some promise someone made him. You wouldn't know anything about that, would you?"

Charley shook her head numbly. A promise? "I'm sorry, I don't."

"Maybe I was wrong, then. See, I've known Jess a lot of years, and he's kind of a funny guy.

You wouldn't believe some of the stuff he's written for me. The guy is short-fuse dynamite when he gets on a story. Nothing distracts him. He even got his arm broken and a fractured skull sniffing up dirt for one piece. Dragged himself around like the walking dead, but he got what he was after. He's one tough customer. The perfect feature man, you'd think. No fear, no conscience, no regrets. I love that guy, Miss Carter. I think of him as one of my few good friends, and I value him as one of the best writers I've ever known. He can do things with words, make them grab right on to your vitals and twist hard. But this last piece he did, it went for the heart, and I didn't understand what made that change in him until yesterday. Read this and maybe you'll understand, too." He passed her an envelope. "And the other thing in there, it's not to the city, but maybe it'll open a lot more."

Charley sat for a long while staring at the magazine she found inside the mailer. It was the latest issue of *Metro Magazine,* the one that had just hit the stands. The one that profiled her life through J.T. Masters's embittered eyes. She didn't want to read his slashing conclusions. It was too personal, too painful. She was too afraid she'd discover exactly what Jess thought of her, and she wasn't ready to have all her illusions shot down just yet. Part of her still wanted to believe, though in a dazed, detached way that had little to do with reality as she now understood it. But part of her had to know. If for no other reason, so that she could go on without him.

She glanced at the cover. The picture had been taken as she left the hospital. How vulnerable she looked. What an easy mark for a hardened journalist. She'd just started to frown when she saw his name. *His* name. Not J.T. Masters. Jess McMasters. And that made her curious enough to open the cover.

When Robert returned, he discovered Charley surrounded by mounds of tissues with the magazine on her lap. She looked up, and her tremulous smile stopped him in his tracks.

"Read this," she said in an achy little voice.

He took the magazine and found himself staring at his sister's face on the cover. Beneath it was the captions "Love's Own Reward" and the name Jess McMasters. He flipped inside and started reading. After the first few paragraphs he glanced up, moved to a shiny-eyed speechlessness. He swallowed hard. "Damn. This is beautiful. This is us. Everything we're trying to do."

Jess had taken the essence of their hearts and souls and distilled it into a poignant story. A story that began with the rescue of one child and ended with the hope of saving thousands. There was nothing sensationalized, nothing exploitive. Just a sensitive portrayal of a woman's courage and her brother's dream. Of promises to keep.

Promises.

Then Charley understood what Jess had meant. A promise. Her promise that she would love him forever and never, ever hurt him.

"Oh God, Robert. What have I done?"

Her hands were shaking as she dialed. Her heart was pounding in her throat as she heard the inanimate voice on the other end.

"McMasters. I can't take your call right now. Leave a message and I'll get back to you." Beep.

"Jess . . ." Would she be just another pleading female voice on his machine? "Jess, call me. Please." She hung up quickly before she started sobbing into the receiver.

How had she missed it? He'd been reaching out to her the only way he knew how—with the artistry of words, with the cautious extension of his trust. And she'd failed him. After all her grand promises. After all her smug confidence. She remembered so clearly the way he'd looked when he'd listened to her make that vow. She could see the fatigue in his unshaven face, his eyes hollow and empty of hope. And that awful, fragile smile, so sad, so sorrowful, as if he'd known all the pain in the world and hadn't the strength to endure any more. She'd had to reach down into his battered spirit to drag up that first grain of trust. And she'd promised him, with her words, with her kisses, with the security of her embrace, that she would never give him cause to regret taking that risk. And she saw again that stark devastation when she'd pushed him away. As if he weren't worth forgiving. As if he weren't worth loving.

She'd ground out the spark that came alive in his spirit, the hope that shone in his near-poetic words. And she was terribly, terribly afraid she couldn't bring it back.

Despondently she picked up the envelope from the floor. Something shifted inside. Curiously she tipped it into her hand. A key. Not to the city, Matthew had said. To Jess McMasters's front door.

And very possibly to his heart.

It took him about five minutes to open his front door. He couldn't see a thing. He was beginning to think he'd go through the rest of his life half-blind. Finally he found the lock and let himself into the emptiness of his house. He closed the door behind him and stood, confronted by the thing he'd feared most. Being alone. He didn't know what to do with himself. There was absolutely nothing left to motivate him from the spot. Dragging the heel of his hand across his face, he made himself move, walking aimlessly into the kitchen. He reached past the tempting remains of a six-pack for a half-gallon of milk, drinking deeply, right out of the carton. It went down hard, being forced past what felt like a baseball lodged in his throat. He screwed the cap back on and smiled ruefully. *See, Charley, I'm taking care of myself. I don't need you to watchdog me.* Then he grabbed a beer.

Out of habit he turned on his answering machine in passing. The sound of Charley's voice snatched him up, seeming to rip his heart right from his chest.

"Jess . . ."

He jabbed stop. The sound of his own breathing was loud and raw. Before he had time to think, he pushed erase, then the instant it started to whir indifferently, his fingertips fluttered helplessly at the buttons as if he could call back the words, the sound. But he couldn't. It was too late. He couldn't call back any of it.

Morosely swallowing a mouthful of beer, he plodded through his darkening rooms in a restless sort of daze. His insides were a quivering mess, so torn up it felt as if he were stoking a furnace with every breath. The merciful thing would be for someone to put him out of his misery. Isn't that what they did to poor dumb animals when they were in so much pain they walked in numb, endless circles unable to comprehend their own agony? Wasn't there someone out there who would kindly do him in with the rap of a five-pound sledgehammer? He glanced blearily at the beer in his hand. Or was he doing a good enough job of it on his own?

Rest. He needed rest. A good, long, peaceful

slumber for the heart and soul and body. His mind had shut down. Physically he couldn't cope with any more. He was running on emotional empty. He tottered into his bedroom and crawled on top of the covers, leaving the open beer on the floor, still fully dressed right down to his jacket and shoes. Curling tight in a fetal position, Jess squeezed his eyes shut and prayed for unconsciousness.

He must have done something good once upon a time because that prayer was answered. It was daylight when he eased his achy eyes open. Somehow he'd found his way under the covers after taking off his coat and shoes. He didn't remember doing it. Or picking up the beer. He half expected to find it spilled all over his carpet instead of sitting safely on his nightstand. If he'd hoped the sleep would make him feel better, he was wrong. It only reinforced the unpleasant news that he was indeed going to survive whether he liked it or not. Life was pretty damn cruel sometimes.

Music. Sam and Dave's "Soothe Me." God, he loved that song. For a minute he simply soaked up the sounds, then awareness sharpened. Either he was crazy or something was on fire.

In an ungainly wobble he made his way to the living room. His leather jacket was there, folded over the arm of the recliner. The lights were on in his entertainment center. Confused into immobility, he stood and stared. Until he heard humming from the kitchen. He couldn't trust himself to breathe let alone to consider the source of that sound. His heart soared.

"Jess? Where do you keep your onions?"

He moved around the corner like a sleepwalker. Either he'd lost it completely or Charley Carter was in his kitchen. He forced a noise past the thickness in his throat.

"What are you burning?"

"Your breakfast." She turned to him then, and a disbelieving frenzy started in his chest. It was Charley. A tired, red-eyed, battle-weary Charley, but her smile held the promise of pure sunshine. And her eyes a plea for forgiveness. Unable to respond to either without turning into a total blithering idiot, he jammed his fists into his pockets and waited for her to explain. "I was afraid you wouldn't take the time to make it for yourself."

"I've been managing."

"Yes," she murmured dryly. "I found the four basic food groups on the floor by your bed."

"Well, it was grain." This was totally nuts, he told himself, this conversation, her being here. But it was a wonderful insanity. "How did you get in?"

Her grin was sassy and sexy as hell. "I'm a resourceful kind of woman."

Something twitched along the parched corners of his mouth, and Jess was surprised to discover it was a weak imitation of a smile. It was then he caught the flash of fire at her earlobes. The diamonds. They'd been in his coat pocket. He hadn't been able to walk away from them. Any more than he could walk away from her.

"I love you, Charley."

For a second he thought she was going to come unglued. Brightness welled in her eyes. Her tender mouth trembled. But she managed to wrestle up a smile and an admirable amount of spunk. "Good, then you'll take me out to breakfast because I don't think you're going to want to eat any of this."

Charley hadn't known what to expect from this pinch-hit decision. She'd been existing on raw nerves and desperate hope since letting herself in with Matthew Bane's key. When she'd seen Jess, it had almost finished her. He'd looked as if a train had run over him and dragged him cross-country. And what had happened to his eye? He'd been in such bad shape that he hadn't moved when she'd undressed him and tucked him in. Not sure he'd even welcome the sight of her, she'd waited. The sound of his deep, full-chested laugh was a reward well worth the anxiety.

"How about we salvage what we can and start over?"

What an open-ended suggestion. It nailed her right through the heart. "Can we, Jess?" That was a hoarse little whisper.

"You're the champion of lost causes. You tell